DRAKON'S PLUNDER

BLOOD OF THE DRAKON

DRAKON'S PLUNDER

BLOOD OF THE DRAKON

N.J. WALTERS

Entangled Publishing, LLC
2614 South Timberline Road
Suite 109
Fort Collins, CO 80525
Visit our website at www.entangledpublishing.com.

Select Otherworld is an imprint of Entangled Publishing, LLC.

Edited by Heidi Shoham
Cover design by Kelly Martin
Cover art from Bigstock and iStock

Manufactured in the United States of America

First Edition July 2017

For my readers. Thank you for being on this journey with me.

Chapter One

This is suicide.

Sam Bellamy stood on the deck of the *Integrity*, a seventy-foot private research vessel currently anchored in the Atlantic Ocean about twenty miles off the coast of Maine. The waves were choppy and the wind brisk, but not too bad considering it was late November.

She sensed someone coming up behind her but didn't turn around. Best no one know just how hyper alert she was.

"Whatcha looking at, Sam?" Aaron Dexter leaned against the railing beside her, getting way too close, as usual. He'd been hitting on her since they'd boarded the vessel.

Aaron seemed to think he was God's gift to women, and since she was the only woman around, it fell to her to be the recipient of his advances. Lucky her.

She was used to being the only woman on board a boat, had spent her childhood fishing with her father and his crew, good, hardworking men who'd never given her any trouble.

Her chosen career had taken her all over the world, from the deserts of Egypt, to the dense, humid jungles of South

America and the mountains of China. She'd run from drug lords, smugglers, and slave traders. But being on this yacht just miles away from the coast of Maine was her most dangerous assignment to date.

"What do you want, Aaron?" She kept her voice level and filled with disinterest. It was better not to encourage him in any way.

He turned and leaned his back against the railing before giving her what she considered his patented seduction smile. She wondered if he practiced it in a mirror. She could have told him it was wasted on her. She'd rather date an alligator— full apologies to the alligator for the comparison.

"Not a friendly sort, are you?" Rather than driving him away, her disinterest only seemed to be encouraging him. Not good.

She supposed most women would find him good-looking, with his thick blond hair being ruffled by the wind and his dark brown eyes watching her intently. He was big and strong. That was his job. He was here ostensibly as security, and she knew he was watching her.

"I'm here to do a job," she reminded him. She was an archaeologist specializing in ancient languages and mythology. Her passion was ancient lore and magic, the things that most other scholars scoffed at. She was interested in mystical artifacts and creatures only whispered about in ancient texts and hinted at in paintings and carvings.

By some fluke of nature, she'd been born with a sixth sense when it came to such items. Being able to find them, even in remote and desolate areas, was what had allowed her to get grants and funding for digs. That had led to a teaching position. Her fellow archaeologists might scoff at her area of study, but there was no denying she got results on a dig.

She'd been chasing such artifacts all her life. They were like a hum in her blood whenever she was near them. And right now, her blood was practically singing. Whatever was beneath them on the ocean floor was important and rare. The kind of thing men killed for.

Aaron reached out and ran his hand down her arm. She was thankful she was wearing a heavy coat with a sweater and thermal shirt beneath. "That doesn't mean we can't be friendly."

Sam refused to give ground. She couldn't afford to. She was stuck on a small vessel rocking on the waves in the vast ocean. There was nowhere she could run to get away from him. "I was hired to authenticate any artifacts brought up from below. I don't know about you, but I don't want to disappoint our employer."

Aaron scowled, but he did remove his hand. Their employer was not the sort of person you wanted to disappoint.

On the surface, Karina Azarov was a rich businesswoman with interests in pharmaceuticals, business, and technologies. Archaeology was her passion, and she often funded expeditions such as this one. She was also a high-ranking member of the Knights of the Dragon, a secret society that had existed for hundreds of years, if not longer.

The *Integrity* was Azarov's boat and was currently salvaging items from the *Reliant*, a vessel that had veered off course and sunk during a storm in the mid-eighteen hundreds. It was one of hundreds that had met their doom off the coast of North America over the years. Not really of note to anyone without family on board. It hadn't been carrying gold or silver when it went down. As far as most people knew it had been a passenger vessel with a small amount of trade goods on board.

Only a handful of people knew the ship had been carrying artifacts belonging to the Knights of the Dragon. Members of the secret society had spent millions of dollars and many years chasing the wreckage, but they'd only recently discovered what they hoped were the ship's remains.

Aaron finally took a step back. "The ROV has located something interesting. The team is getting ready to retrieve it and bring it on board."

Sam nodded but said nothing. Finally Aaron turned and stalked off, allowing Sam to breathe freely once again.

The ROV, or remotely operated vehicle, was a godsend in recovery efforts like this. It allowed them to go deeper than a diver could go and to stay down longer. It could also retrieve small or light items. This expedition was well funded, and the ship was outfitted with some of the best equipment available, as well as experienced divers.

It was a dream job, or would be if she wasn't working for some of the nastiest people on the face of the planet. The Knights of the Dragon were obsessed with dragon lore, believing the creatures were real. It was rumored that among the cargo was a scroll or tablet that contained information on how to control one of the mythical creatures.

Of course, she wasn't supposed to know anything about the Knights or their true mission. As far as everyone was concerned, she was an archaeologist here to oversee the authentication of any artifacts. She had to keep it that way. If they knew she was aware of their secrets, she probably wouldn't make it back to port alive.

Sam didn't believe in dragons. They were interesting and fascinating to study, to be sure, but nothing more than myth.

What she did believe in was justice. And the Knights had killed her mentor, the one man who'd taken her under his wing and guided her when other archaeologists and scholars had scoffed at her passion for the mythical, deeming it unimportant.

And for what? A book.

Brian had stumbled onto a one-of-a-kind leather-bound book detailing the secret society, and they'd killed him in order to get it. Not that she had any proof. The police had called it a home invasion gone wrong.

Sam believed otherwise.

After Brian's funeral, she was approached by a rare book dealer, Gervais Rames. He'd claimed to know Brian and had told her a crazy story about the Knights and a rival group he claimed to belong to—the Dragon Guard, whose mission was to oppose the Knights and protect dragons. She'd ignored him at first, but unable to let Brian's death go unsolved, she learned more from Gervais, and her search for answers had led her to this job.

She shivered, suddenly colder than she'd been only seconds before. She pulled her coat more securely around her and her black watch cap more snugly against her ears. Turning away from the ocean, she headed back to the cabin.

Whatever happened, she was going to make certain the Knights didn't get their hands on any artifacts discovered. It was the least she could do for Brian.

• • •

Karina Azarov picked up her silver teaspoon and tapped the expensive silverware against the edge of her crystal wineglass. The murmur of voices lessened and finally stopped. She stared down the table at the dozen other people who had been invited to this meeting. This was the inner circle of the Knights of the Dragon.

Some of them, like her nemesis, Herman Temple, were more than a hundred years old, kept alive by the blood of a dragon. But Temple was beginning to show his age. He'd managed to allow the dragon in his care to die and had lost his supply. Dragon blood lost its potency once it was removed from the creature and couldn't be stockpiled, which was what made dragons so valuable.

These were dangerous creatures with a vast intelligence

that was not to be underestimated. There were books that contained recipes for potions that allowed them to capture and contain the beasts, incantations and spells that were rumored to do the same. Karina preferred to stick with the potions. That was science, pure and simple. Drugs, heavy chains, and titanium enclosures were their best weapons.

Thanks to Temple's now-deceased son, they'd lost one such valuable book. They'd also lost Darius Varkas, whom they all believed to be a dragon. It had been several weeks since they'd had any real lead on his whereabouts. The trail had gone cold. But he'd have to surface eventually, and when he did, they'd capture him and the little nobody of a librarian who'd stolen the book and tipped Varkas off.

"Thank you for inviting us to your home." Anton Bruno from Russia stood and lifted his glass. "To your gracious hospitality and your enduring beauty."

The others lifted their glasses and drank. Karina was not moved in the least by his toast. Anton would slit her throat in a heartbeat if he thought it would gain him what he wanted the most—immortality.

That's what they were chasing, the longevity that came from ingesting dragon blood.

Karina was ambivalent about the whole idea of living forever, but she figured she'd change her mind when she started to age. She was currently in her thirties, healthy and strong. For her, this was all about power and money.

Karina waited until Anton had retaken his seat before standing. "Thank you, Anton. And thank you all for coming." This was the annual meeting of the Knights. They often spoke over secured lines, or met one-on-one, but having them all together happened only once a year.

None of them would dare to refuse to come.

"I have located the *Reliant*." Voices were raised in disbelief and excitement. Karina remained quiet until they settled down once again.

"Where?" Herman Temple demanded.

Karina arched one finely delineated eyebrow at him and then turned her attention back to the table at large. "I have a vessel on site pulling up artifacts as we speak. I'll hear as soon as they find something."

"Are you sure it's the *Reliant*?" Jeremiah Dent asked. Dent was a close associate of Temple and, like him, bore watching.

"My people assure me it's the right ship."

"Who do we have on board to authenticate?"

Karina was getting tired of being questioned by Temple. "If you'll be quiet long enough, I'll share the details." That shut him up and drew some snickers from other members. No, Temple wasn't well liked in some quarters. Something to remember in case she needed allies down the road.

"I hired Sam Bellamy for the job." She waited and watched as several members frowned.

It was Anton who spoke. "Wasn't she associated with that archaeologist we had to dispose of last year?"

Karina inclined her head.

Anton tipped his glass to her once again. "My dear, once again you seem to have everything well in hand."

"Isn't it dangerous to have her on board?" Temple asked.

Karina sat back down and picked up her fork. Her dinner was getting cold and the chef had outdone himself with the crab soufflé. "I get the artifacts authenticated and then poor Dr. Bellamy will have an accident. So sad really, but these things happen."

Temple slowly began to smile. Really, for a man who'd lived as long as he had, he could be incredibly dense at times.

But Anton wasn't. He was watching her, assessing her every move. He'd already figured out what most of the rest of them hadn't. She was the only one who would have control of the artifact once it was recovered.

When it came to moving dangerous artifacts, secrecy was paramount. It was the same now as it had been when the *Reliant* had gone down. No one knew exactly what the ship had been carrying, only that it had been valuable to the Knights. If it was a book, it might have been destroyed or damaged beyond use after years on the ocean floor. Karina was hopeful that maybe it was a stone tablet or a scroll stored in an airtight jar or some other container that might protect it. She wasn't sure how much use it would be if it was an amulet or bowl or something of that nature.

Either way, destroyed or intact, she'd know and knowledge was always power.

Karina discreetly glanced at the diamond studded Piaget that graced her wrist. It had cost more than most people make in a year, but she had a weakness for pretty things and occasionally indulged herself. The expensive watch told her it would be at least another hour before she could get rid of this bunch. Their meeting had run long and they had yet to be served dessert and coffee.

A slight movement brought her attention to the door. Birch, her private bodyguard and most trusted man, slipped into the room. He gave his head an almost imperceptible shake to let her know there was no news from the site of the *Reliant* yet. It could be days before they discovered anything of interest. These things took time. Fortunately she was patient when it came to getting what she wanted.

Chapter Two

It had been two days since they'd started recovering artifacts from the seafloor. Sam knew if she wasn't here to keep an eye on things, many of the discoveries would have ended up back in the ocean. The other members of this expedition were after one thing and one thing only—whatever pertained to the Knights of the Dragon.

The phone on her desk rang, startling her from her work. Her heart began to pound, although she tried to remain calm outwardly. "Yes."

"They're bringing up another load from the seabed," Aaron told her. "I'll make certain it's brought down."

"Fine." She hung up the phone and went back to working on her notes, but the computer screen blurred in front of her, the words all running together. She rubbed her eyes but didn't relax her guard, not for one second. She was almost 100 percent sure this room was under surveillance. It only made sense, since she was handling potentially priceless artifacts.

About ten minutes later, Sam took a deep breath, closed her laptop, and headed to the galley to get a cup of coffee.

Mug in hand, she headed topside. She really needed a coat, but she wouldn't be staying outside long. All she needed was a breath of fresh air and a few moments alone.

She stepped out onto the deck and huddled beside the door, using the wall of the cabin to block the wind. Voices were raised and a mechanical *whir* filled the air as the winch brought up the latest batch of artifacts.

Sam watched the choppy waves rock the boat. So far, the weather had been exceptionally good, a rare occurrence for this time of year. She prayed it would hold, at least until she was able to take a dinghy and get off the ship. That was her plan. It wasn't much of one, but there really weren't any other options.

If she found something that belonged to the Knights, she'd take it and run. If they found her, she'd try to destroy it. Whatever worked. There was no way she could let them get their hands on anything that might give them even more power.

Maybe she was delusional to believe her small efforts, taking and destroying one or two small items, might have any effect on the operations of the Knights of the Dragon, but it was all she had. The only way she could possibly enact some kind of justice for her mentor.

And if they didn't find anything? She might still have to make a run for her life. She had a sinking feeling she wasn't meant to survive this trip. She'd been watching and learning about the Knights for the past year, and all the while they'd been monitoring her.

This deadly game of cat and mouse would soon be at an end.

Sam ducked inside and headed back to her temporary lab. She was settled in and working once again when two workers brought in a plastic tub filled with encrusted items under Aaron's watchful eyes.

She waved them over to her right. "Put it there. I'll get to it when I'm done with this." She continued her inspection of the corroded remains of a dueling pistol before logging it into the records she was keeping of each item salvaged from the *Reliant*.

Aaron scowled but simply nodded and jerked his head at the other men. They hurried back out of the room, leaving her alone with the head of security.

"Anything?" Aaron stood in the doorway to her workspace, filling it completely. Even though the dueling pistol had long since passed its useful stage, she picked it up. Having the weapon in her hand made her feel marginally better. It might not fire a bullet, but she could use it to bludgeon him if necessary.

"This is a common dueling pistol dating about twenty years before the sinking of the vessel. We have to assume it was either a family piece or someone bought it to be used."

He swore and stalked over to the table where she had all the artifacts displayed. Most of it looked like encrusted clumps of metal that would have to be cleaned further. Other items, like the pistol, were easily recognizable.

"I don't care about the damn gun." He picked up the remnants of a dagger and ran his finger along the flat edge of the corroded blade before dumping it back on the table.

"What do you care about?" It was bold and brazen of her to ask, but she wanted to know if he was hired muscle or if he had a higher stake in the game the Knights were playing.

His eyes flashed and his expression turned from one of frustration to his patented smile. "Why, treasure, Dr. Bellamy. Isn't that what everyone wants when they go treasure hunting?"

"Depends on your definition of treasure," she retorted. "What we've uncovered so far says a lot about the people who died on board the *Reliant*." She reluctantly set the pistol down on the top of her workspace. "If you mean gold, silver, and jewels, you may be disappointed. Those kinds of discoveries are rare."

Aaron ambled over to stand beside her. It took everything in her not to tense at his closeness. The bastard knew he made her uncomfortable, and he liked it. Damned if she'd give him even more satisfaction by showing him.

"Our boss will want an update later tonight. Make sure you have a general idea of what's in the latest haul." With that, he left her alone.

Thankful for small favors, Sam went back to work. As much as she wanted to rush to the latest finds and dig through them, she forced herself to continue cataloging the pistol. When it had been tagged, photographed, logged, and set on the table with the other artifacts, she decided enough time had passed. If anyone was watching her, she wouldn't seem too eager.

She went to the plastic tub where they'd piled the latest items and began to pull them out one by one and set them on another table to better view them. She was surprised to see a glint of gold. She rubbed the spot of what appeared to be part of a chain, revealing more of the precious metal. It was a necklace.

At least she'd be able to tell Aaron he was getting some gold out of the trip, even though she didn't think he'd appreciate it.

There was something totally unexpected near the bottom of the tub. A fairly large pottery urn with a broad top. She set it carefully on the table, her excitement mounting. It was still sealed. Whatever was inside could be preserved.

Of course, it might be nothing. But she didn't think so. Her senses were humming so loudly she was practically vibrating. She'd ignored the sensation because they'd been humming ever since the *Integrity* had arrived at the search site.

This was different. Whatever was inside this urn was significant. Still, she forced herself to go through her normal routine of tagging, snapping pictures, and logging it into inventory before she reached for a sharp knife to break the seal.

She shouldn't be doing this so quickly. Not without extensive consultation and thought. She could potentially destroy whatever was inside. If this were a normal marine recovery, she'd set it aside until she was back on shore and had more equipment available.

But she couldn't wait. This might be the only chance she would get to see what was inside before Karina Azarov took possession of the artifact. She took a deep breath, slipped the knife around the edge of the opening to the pottery jar, and carefully cut through the heavy wax seal that covered the entire top and several inches down the sides.

It wasn't easy. Even after all this time, the urn did not want to give up its secrets.

Once she'd loosened the seal, she jammed the knife downward and pried the layer of wax off. It revealed another stopper. This one was metal and took even more effort to maneuver.

She was sweating by the time it finally gave way. She set the knife down and lifted the metal stopper, carefully placing it on the table. Her heart pounding, she grabbed a flashlight and shone it into the opening. It was empty except for another smaller jar and the straw padding used to cushion it.

Sam took a deep breath and then another. When she was calm enough, she lifted the urn onto its side and carefully tipped the contents onto the table. The smaller jar rolled out, and she caught it before it could fall off the table.

When she had the larger urn upright once again, she turned her attention to the jar. It was more ornate than the larger one, with symbols from different cultures running all around the side. The markings confused her. They were a combination of protection and warning that what was inside was extremely powerful.

She didn't need any symbols to tell her that. The jar was pulsing with energy. Anyone else might not be able to feel it, but there was no hiding it from her gift.

A more primitive part of her psyche screamed at her to destroy whatever was inside. It was dangerous. That much she knew for sure.

Her timetable had just been moved up. She had to get out of here tonight.

• • •

Ezra raked his hair back from his face, squeezing the water from the thick strands. The ocean always invigorated him. Naked, he stood on his dock and watched the waves. Thirty feet from shore, a whale breached the surface before disappearing once again into the depths. The forty-foot female humpback had raced alongside him for a time, and he'd slowed so she could join him in their mutual enjoyment of flying through the water.

He padded back up to the house, his stomach grumbling all the way. Definitely time to eat. Drakons burned a lot more calories than humans did. And after a two-hour swim, Ezra was starving.

Not bothering with clothes—one of the perks of living alone—he went to the kitchen and opened the refrigerator door. He'd put four large flank steaks in there to marinate while he was gone.

The grill pan was already on the stove, so he turned it on to heat it up. While he was waiting, he helped himself to a bottle of water, grabbed his phone off of the counter, and checked his messages.

There was only one, and it was from Tarrant, asking him to call back. It was answered on the first ring. "What's up?" he asked.

"Picked up some chatter." Tarrant was a world-class hacker. He'd been fascinated with technology since its inception and owned the largest telecommunications company in the world.

"About?" He took a swig of water and wandered back to the stove. Deeming the pan hot enough, he grabbed a set of tongs and put the steaks on the grill.

"Seems Karina Azarov has a boat off the coast of Maine not too far from you."

"That so?" He hadn't noticed any unusual boats to the northeast, so it must be more south.

"That's so. And according to Valeriya, this particular boat is a research vessel, one that salvages shipwrecks." Now that was interesting, and Valeriya would know. Ezra still had a hard time wrapping his head around the idea that his brother was involved with the sister of the head of the Knights of the Dragon, but there was no doubting Valeriya's devotion to Tarrant.

"Any idea what the Knights are looking for?"

There was some tapping in the background, and Ezra knew his brother was doing some sort of search with his computer. He took the opportunity to flip the steaks.

"According to what I've been able to access, which isn't a lot, it's a passenger ship that went down in the eighteen hundreds."

"Must have something pretty special on board for them to go to all that trouble." Karina Azarov didn't do anything unless there was some gain in it for her.

"That's what we need to find out. If they're up to something, you can stop them. I'm texting you the approximate coordinates."

Ezra checked the steaks on the grill, deemed them done, and lifted them onto a clean plate. "What exactly are you saying, Tarrant?"

The war between the Knights and the drakons had been ongoing for centuries, but in the past few weeks, it had ramped up to a whole new level. Darius was being actively hunted, and Tarrant's home had almost been destroyed. The drakons had been content to live and let live. That had proved to be a mistake. It had made the Knights bolder and deadlier.

But the time had come to take a stand. The Knights didn't care who they hurt in their hunt for power. They'd killed thousands of innocent humans over the centuries, and most recently a good friend of Tarrant's, and his brother didn't make friends easily.

"Find out what the Knights are doing out there, get any artifacts if there are any to get, and scuttle the ship."

"You want me to kill them?" It was one thing to protect himself, quite another to murder people in cold blood. "What if some of the crew is innocent?"

Tarrant swore. "Just sink the damn ship. They can get back to shore using their lifeboats. But at least they won't be able to use that particular ship again."

Ezra could live with that. "I'll check it out tonight."

"Make sure you're not seen. They don't need to know who you are."

"I know how to go undetected in the water," he reminded his brother. "I am a water drakon."

Tarrant sighed. "I know. I'm on edge with everything going on right now."

"How is Valeriya?" That was the one subject guaranteed to take his brother's mind off his troubles.

"She's doing great. Almost finished work on her latest book." Valeriya wrote and illustrated children's books.

"Tell her I'm looking forward to reading it." It might be

for kids, but Ezra had ordered copies of her books about a friendly little dragon. He'd read them and liked them.

"I will. I gotta go, but let me know how things turn out."

"Will do." Ezra ended the call and tossed his cell phone on the counter. He could check the coordinates of the ship before he left. Right now, the steaks were done. He should have baked some potatoes to go with them, but he was too hungry to wait.

He carried his meal to the table, dug up a fork and knife, and began to eat. By the time he finished the last one, the worst of his hunger was sated. He carried his dishes to the kitchen and tucked them into the dishwasher.

The house was quiet. He didn't own a television. Anything he wanted to watch, he streamed on his laptop. He had a large sectional sofa and a couple of large chairs flanking the stone fireplace, but he usually sat at the window seat. He liked being able to see the water.

He mounted the stairs and went to the master suite. Drakons didn't need a lot of sleep, but he was tired. He'd been pushing himself hard since his family had left. Seeing his brothers with their women had made him realize just how empty his life was.

He stretched out naked on the bed, stacked his hands behind his head, and stared up at the ceiling. Fluorescent stars glowed out of the darkness. He'd put hundreds of the stickers up there for nights when it was foggy outside and he was unable to view the real stars in the sky through the two skylights.

He closed his eyes and took a deep breath. He'd rest for an hour or two and then he'd head out.

Chapter Three

Sam held her breath as footsteps sounded in the corridor just beyond the workroom. It was after midnight, and everyone was in their bunk except for the two men on duty. One was in the wheelhouse, and the other was walking the decks.

Once the footsteps receded, she turned on the tiny penlight she clutched in her hands. Her heart was pounding so loudly she was surprised the guard hadn't heard it and come to check on the noise. She wasn't cut out for this cloak and dagger stuff, but she was determined.

She crept over to the table where she'd left the smaller of the two jars earlier. Such a tiny thing to hide such a dangerous artifact. Inside had been a book, no more than five inches long and four inches wide. It was small. The kind of thing a man might keep tucked away in the inside pocket of his coat. It had been wrapped in oiled cloth before being deposited in the jar. Whoever had owned this book had gone to great lengths to protect it.

Now, Sam was taking desperate measures to make sure it stayed out of the hands of the Knights. When she'd unwrapped it earlier, she'd stuffed a necklace inside and hid the book in a desk drawer. It had been a gamble, but it had paid off.

Aaron hadn't been pleased to discover the seals on the urn and vase broken and only a gold necklace hidden inside. At least that was the story she'd told him. Thankfully, he'd seemed to accept it.

Now she was back in the middle of the night to retrieve the book. She had to get off the ship with it or destroy it.

She eased the desk drawer open. The tiny volume sat there looking inconspicuous with the plain brown leather cover. There was nothing particularly exciting about it from the outside. Sam hadn't even risked opening the cover of the thing. She didn't have to. It positively radiated power. She didn't question her instincts. They'd never been wrong.

She hesitated before lifting the book. The oils from her skin could damage the binding. She grabbed a latex glove but didn't bother to put it on, using it to cover her skin as she stuffed the book into a small plastic bag. When it was secure, she shoved it into the inner pocket of her coat. She had much bigger things to worry about than damaging the cover of the book.

She'd debated whether or not she should wait to see if any other artifacts were brought on board before making an attempt to escape. But she sensed Aaron was getting impatient, and that probably stemmed from their employer also losing patience. Sam didn't know how much longer they'd be here, or if she'd even make it back to shore alive if she stayed longer.

It was now or never.

She'd spent every day since she'd first stepped onto the *Integrity* studying the layout of the research vessel. She knew where the lifeboats and dinghy were and how to access them. It was crazy to think she'd be able to steal one without anyone noticing, but it was a chance she had to take.

She tucked her flashlight away and listened at the door for several minutes before cracking it open. The dim light shone in the hallways, showing her it was empty. Sam hurried toward the opening at the far end. The rubber soles of her sneakers allowed her to move silently.

The book in her pocket felt incredibly heavy for such a small thing. It would lead to her death if she was caught, of that she had no doubt.

She stepped out onto the deck and immediately slid to the left into the shadows. The closer she got to freedom, the more anxious she became. She was sweating now, her thermal shirt beneath her sweater and coat was stuck to her skin.

She shivered in the cold night air.

This was crazy. It was late November and she was contemplating escaping in a dinghy. If she fell in the water without a survival suit, she wouldn't last long.

"Don't think about it," she whispered under her breath. She had to think about Brian, her mentor, and the other innocent people the Knights had murdered. This was some small measure of justice for them.

In the back of her mind, Sam knew there was no going back to the life she'd known. The Knights would be searching for her and wouldn't stop until they found her. Her life had been forfeit the moment she'd agreed to take the position aboard this ship. Maybe it had been forfeit when Brian was killed, and she'd been living on borrowed time ever since.

She'd moved money into an offshore account under an assumed name and had a new passport and other identification with that name. All she had to do was get back to shore, grab her escape bag from the storage unit where she'd stashed it, and get out of the country before the Knights realized she'd left. A tall order, for sure.

At the very least, she could try to get the book to the people who'd recruited her in the first place. She didn't know much about the Dragon Guard, but she knew they'd protect the book or destroy it after they'd studied its contents. Her contact at the Guard, Gervais Rames, had gone missing several months ago. She had no idea if he was dead, hiding, or on some mission of his own, but if she couldn't find him, she'd destroy the book herself.

All this thinking and speculating wasn't getting her off the ship.

She glanced around and found the sentry having a smoke up near the bow of the ship. She knew the man in the wheelhouse spent most of his time reading unless something came up. It was now or never.

She hurried down the port side toward the stern. She ignored the larger lifeboats and focused on the small inflatable dinghy the divers used. It was lashed to the ship just where she'd expected it to be.

She glanced over her shoulder as icy fear snaked down her spine. She couldn't get over the sensation that someone was watching her. The rope was slippery from the water that occasionally splashed against it. Her fingers slipped, and she struggled not to start swearing.

This was taking far too long.

Finally, the knot gave way, and she lowered the boat into the water. It hit with a splash. Still, no one called out or raised an alarm.

She quickly went over the side of the boat, landing hard in the dinghy. Where was the paddle? She was almost blind here in the darkness. Why hadn't she secured the paddle before lowering the boat?

She frantically patted the side of the dinghy. A wave of relief hit her when her fingers wrapped around wood. She lifted it and dipped it over the side and into the ocean. Then she began to paddle as though her life depended on it. Because it did.

• • •

Ezra was in his human form about twenty feet from the boat, trying to decide on the best way to sneak onboard, when he first caught sight of the woman creeping along the port side. With his preternatural vision, he could see perfectly. It was obvious she was trying to hide. She had a black wool hat pulled down over her head, was swathed in a large dark coat, and moved furtively along the deck, keeping to the shadows.

He glanced at the bow of the ship where the lone guard stood, cigarette in hand. Ezra had circled the boat twice already, and this seemed to be the only man keeping watch outside.

Who was the woman, and what was she doing?

His dragon stirred inside, wanting him to move closer. He glided until he was only about fifteen feet away. She glanced over her shoulder, but he knew she couldn't see him in the dark.

He watched while she untied the rubber dinghy and dropped it into the water. Was she leaving? Curiosity piqued, he drifted closer and watched her frantically trying to find the paddle. He sensed her relief when she finally found it. Seconds later, she began to paddle.

A spotlight came on, shining right at the dinghy. Ezra managed to duck beneath the waves and swim into the shadows before it caught him in its glow. By the time he surfaced, a man was standing on the deck with a gun pointed at the woman.

A slow anger began to burn inside Ezra.

"You didn't really think I bought the whole story about there being nothing in the urn but a necklace, did you, Sam?"

To give the woman credit, she didn't stop paddling. "You wanted gold, Aaron. Now you have some. That necklace is worth a small fortune."

"But it's nowhere near as valuable as what you have in your pocket." He laughed when her hand went to her jacket. "I knew the second you went back to the lab. There's nowhere on this ship you can go without me knowing about it. Now stop." He fired a shot that landed just in front of the dinghy. Sam set the paddle down on the floor of the boat.

"I can't let you have this."

Ezra could tell the woman was terrified but was trying to appear brave. He wondered what she had that was more valuable than gold. Whatever it was, it was probably what he'd come here to retrieve.

She pulled a small plastic bag from her pocket and opened it. The angle she held it at made it impossible for Ezra to see what was inside. The man on deck began to swear. "Don't do anything stupid," he warned her. "We can talk about this."

She laughed, but there was no humor in it. "I've always known you planned to kill me. Just like you killed Brian."

"Who the hell is Brian?" the man demanded.

She held the open bag out over the rim of the dinghy, perilously close to the waves. "Brian was my mentor. He was the only family I had. Well, you can all rot in hell before I'll give you this book. If I can't have it, no one can."

What had Ezra stumbled into? A power play among members of the Knights? Those in the lower ranks of the society frequently jockeyed for position, often killing one another to move upward. There was little honor among them.

He didn't like thinking that about the woman, but he didn't know what else to believe. His dragon didn't like her talking about another man, even if she spoke of him as though he was family. He struggled to keep the creature in check and stay in his human form. Now was not the time to shift. Not yet.

"Come on, Sam," the man called Aaron cajoled. "We can work this out. There's no reason for you to do this."

"I can't." She shook her head and looked resigned.

"That's really too bad." Aaron raised his weapon.

Ezra realized what he was about to do and rocketed through the water, shifting on the fly. His dragon became a living torpedo with a single target.

A shot rang out just as he rammed the *Integrity*. He heard men yelling as the boat shuddered and shook and began to take on water from the huge hole in the bow. Ezra circled and rammed the ship again, this time driving it onto its side.

He used his powerful wings to propel him underwater and back to the side of the dinghy. It had also taken on water when the bigger vessel faltered. The woman—Sam—lay on her side on the bottom of the small boat, blood mixing with the seawater puddled around her.

There was no time to waste. He grabbed the line from the dinghy in his mouth and began to swim, cutting through the water. He had no idea how badly she'd been wounded. He wasn't even quite sure why he cared, but he did.

He couldn't let her die. He needed to know more about her, why she was with the Knights, and what was in that bag she'd been holding. He hadn't noticed the plastic bag in the boat. Oh well, if it was there, he'd find it, and if she'd dropped it overboard, it had already sunk to the bottom of the ocean.

The crew from the *Integrity* wouldn't be retrieving it tonight. They'd be too busy trying to save their own lives.

Once Ezra had Sam settled in his home, he could swim back and check on the wreck and the artifact, if need be.

Chapter Four

Ezra grabbed the edge of the wharf and hauled himself out of the water. It had taken him almost an hour to get here even at top speed. He was exhausted, but he ignored the fatigue in his limbs.

Had Sam died on the way here? He'd stopped out of sight of the wreck long enough to check on her, but it had been impossible to tell just how badly she was injured. He hadn't wanted to remove her jacket to examine the wound because it was cold, and she needed all the layers she could get. In the end, he'd found a man's sweater on the floor of the boat, ripped it enough to form a bandage, and wrapped that on the outside of her coat. It was all he'd been able to do while they were at sea.

He reached into the boat and lifted her limp body. His fatigue slipped away only to be replaced by worry. Her skin was cool and pale. He placed two fingers on the side of her neck and found a fluttering pulse.

She was still alive.

He hurried up the dock toward the house. He only had a

couple of hours until dawn, maybe less. Before the sun rose, he needed to get Sam settled and sink that dinghy far away from his island.

He shoved the door open. It was never locked since he lived by himself on an island. Dripping water everywhere, he carried her up the stairs. He hesitated outside one of the guest rooms before heading to the master. He carefully set Sam down on his bed and turned on the bedside light.

She moaned and moved restlessly. The corners of her mouth turned down. She was obviously in pain.

He unwrapped the makeshift bandage, but it wasn't easy. The water had made the knot tight. Sam moaned when he accidentally hurt her. "I'm sorry." He hated causing her more pain, but there was nothing he could do.

He tossed the soggy mess on the floor and started on her coat next. He swore under his breath as he removed her outer layer and then the sweater underneath. The left side of her thermal shirt was splotched with blood.

He left her long enough to grab the first-aid kit from the bathroom. Placing it on the bed beside her, he popped open the top. He didn't have much experience with this kind of thing. He was hard to injure and quick to heal.

Sam was human and much more fragile.

He grabbed the scissors and cut the sleeve of her shirt, exposing a seeping wound. He leaned closer to inspect it. It was just a flesh wound. She'd gotten lucky, and he didn't think it was because the man who'd shot her was inexperienced. It was most likely because she'd moved just in the nick of time.

He left her long enough to get a pan of warm, soapy water and a clean cloth. Working quickly, he cleaned the wound, being careful to remove all the fibers embedded in it from her shirt. It had stopped bleeding, but it was doing so again by the time he was finished. Once he was sure it was free from any debris, he disinfected and covered it with a thick bandage secured with gauze. It was the best he could do.

Now that the worst had been taken care of, Ezra took a good look at his houseguest for the first time.

She was still wearing the dark watch cap on her head. He pulled it off and was surprised to find a shock of red hair hidden beneath. The curls seemed to explode from beneath the cap. He hadn't expected her to be a redhead, not with her porcelain skin and no freckles in sight. Her face was more heart shaped than round, and she had a stubborn chin and straight nose.

His breathing quickened when he realized he was becoming aroused just looking at her. And he was still naked. If she woke now, she'd probably scream the house down.

He left her long enough to drag on a pair of sweatpants. That would do for now.

She shivered, and he felt like smacking himself in the head. She was still wearing wet clothes. She had to be freezing. She couldn't regulate her body temperature like he could.

He started at her feet and removed her water-logged sneakers first. He'd have to take them downstairs and put them somewhere to dry. He removed her jeans next. That wasn't an easy task. They were soaking wet and stuck to her like a second skin. He thought about just cutting them off, but that would leave her with nothing to wear.

He set to work, patiently drawing the cold fabric down her legs.

• • •

Sam's arm throbbed and felt as though it were on fire. What had happened? She lay trying to get her bearings when she felt someone tugging on her jeans. Fear tasted acrid and sour in her mouth. Had Aaron done something to her?

Why couldn't she remember what had happened? And

where was she?

Feigning sleep, she opened her eyes a slit and immediately slammed them shut. It wasn't Aaron touching her, but a man she'd never seen before.

He was big. Maybe the biggest man she'd ever seen. He was naked from the waist up and had broad shoulders and rippling abs, the kind she'd never seen outside of a magazine cover.

His shoulder-length brown hair was damp and framed a ruggedly handsome face. His lips were compressed into a hard line as he worked her jeans off. Why the hell was he removing her clothing? Why were they wet? And why was she so cold?

"I know you're awake," he told her.

Her eyes flew open before she could stop herself. A gaze as turquoise as a Mediterranean sea studied her. She'd never seen anyone with eyes quite that color before. She licked her salty lips, suddenly not nearly as cold as she'd been only moments before.

Then sanity returned, along with a shot of adrenaline, and she kicked him, or tried to. She was so damn weak. "What do you think you're doing? Leave my clothes alone."

"You need to get warm. They're not helping." Ignoring her feeble attempts to stop him, he dragged her jeans off and tossed them aside.

Her shivering increased. "Where am I?"

"You're in my home." He seemed to hesitate, his brows lowering and his features settling into a fierce glare. "You were drifting in a dinghy." He watched her as if waiting for something, some recognition.

She surged upward and then cried out as pain bolted down her left arm.

"Whoa." He caught her and eased her back down. "You're not going anywhere at the moment. You were shot."

Aaron. Her attempted escape. The sound of gunfire.

"You—" She ignored the fatigue pulling at her and pushed beyond the pain throbbing through her arm and down her shoulder. Sweat beaded on her forehead. "You have to let me go." It was too dangerous for her to be around this man, whoever he was. "Not safe." Aaron and the Knights would be searching for her.

The book.

Ignoring the pain, she surged upright and began frantically searching for her coat.

"What are you looking for?" His deep voice shocked her from her panic.

It occurred to her she was in a strange place with a strange man and no idea how she'd gotten here. She didn't know if he was with the Knights or not. "Nothing." She couldn't afford to trust anyone. "Who are you?" she demanded.

"Ezra," he told her as he reached down, picked up her coat, and began to methodically go through the pockets.

"Leave that alone." She tried to sound assertive, but she was too weak for it to come out as more than a whisper. She was shivering harder now and her teeth began to chatter.

Ezra yanked the baggie out of the inside pocket of her coat. "Is this what you're looking for?" He was watching her, not looking at what he was holding.

She gave a curt nod. "Dangerous. Have to keep it safe."

He studied her intently, and in spite of the chills wracking her frame, she began to feel warmer. He opened the bedside table and tossed the book still in the bag into the drawer. "It's safe enough there."

As though she were a child, he worked the tattered remains of her thermal shirt off, leaving her only in her underwear. She was very conscious of being nearly naked around a stranger, a stranger who'd seemingly saved her life, but a stranger nonetheless.

When he reached for the strap of her bra, she jerked back.

He crossed his arms over his extremely large chest and pinned her with a glare. "You can't rest in wet clothes."

"I'm not getting naked in front of you." She might be weak, but she was still a fighter. One corner of his mouth quirked upward, softening his harsh features and making him look even more handsome. There was something primal and compelling about him.

"You're weak and need help," he needlessly pointed out.

"Bully," she countered.

"I'm concerned about your health. You're borderline hypothermic." She knew he was right, but she still couldn't make herself get naked in front of a stranger.

Finally, he sighed and walked over to a large closet door. He yanked it open and pulled out a flannel shirt. "Put this on." He brought it to the bed and handed it to her. Then he turned his back.

Sam figured this was as good as it was going to get. And honestly, she was too tired to argue further. She tried to reach around and unhook her bra, but it was difficult with only one good arm. And when she tried to twist, she hurt her injured one.

As soon as she moaned in pain, Ezra whirled around. Without saying a word, he unhooked her bra and eased the straps down her arms before tossing the plain cotton garment aside.

She was blushing. She could feel the heat creeping up her cheeks. Ezra ignored her bare breasts and concentrated on maneuvering her arms into the armholes of the shirt. When it was on, he buttoned the garment. It was so large it was more like a flannel nightshirt. It was warm and cozy and made her feel safe. It also smelled slightly of him, like salt air on a crisp day.

The backs of his fingers brushed against her skin as he worked his way to the last button. Sam sucked in a breath but didn't say a word. She wasn't sure she could speak.

She couldn't remember the last time she responded so quickly and completely to a man. He had big hands that could snap her like a twig, but he was incredibly gentle as he finished securing the garment.

Before she could relax, he thrust his hands under the hem. Sam shrieked and tried to bat his hands away, but he grabbed the waistband of her underwear and peeled them off. Now she was naked but for the shirt.

As much as it pained her to admit it, it felt good to have the wet clothes away from her skin. She was already feeling warmer.

Ezra lifted her enough to pull the covers out from under her. Then he tucked her beneath them. She automatically curled onto her side and almost saw stars when she put pressure on her wound. How could she have forgotten to be careful of a gunshot wound?

Panting hard, she rolled onto her back. She felt Ezra hovering over her, but thankfully, he didn't ask any questions. Finally, the pain and the sick feeling in her stomach passed enough for her to open her eyes.

"How bad is it?" She gestured to her bandaged arm.

"Flesh wound. Could have been worse. Infection is your biggest problem."

Sam nodded. She couldn't go to a hospital. Come to think of it, why hadn't Ezra taken her to a hospital? "Where am I?"

"My home."

She frowned. That told her exactly nothing. Fatigue swamped her, and she yawned before she could form her next question.

"Sleep. You're safe here."

Oddly enough, she believed him. She'd travelled all over the world, relying on her instincts to keep her safe. They'd never steered her wrong. Getting in trouble with the Knights had been her own doing. She'd ignored her instincts in her search for justice. If Ezra wanted to hurt her, there was nothing she could do to stop him in her condition. He'd done just the opposite, taking care of her in spite of her protests.

Her eyes fluttered shut and she sank into the warm bed, letting it cradle her. She thought she felt his hand brush her hair. It was a totally unexpected gesture of kindness and made her eyes prickle with unshed tears.

The stress from her attempted escape, from living and working under pressure for so long coupled with the trauma of her injury and the cold, pulled her under. She should warn Ezra about the Knights of the Dragon. She was leaving him vulnerable.

She tried to open her mouth to speak, but darkness swept her away before she could utter a single word.

• • •

Ezra knew the moment Sam lost consciousness. Her entire body relaxed and the hand clutching the covers released its death grip. She was like a flame with her red hair vibrant and alive against his plain white pillowcase. Her eyes were a brilliant green and filled with intelligence and strength.

He glanced down at the front of his pants and shook his head in wonder. He was as hard as a rock. That was unusual. Sure, he had a healthy sex drive, but he'd always been in control of it. He'd met some of the most beautiful women who'd ever lived during his long lifetime. Some he'd watched from a distance, others he'd shared more intimate relationships with, but never had he been in anything less than perfect control.

Why Sam? Why now?

He gathered her belongings and started to leave the room, hesitating at the doorway, not wanting to leave her. He should be more worried about what was in the book she'd stolen.

Whatever it was, it was dangerous and should be locked in his safe until it could be examined properly.

But he'd promised her it would be safe in the nightstand drawer.

"And if she's a Knight?" he muttered. Just because she'd been shot by one of them didn't mean she wasn't one. It could have been a falling out among the ranks.

He silently padded back to the nightstand and withdrew the book. The feeling he was betraying her nagged at him. "Best to keep it safe." He left the room before he did something stupid like return the book to the drawer and curl up alongside Sam.

With the soggy mass of clothes in one hand and the book in the other, he headed to his office long enough to deposit the book in a titanium floor vault with a retinal scanner and a twenty-four-digit code. He'd laughed at Tarrant when his brother had insisted he install it. He wasn't laughing now.

When the book was secured, he took the clothes to the laundry room. The thermal shirt and the garment he'd used as a bandage were only fit for the garbage. He studied the sweater she'd been wearing and decided that belonged in the garbage, too. That left her jeans, socks, underwear, and coat. Shrugging, Ezra threw it all into the washer and set the cycle.

Now it was time for him to dispose of the evidence.

He carried her sneakers to the front entrance and set them on the mat to dry. Then he carried the bloody garments down the path to the dinghy. He hated leaving Sam alone, even though he knew her body needed rest and she'd probably sleep for hours.

He dumped the clothes into the dinghy and stared out over the water. Dawn was starting to break as he removed his track pants and set them on the dock. He dove into the ocean, grabbed the rope of the dinghy, and began to swim. He cut quickly and efficiently through the water, heading toward the perfect place to dump the boat and clothes. There could be no trace of Sam to lead back to him.

Maybe the Knights would think she'd died at sea. He snorted. Not likely. They'd search until they found a body, watch for reports of a body washing onshore, or if there was activity in any of her bank accounts, but eventually they'd decide she was either dead or gone.

He paused when he reached a particularly deep chasm in the ocean floor. It wasn't large, but it was more than big enough to hide a dinghy. He embraced the creature inside him, allowing his dragon free rein. Even after all these years, it was still a rush to feel his body changing. Even his mental processes were different. He was still present, but he was ruled by a more primitive mind and primal instincts.

He caught the dinghy between his teeth and spiraled down into the water. All around him, smaller fish fled. A great white shark started toward him, only to have second thoughts and veer away, heading toward open water.

Ezra went down to the depths of the ocean that would crush a man, to the dark where no light penetrated. He shoved the remains of the dingy deep into a crevice. Then he moved several boulders on top of it to keep it in place. It would never be found.

He turned away from the darkness and shot back toward the light of dawn. Sam was waiting at home for him. His dragon half was as eager to get back to her as his human side. Both parts of him yearned to be closer, to protect her.

She was his. He'd found her in the ocean, plucked her from the sea. By the laws of maritime salvage, that meant she belonged to him now.

• • •

Karina Azarov was not happy. "What do you mean, the

Integrity is gone?" Her personal bodyguard, Birch, had woken her in the middle of the night to inform her she had an emergency phone call. It was not news she wanted.

"Something hit the ship. Hard. And not just once. Rammed it right over on its side."

She tightened her fingers around the phone, when what she really wanted was to wring Aaron Dexter's neck. Why was she surrounded by incompetence? "A whale?"

"Uncertain. One of the men managed to take a grainy video."

"Send it to me." If there was a way to determine what had happened, she'd find it. Maybe it was nothing but bad luck, but Karina didn't believe in luck, good or bad. She forged her own path in the world. Hard work and determination were the keys to success. And she'd be damned if she didn't get what she wanted, what she'd worked her entire life for.

"Already done?"

"And Sam Bellamy? Is she alive or dead?"

"Unknown. No body."

A tiny niggling began in the back of her mind. It was a sign she didn't ignore. Aaron Dexter was holding out on her. "Was anything of significance discovered from the shipwreck before the *Integrity* was hit?"

Again, there was a slight hesitation before he replied. "Uncertain. There were artifacts that hadn't been examined yet."

"So what you're telling me is that both the good Dr. Bellamy and a possible artifact are both missing?" She knew it in her gut. "Don't lie to me, Aaron. I'll know if you do."

There was silence, and then he finally relented. "There was something, an artifact of some kind. She was trying to get off the ship with it when we were hit. By the time we got to the lifeboats, the dinghy she was in was gone. I assume it got dragged down with the *Integrity*."

Idiot. "Assume nothing. Get out there and find her, or at least her body. I want whatever she found recovered."

"I'll take care of it."

She ended the call before he could say more. Birch was waiting, silent and patient. "Aaron Dexter is a problem. He let Dr. Bellamy get off the *Integrity* with an artifact, one that might be important. Even now, it may be lost because of his incompetence."

Karina carefully set her phone down on her nightstand and began to pace her bedroom. Normally she would do anything not to appear weak in any way, but this was Birch. He'd been with her since she was a child. He was more mentor and father to her than her own had been.

She turned to him. "I need to see what's on that video." Maybe it was nothing, but it was better to be sure.

"I've already got our best tech working on it," he assured her.

His calm demeanor settled her. She could always count on Birch. "Dexter is not reliable." She'd suspected that for a while now.

"No. He probably spent more time trying to get Dr. Bellamy to sleep with him than watching her."

Karina walked toward him. "Why didn't you tell me?"

"You already knew." That was Birch. Others might cower in fear from her, but he kept her honest.

"You're right. I knew he fancied himself a ladies' man, but I still thought he could do the damn job. It was simple. The woman is an archaeologist and was confined to a ship in the middle of the ocean. How hard could it have been to watch her? He'll have to be dealt with when we're sure we know everything that happened. Until then, we keep a close eye on him."

"Temple will cause problems," Birch reminded her.

"We'll keep this quiet until we know more." She headed

to the bathroom. There would be no more sleep for her. She might as well shower and start her day.

"Do you want it salvaged? I can contact a local company and have them try to refloat the *Integrity*. We don't know if there was more than one artifact and what else might be on board."

Karina paused in the bathroom door. "You're right. Get the best in the business. I want them out there assessing the situation today. There's no time to waste."

She closed the bathroom door and allowed herself a moment to sigh. She didn't need complications, not with Herman Temple and a few others making trouble for her. Her sister's disappearance hadn't helped matters. Valeriya vanishing had caused her unwanted problems, and she already had enough to deal with.

She squared her shoulders and headed to the shower. She would find Darius Varkas, find and dispose of her sister, deal with Temple and his cronies, and recover whatever it was that Dr. Bellamy had stolen from her.

She was the leader of the Knights, and she would have what she wanted—power and revenge. They were great motivators.

Chapter Five

The sun was making the ocean waves sparkle like diamonds by the time Ezra made it back to the dock. He usually liked to sit outside and watch the ebb and flow of the tide, listen to the seabirds, and feel the wind against his skin when he returned from a swim.

Not today.

Today, he grabbed the pair of sweatpants he'd left on the dock and hurried toward the house. It was no longer empty. She was waiting for him, in his bed.

He was practically running by the time he hit the porch. He paused and laid his hand against the front door. What was he doing? Sam wasn't waiting for him. She was injured and sleeping.

Ezra raked his fingers through his wet hair, not bothered by the droplets of water running down his back. He needed to proceed with caution. He knew nothing about this woman. The fact that he was so attracted to her was a red flag. He'd never felt so attached to a woman so quickly in his long life.

He took a deep breath, opened the door, and stepped

inside. Silence met him. Good, that meant she was still sleeping. He climbed the stairs, keeping his tread light. Unable to stay away from her, he went to his room and stood next to the bed.

Sam's eyes were closed, hiding the vibrant green color. She still looked pale, but that wasn't surprising considering she'd lost quite a bit of blood from the wound on her arm. Or maybe she was normally pale. There was so much about her he didn't know, including her last name. If she'd had any identification on her, it had been lost at sea.

Time slipped by, and it was only when his stomach growled that he realized he was just standing there watching her. He forced himself to turn away when what he really wanted to do was pull back the covers and climb in beside her.

After collecting jeans and a long-sleeved shirt, he went to the bathroom and closed the door. He needed to shower off the salt water and then get something to eat. Maybe by then Sam would be awake and ready to talk.

• • •

Sam's eyes snapped open the second she heard the door close. She sat upright and looked around.

Where am I?

Everything was vague. She'd escaped from the *Integrity*, or had she? No, Aaron had shot her. Then something had rammed the salvage vessel. It was all a bit of a blur after that. She had no idea how she'd ended up here.

And where exactly was *here*?

The sound of water running made her turn her head toward a closed door. An image of a man popped into her head. A very big, ruggedly handsome man with brown hair and turquoise eyes and… She closed her eyes and formed a mental image. Tattoos. He had vibrant swirling tattoos covering his left arm and torso. He'd said his name was Ezra.

She opened her eyes again and lightly touched her injured arm. It was bandaged beneath the oversize flannel shirt she was wearing.

The book!

Ignoring the pain in her arm, she reached toward the nightstand. He'd put the book in there, told her it would be safe. She yanked it open and gave a small cry of dismay. It was gone.

"Stupid," she muttered. Stupid to have trusted him. Had he really rescued her, or was she a prisoner?

Not willing to take a chance, she eased off the bed. The world spun, but she used the mattress and nightstand to keep herself upright. When she figured she wouldn't collapse in a heap, she took her first step toward the door. She glanced at the bathroom, half expecting Ezra to come charging out to stop her.

When that didn't happen, she moved faster. She was weak, but at least her knees weren't in as much danger of buckling. She clung to the banister to make sure she didn't fall down the stairs. The main floor was mostly open with the living and dining area flowing into a kitchen.

Sam headed for the front door.

When she opened it, the cold November wind blew under the hem of the shirt she was wearing, reminding her that she was naked beneath it. She stepped out onto the porch, ignoring the way the chill seeped into her bones.

She glanced back inside and almost yelled with relief when she noticed her sneakers sitting on the mat. She stuffed her feet into them, ignoring the fact they were still wet and her feet squished when she walked. They were better than going barefoot.

There was nothing for as far as she could see beyond the dock at the end of the path. Ezra's home was obviously isolated. Did he have a car of truck she could borrow? It wasn't really stealing, she assured herself. She'd leave it somewhere safe once she was away from here.

The wind snapped through her hair, sending the tangle of curls over her face. She impatiently brushed them away and hurried down the steps. Ignoring the biting cold, she began to pick her way around the house, careful not to trip on anything. She couldn't afford any more bumps and bruises. Her body had already taken a beating.

It was insanity to try to get away from here wearing nothing but a man's shirt and a pair of wet sneakers, but there'd been no sign of her clothes. She focused all her attention outward as she circled the house. There was nothing but trees and ocean. By the time she'd reached the front porch again, she had a sinking feeling in her stomach.

She was on an island. Ezra lived on an island. She had no idea if there was anyone else living here, but she hadn't seen any other signs of habitation. The dock directly in front of his home was the only one she could see, and there was no boat there.

What had happened to the dingy she'd been in? And how did he get on and off the island? Did someone else live here with him? Maybe they had the boat.

For the moment, she was stuck here.

She sank down onto the step, pulled her legs toward her body, and wrapped her arms around them. She knew she should go inside, but she no longer felt the cold. She didn't feel anything.

The book was gone. Ezra had taken it. That could only mean one thing—he worked for the Knights of the Dragon. She was trapped as surely as if she were in a prison cell. There was nowhere to go.

• • •

Ezra stepped out of the bathroom already thinking about breakfast and came to a complete stop. She was gone.

He raced out of the room and down the stairs. "Sam?" Where had she gone? Had someone taken her?

No, that was impossible. He hadn't been in the shower long enough for someone to have gotten onto his island and taken her. She had to be here somewhere.

He started to head toward the kitchen but changed direction when he noticed her sneakers were no longer on the mat. The front door was partially open. She'd gone outside.

He charged out onto the deck only to find Sam sitting there with her arms wrapped around her legs, staring out at the water. He fell to his knees beside her. "What's wrong? Why are you out here?"

He touched her face and swore. She was freezing. Not waiting for her reply, he pulled her into his arms, stood, and carried her back inside. He kicked the door shut behind him.

She needed to get warmed up right away. She was a fragile human and couldn't handle the cold the way he could. He set her on the sofa nearest the fireplace and yanked a cashmere throw over her. Darius had bought it for Sarah, to keep her warm on chilly nights. He was glad they'd left it behind.

He removed her sneakers before tucking the ends around her cold, damp feet. He went to the fireplace and lit the kindling there. He might not need a fire to stay warm, but he liked the ambiance one provided. It would be much faster to just breathe drakon fire on the wood, but he wasn't willing to share that secret with her. If she didn't know what he was, he wasn't about to enlighten her. Not yet, at any rate.

When the flames caught and the logs began to crackle, he turned back to Sam. She was sitting there watching him with a blank expression. She looked...defeated. Not at all like the woman who'd stood up to a gun-wielding man.

He went back to her side, crouched down, and began to

rub her legs. The cashmere was soft against his hands, but not as soft as he knew her skin would be. "What were you thinking?" He lowered his voice, kept it quiet and unthreatening.

She sighed and closed her eyes for a brief second before opening them once again. "I don't know who you are or where I am. And the book is gone." The last was said like an accusation.

"I didn't think it was safe sitting in a drawer. Not when it obviously meant so much to you." He was walking a fine line here. He couldn't tell her he knew she'd been shot stealing it. He was supposed to have found her washed ashore in her dinghy, not have actually been there to witness the entire event. "As for your other questions, I told you before, you're in my home, and my name is Ezra."

"But where is your home? And exactly who are you, Ezra?"

He ignored her questions and countered with some of his own. "What happened? How did you end up shot and adrift at sea?" He kept up slow, steady pressure on her legs, pushing the warmth of his palms into her. He really wanted to lie beside her and have her snuggled close, but it was way too soon for that.

She sighed and shrugged, wincing when the movement aggravated her injury. "It's better you don't know."

"Do you want me to call the police?" he asked. Maybe if she thought he was willing to do whatever she wanted, she'd be more open.

She shook her head. "No. It's too dangerous."

"Just what are you involved in, Sam? And why is a book so valuable?"

• • •

Sam studied Ezra. He wore a pair of faded jeans that clung

to him like a second skin and a long-sleeved thermal shirt the color of oatmeal. Nothing special, but he could be on the cover of *Rugged Outdoorsman* or whatever magazine catered to that kind of audience.

He hadn't hurt her when he'd discovered her outside. Quite the opposite. She was ensconced on a comfortable sofa, covered in a soft throw, with a fire adding warmth. And he was rubbing her legs.

Could she trust him? Or would that only put him at risk?

She couldn't take the chance either way. "It's better you don't know."

She sensed his frustration, but he nodded. "You'll tell me when you're ready." His certainty was both annoying and amusing.

Then something that had been niggling at the back of her brain suddenly occurred to her. "How did you know I was shot?" He'd mentioned it twice. How could he know? He certainly hadn't been a member of the crew. She'd have remembered him. And there'd been no other ship in the vicinity last night. He'd said he found her washed ashore.

"You mentioned it." He frowned, appearing concerned.

"I did?"

He shrugged. "You must have. In the meantime," he continued before she could dispute his words, "what's your full name?"

She supposed it didn't really matter if she told him. Once she left here, she was going to grab her new identification, assume a new name, and disappear. "Sam Bellamy."

Ezra stopped rubbing her legs and sat back on the large wooden coffee table. She missed the contact. He crossed his arms over his massive chest and scowled. "If you don't want to tell me the truth, I can accept that. Just don't lie to me."

She frowned. What was he talking about? "I'm not lying."

He shook his head. "You want me to believe you're

named after a pirate, or did you think I wouldn't recognize the name? Black Sam Bellamy is a legend around here. The Prince of Pirates."

This wasn't the first time in her life Sam had been embarrassed by her name. Not everyone recognized it, but Ezra certainly did.

"What does Sam stand for? Samantha?"

She hated having to explain. Her father loved her, she'd never doubted that, but he'd wanted a son. After the delivery, the doctor had informed her parents that her mother wouldn't be able to have more children. A complication with her birth had resulted with her mother having a hysterectomy. Her father had named her for the son he'd wanted.

"Sam?"

"My father wanted a son, okay? He loved the pirate legends and often bragged we were related to *the* Sam Bellamy. I have no idea if it's true or not and don't care. But my name is Sam Bellamy. Sam is short for Samuel." She stared into the fire, unwilling to look at Ezra.

Powerful fingers wrapped gently around her jaw. She tried to resist the light pressure but finally gave in. "Are you happy now? And what's your last name?" Better to be belligerent than to feel sad.

"Thank you for sharing that with me." A slow smile curved his lips upward. "My last name is Easton. Ezra Easton."

Why was he smiling? It took her a second to make the connection. "Easton? After the pirate, Peter Easton?"

He nodded and chuckled. Sam smiled and soon joined in. It was too crazy to be believable, but life was like that.

And she owed this man a debt of gratitude she could never repay. "Thank you for saving my life, for bringing me here, wherever here is, and for tending my wound. I'd be dead if you hadn't found me."

"You're welcome." He took her hands in his. They were

big and strong. Warm. "What happened, Sam? What are you afraid of?"

She couldn't tell him, even if she wanted to. And she discovered she *did* want to share her burden with him. But he wouldn't believe her. The story was far too crazy. Plus, the less he knew, the safer he'd be.

"I can't." She swallowed, suddenly aware she was very thirsty.

Rather than get angry, Ezra nodded. "It's okay. We've got time."

Maybe, or maybe not. The Knights would not give up. If Aaron was alive, he'd be looking for her. Karina Azarov would demand a body as proof of her death. She'd taken something valuable from the Knights. That couldn't be allowed to happen, not without retribution.

She had no family, no close friends. There was only Ezra, the man who'd rescued her from the cold, unforgiving ocean.

She squeezed his hands and then released them. Best not to become any more attached to him than she already was. She was just so damn tired, and he was so big and strong. So solid.

The past year, she'd been living on nerves and dreams of justice. Now it had all fallen apart. Unless she could get away from here before the Knights tracked her to Ezra's home, he would pay the price for her actions.

"I need to leave. It's not safe for me to be here."

"I'll protect you," he promised.

"It's not me I'm worried about." His expression became so fierce she actually leaned away from him. Not that she thought he'd hurt her. After all, he'd had plenty of opportunity, and all he'd done was take care of her.

"Me? You're worried about protecting me?" It was as though the concept was foreign to him. Maybe because he was such a large man, he'd never had to worry about being in danger before.

He'd never dealt with people like the ones after her.

"You have no idea who is looking for me." She shoved the blanket aside and sat up. It was time to get dressed, if she still had any clothes, and get out of here. "These people are dangerous and will stop at nothing to find me. If they don't find a body at the wreck — " She broke off before she said too much.

"So you were in a wreck. I wondered why you were alone in the dinghy. And who is after you?" He stood, looming like a large, avenging angel over her. "You can trust me to protect you."

"You might be willing to risk yourself, but I'm not. I need to leave. Where are my clothes?"

As though she hadn't spoken, Ezra continued. "You must be thirsty. Hungry, too. I'm starving. How about I make some bacon and eggs? Maybe some pancakes and toast." He left her standing there and padded barefoot into the kitchen. Why did she find it so sexy that he was barefoot?

She was obviously not thinking straight, otherwise she wouldn't notice the way his long hair brushed his shoulders, or the way the soft denim cupped his behind as he walked away. Her toes curled against the rug.

She snatched up the throw blanket, wrapped it around her, and hurried after him. "Didn't you hear anything I just told you? It's not safe for you if I'm here. The people looking for me will kill you."

Ezra pulled a carton of eggs, butter, and a package of bacon out of the refrigerator and set them on the counter. He added a box of pancake mix and a bowl to his collection before getting several large skillets out of the cupboard.

"Did you hear me?" she demanded. "They'll kill you."

Ezra propped his hands on his hips and faced her. "Not if I kill them first."

Chapter Six

Ezra had meant to reassure Sam, not scare her. From the look of horror on her face, he hadn't done such a great job. Maybe blurting out that he had no trouble killing anyone who came for her was a mistake, but he wouldn't take it back. He would protect her, no matter what it took.

Tarrant would call him crazy. After all, she could be a member of the Knights. Just because she was running from some of them didn't mean she wasn't working for another faction.

And that was another thing. His brothers needed to be updated. He was surprised Tarrant hadn't already called, demanding to know what was going on.

"Why don't you get a shower?" She had to be feeling less than fresh after everything she'd been through. Her skin and hair would still have residue from the salt water. "I'll whip up some breakfast while you're gone."

She yanked the colorful throw more tightly around her. "Fine. But when I come down, we're going to talk, and you're going to give me some answers." She spun around and stalked toward the stairs. Ezra watched her all the way.

"And you're going to give me some answers, too," he muttered under his breath. The beast inside him growled, not liking the fact that Sam was leaving. He'd never been possessive over a woman before. It was unsettling.

As soon as she was out of sight, he grabbed his cell phone and called his brother. Tarrant answered on the first ring. "Where the hell have you been? I've been calling for hours."

He'd meant to leave the phone on. Obviously, he hadn't. No wonder he hadn't heard from his brother. "I had the phone turned off. You know I'm not fond of all that ringing."

Tarrant growled at him. Ezra couldn't help but grin. "All that ringing? Only three of us have your number."

"And telemarketers," Ezra reminded him. "Those people can find you anywhere. No number is safe from them."

Tarrant made a rather rude and anatomically impossible suggestion. Ezra held the phone away from his ear and chuckled. "Listen, I'm going to put you on speaker, and I don't have a lot of time."

His brother was all business. "What happened? What do you need?"

It was a reminder that his brother was there for him, no matter what. They all were. The bond the four of them shared was unbreakable. "I need to know everything there is to know about a Samuel Bellamy." He could hear computer keys clicking in the background as Tarrant worked. Ezra began to measure out pancake mix for the batter, then decided he should start the bacon frying first.

"There are dozens of people with that name. Can you narrow it down for me? Any idea what this guy does for a living? And where did you meet him? Was he on the *Integrity*?"

Ezra sliced open the package of bacon and began to lay strips out in the pans he'd set out. "First of all, Samuel is a woman. And secondly, she was escaping the *Integrity* in a dinghy when I first saw her."

"What the hell happened, Ezra? No more beating around the bush. Tell me everything."

Keeping one ear out for Sam, Ezra told his brother about watching the fight between Sam and the man aboard the *Integrity*, her getting shot, Ezra sinking the ship, and then bringing Sam back with him.

All the bacon was cooked, and he was starting on the pancakes by the time he was finished recounting the tale.

"Fuck. You should have called me immediately."

"Sorry." He was, but he couldn't have done anything differently. "I had to tend to Sam and sink the dinghy so there'd be no trace to lead anyone here."

The clicking of computer keys hadn't stopped while they were talking. No one on the planet could access information like Tarrant could.

"Okay, here's what I can tell you. Samuel Bellamy is twenty-nine years old. Both her parents are dead, and she had no siblings and no other immediate family."

Ezra wanted to ask if there was a man in her life, but he figured that would make Tarrant lose his mind with worry. Best to ask her himself.

"She's an archaeologist. Has lectured at several universities." Tarrant paused. "This is interesting."

"What?" Ezra poured batter onto the hot skillets and began making pancakes.

"She had a mentor who was killed in a home invasion about a year ago. She was the one to discover the body."

The thoughts of Sam finding the body of her mentor made his heart ache. Sam seemed to be truly alone in the world.

"Do you know if the Knights found anything in the wreckage? Was there anything there we need to be concerned with?"

Ezra scooped six pancakes onto a plate and began to cook the next batch. Once he had them sizzling, he stuck the plate in the warm oven alongside the platter of bacon.

"That's the thing. Sam was trying to get off the ship with a book."

This time, Tarrant's cursing was extra inventive. It was also in several languages. "Have you lost your mind," his brother demanded. "You know how dangerous books belonging to the Knights of the Dragon can be."

"It's secured. I put it in that safe you insisted I needed."

"That's something."

"I've got to go."

"I'm worried, Ezra. You sound way too involved. You should have left the woman with the rest of the crew of the *Integrity*."

Ezra tried not to be angry with his brother. Tarrant didn't understand. "We'll talk more later. Get me everything you can about the crew of the *Integrity* and what's happening with it."

"I'll call you back as soon as I can." Tarrant hung up on him, but Ezra didn't take it personally.

He glanced toward the base of the stairs to find Sam standing there with a look of horror on her face. "What have you done?" she whispered.

• • •

A shower had perked Sam up considerably. It had been awkward and a bit painful to bathe, but well worth it. Just that small amount of activity had exhausted her. What she really needed was some food and about eight solid hours of sleep. But what she needed most was answers.

With none of her own grooming products on hand, she'd been forced to use Ezra's. Unfortunately, that didn't run to conditioner and control serum for curly hair. Still, being clean made up for the wild profusion of curls that bounced around her shoulders. She'd even raided Ezra's closet and dug up a clean flannel shirt, socks, and a pair of sweatpants to go with them. The pants were much too big, but the drawstring kept them up, and she cuffed the legs. The sleeves of the shirt needed to be rolled back several times. She looked ridiculous, but she was warm, clean, and covered. That was all that mattered.

She really needed to find out what Ezra had done with the rest of her clothes. Maybe they hadn't been salvageable.

She started down the stairs, once again clinging to the banister for support. When she heard male voices, she slowed and listened intently. Ezra was talking to someone. And they were talking about the *Integrity* and her.

"What have you done?" she asked when he turned to face her. He tossed aside the phone and started toward her. She held up a hand, surprised when he actually stopped. "You've put both of us in danger."

"How much of the conversation did you hear?" he asked.

"Enough to know you told someone about the *Integrity*. Whoever you were talking with was probably right. You should have left me there." Then he wouldn't be in danger. Then something even scarier occurred to her. "How did you know it was the *Integrity*? I didn't tell you the name of the boat."

She had to get out of here now. Who exactly was Ezra Easton? How did he know about the *Integrity*?

"I have to leave. Now." She turned toward the front door and stopped short. She was on an island with no way off.

Strong arms wrapped around her from behind and Ezra's warmth surrounded her. "First of all, it wasn't hard to find out the name of the ship you were on. My friend is good at finding out information, and there are only so many ships out on the water nearby. When you narrow it down to those involved in a wreck, it's a very short list."

His explanation did make sense. She had no idea if anyone from the *Integrity* had contacted the coast guard. If they had, it might have even made the news.

He scooped her right off her feet as though she weighed nothing at all. "Come and have something to eat and we'll talk." She fought the urge to rest her head against his shoulder. She wanted to burrow close and never leave.

Ezra set her on one of the stools next to the large peninsula separating the kitchen from the dining area. She rubbed her hand against her forehead, ignoring the throbbing in her arm and the pain in her head. "You have no idea what you've done. The people who will be looking for me have more power than you can imagine." She had to make Ezra understand. "They have tentacles everywhere."

"Why do you work for them?" As though he had no worries in the world, he removed some golden-brown pancakes from a pan and poured in the last of the batter.

God, she ached everywhere but forced herself to concentrate. "I don't. Or I did, but not really." She sighed. "It's hard to explain."

"Try me." He obviously knew his way around a kitchen. He had plates of food warming in the oven, pancakes bubbling away on the stove, and now he was cracking eggs into a large bowl. When he had a full dozen, he picked up a fork and whisked them quickly. His movements were economical and oddly graceful for such a large man.

"I'm an archaeologist." For some reason, she didn't want to lie to him. "I was onboard the *Integrity* to handle the salvage from the shipwreck that was being excavated."

"What were you looking for?"

She leaned her elbows on the counter and propped her chin on her hands. "That's the thing. Even my employer didn't know what we should be looking for, only that there was something rumored to be valuable on the vessel when it went down."

"Gold?" The way he asked made her think he already knew the answer to that question.

"No, not that kind of treasure."

"Ah." He opened the oven and scooped the last of the pancakes onto the warm plate before shutting the oven door. The delicious aromas made her stomach growl.

"What do you mean by that?" she demanded.

He divided the eggs between the two skillets, pulled a container of orange juice out of the refrigerator and poured two large glassfuls, then handed one to her. She took it and drank deeply.

"Do you have any coffee?" She'd kill for a mug.

"After. You need to hydrate first. You lost a fair amount of blood." He retrieved a bottle of water and set it beside her before tending to the eggs. "Back to the treasure. I take it the book was what they were looking for."

This is where things got tricky. "I'm not entirely sure."

Ezra faced her, spatula in hand, and a look of disbelief stamped on his face. "You're not entirely sure?" He set the spatula down and stalked toward her, his turquoise eyes snapping with temper. "You risked your life. You were shot for the thing, and you're not sure?"

Sam sighed and shook her head. "All I know is that whatever is in that book is powerful." She took the plunge, knowing he'd either believe her or not. Maybe if he thought she was off her rocker, he'd be glad to be rid of her. She ignored the tiny part of her that mourned the thought of leaving him. "There's like a hum in my blood when I'm around certain items."

He stood there staring at her until she motioned to the stove. "Your eggs are burning."

. . .

Ezra didn't know whether to shake Sam or kiss her senseless. How could he be expected to think straight when she was sitting there looking adorably mussed in another of his too-large shirts with her red curly hair bouncing around her shoulders?

As a man, he was drawn to her on many levels. Physically, it went without saying. There was a vibrancy about Sam that made him want to be near her. He wanted to strip the clothes from her body and spend hours mapping every hollow and curve. He wanted to kiss and stroke her soft skin until she begged him to do more.

But it was her eyes that really tugged at him. They were green pools of emotion. Whoever Sam was and whatever she'd done, she was not very good at hiding what she was feeling. And if that were the case, why had the Knights hired her?

He grabbed the pan off the stove and turned off the heat. It was time to eat. "What do you mean there's a hum in your blood?" He found it interesting that Darius's Sarah had a talent for psychometry, most specifically for books. Tarrant's Valeriya had a sixth sense for danger, always knowing when it was near.

Now Sam was telling him she had an unusual ability as well. Was that what attracted the other side of his nature, his dragon side? Definitely something he needed to share with his brothers. If the Knights ever discovered this weakness, they'd exploit it to the max, using it to trap an unwary drakon.

They couldn't let that happen.

Sam shrugged. "I can't really explain it. I can always find objects of a certain nature if I'm near them."

He set the platter of pancakes and the pan of bacon on the counter. He picked his words carefully as he got down plates and dug out cutlery. "What kind of objects?"

Sam tucked her hair behind her ears, but the curls didn't stay there longer than a few seconds. "The kind most other archaeologists aren't really interested in. I find things linked with myth and legend. Many of my colleagues consider such things inconsequential, but I believe myths and legends have a basis in reality if we search long enough."

Ezra piled food on Sam's plate and then heaped even more on his own. He'd just taken his first forkful of eggs, when she added, "Take dragons, for example."

He choked and began to cough. Sam jumped off her stool, hurried to his side, and began to pat him on the back. His eyes watered, but he cleared his throat. "Dragons?" How much did she know about him? Could she sense he was different?

When he waved her away, she slid back onto her stool and had a sip of juice. She was blushing, both her cheeks a soft shade of pink. "I know it sounds crazy. I'm not saying there are dragons. I'm just saying they probably had a basis in fact. My theory is ancient man stumbled across the bones of a winged dinosaur and thought it belonged to a living creature."

"A dragon."

She nodded. "Exactly. I find artifacts relating to such things—pottery, tablets, scrolls, jewelry." She gave him a pointed look. "Books."

"Just dragons?" Was that why he'd been so drawn to her?

She shook her head, and he was briefly mesmerized by her bouncing curls. They were like fire in the morning sunlight. "No, all myths and legends—phoenix, dragons, unicorns, the kraken, mermaids, and a bunch you probably never heard of. What people fear, what they revere, that really speaks to the heart of who they were and what drove them in their daily lives."

She frowned at her pancakes. "Do you have any syrup or butter?"

He went to the refrigerator and retrieved the butter. "No

syrup. Sorry." He wasn't overly fond of sweet things, although Sam was sweet, and he had a feeling he could easily become addicted to her if he wasn't careful.

"So you found this book," he prompted.

Sam sighed. "I really shouldn't be telling you this. The people I work for are nasty. My boss belongs to a secret society." She paused and leaned forward, as if imparting a great secret. "The Knights of the Dragon."

"Dragons again?"

"Scoff if you want." She picked up her knife and spread some butter over the pancakes before cutting a piece. "But they believe it, and that's what makes them dangerous."

He couldn't picture Sam being involved with the Knights. "So why are you working with them?"

She carefully set her fork down on the side of her plate and swallowed her mouthful of food. "I know I can't stop them. They're too large a group. Too powerful. I'm just an archaeologist." Her gaze sharpened, and he caught the edge of old pain reflecting in them. "They killed a dear friend of mine about a year ago."

That had to be the mentor Tarrant had mentioned. "Why?"

"He was so excited. He'd discovered an old book from the eighteen hundreds about an arcane society, one that believed dragons were real. He wanted me to come by so he could show it to me."

Ezra had a sinking feeling he knew how this story was going to end.

"When I arrived and he didn't answer the door, I got worried and used the key I had. He was lying on the floor. At first, I thought he'd had a heart attack or maybe gotten dizzy and fallen. Then I saw the blood on his chest. He'd been shot in the heart."

Ezra shoved aside his plate and reached for Sam. He felt

utterly helpless when her voice broke on a sob. "The police investigation pegged it a home invasion gone wrong. I looked for the book, the one he'd told me about, but it was gone."

There was more to the story. Ezra needed to know how she'd gone from her mentor's death to discovering the Knights. But that would come later. Right now the only thing that mattered was comforting Sam.

. . .

Karina Azarov sat at her desk and viewed the video footage that Birch had brought up on his laptop. "Is this the best they can do?" she demanded.

"Unfortunately, it is. It was dark and there's only about fifteen seconds of footage. If we had more, we might have been able to get something out of it." Birch hit the play button without her having to ask and she watched it again.

"It's big." She leaned forward. "It could be a whale."

"It most likely is." Birch closed the cover and tucked the laptop under his arm. "It's big and fast. There were whales sighted in the area earlier that day."

"So it's nothing more than bad luck." Karina sat back and rubbed her forehead. "Why doesn't that surprise me? Nothing has been going the way it should these past weeks."

"The best we can do is salvage what's left of the *Integrity* and send another vessel to keep excavating the *Reliant*. We need to know if there's anything else of value in the wreckage. Dr. Bellamy is missing. We don't know if she's dead or alive, if she had the artifact on her, or if it's lost."

"You're right." She straightened in her chair and picked up her phone to make some calls. "You deal with Dexter. Let him know I won't tolerate any more failures. His only job is to find out what happened to Sam Bellamy and to recover anything she might have found. Tell him he has a week. After that, I'll send someone else to do the job."

Birch nodded and left, not surprised by her ultimatum. After all, he was the one who'd taught her how best to deal with the people in her employ. Results were rewarded. Failures were dealt with swiftly and brutally.

Chapter Seven

All the pent-up pain and sorrow of the last year seemed to pour out of Sam at once. Maybe it was because for the first time since she'd discovered Brian's body, she felt safe. Her mentor had been her only true friend, her family. She barely knew Ezra, but he'd saved her life and given her a temporary safe haven. It was more than she'd expected when she'd set out on this mission.

There was something so solid about him. It didn't hurt that he was sexy. He felt…right. She didn't know quite how else to phrase it.

"You're safe." His deep voice seemed to surround her before it seeped into her very bones. Ezra was just one man, but she felt as though nothing could harm her as long as he held her in his arms.

This surcease of fear was temporary. She knew that. She couldn't hide here forever. That would only endanger him. He might think he understood the danger, but she honestly didn't think he did. No one could unless they'd seen firsthand just how far the Knights would go to protect themselves and their secrets.

Ezra scooped her into his arms and started moving. She lifted her head long enough to see him heading toward the stairs. "Where are we going?" She sniffed back the tears, hating that she'd succumbed to them. She'd cried endlessly after Brian's death. Then she'd been approached by Gervais Rames with his claims about the Knights of the Dragon. Her sorrow had quickly turned to anger.

She'd been on enough archeological digs, discovered enough artifacts, that she understood certain items had a particular energy, an even mystical power about them. It wasn't that she didn't believe such things existed. Many would consider her gift for finding such things to be magical. But her beliefs didn't extend so far as to believe dragons were real.

Throughout the annals of time, people had killed to get their hands on these mystical amulets, statues, and texts. She'd just never thought her mentor would die for one of them. His life had been worth so much more than any book.

She hadn't cried since, until now.

"To bed."

She didn't know if he meant to put her to bed to rest or if he planned on joining her there. Funnily enough, the idea of getting naked with him didn't bother her at all. In fact, it was exciting.

She'd almost died. Had expected to die. For the past year of her life, she'd been insulated from the rest of humanity, living in a dark world where secret societies killed and got away with it because they had money and power. Most people lived their entire lives in ignorance, never knowing such people existed.

Sam wished she could go back to a time when she'd been blissfully unaware of such things. But there was no turning back the clock. No way to forget the things she'd seen and learned this past year.

Gervais had introduced her to a world of influential people, money, and deadly games all driven by their belief in dragons. He had a vast knowledge about the Knights, and when she began to look into it herself, she'd finally been forced to admit he didn't seem to be as crazy as she'd first assumed. Not that she believed dragons were real, but there were powerful, dangerous people who did.

Ezra placed her in the center of the bed and then stretched out beside her. He watched her intently with the most mesmerizing eyes she'd ever seen. She had her hand halfway to his face before she stopped herself. What was she doing?

"No. Don't stop." He clasped her hand in his much larger one and pressed it against his cheek. He closed his eyes and inhaled sharply.

His features, like the rest of him, were bold and rugged. She ran her thumb over his bottom lip. He growled and nipped at the tip. A blast of heat jolted through her. Sam knew she was playing with fire but didn't care.

There could be nothing between them but these stolen moments in time. She had to leave. Staying in one place would only make it easier for the Knights to find her. Aaron Dexter was out there somewhere, looking for her. She could feel it in her bones.

"What are you thinking about?" He took hold of her hand and brought her palm to his lips. He kissed it and then nibbled on the tip of one of her fingers. "You seem so far away."

And she didn't want to be. She wanted to be right here with Ezra Easton, the stranger who'd plucked her from the sea.

"It's not important." He frowned and then nipped her finger, not hard enough to hurt, but enough to startle her. "Ouch! What was that for?"

"Don't lie to me." He rolled, covering her with his

enormous body. He held his weight on his forearms so he didn't crush her. His wild, vibrant scent surrounded her. There was no mistaking the hardness pressing against her leg.

"I'm not lying." She shrugged when he frowned. "There's just no point in talking about it." A tear trickled from the corner of her eye and down her temple, disappearing into her hair. She hated the weakness.

Ezra groaned and licked the next salty tear before it could slip away. "We'll talk, but later." He brushed light kisses over her cheekbone, angling toward her lips.

This was a mistake. There was no place in her life for any kind of relationship. But this wasn't a relationship, was it? This was two people coming together in extreme circumstances.

What did it matter how she justified it to herself? She wanted Ezra. There was an empty spot deep inside her she suspected he could fill. She'd been cold and afraid for so long. She wanted to reach out and grab some heat, some human comfort, some sense of connection.

Their lips met, and the cosmos exploded. It was the briefest of touches, but it totally rocked her world, changing it forever.

He stared down at her, and she imagined the shocked expression on his face mirrored the one on hers. "Ezra."

"Later." He sealed his lips to hers, stealing her breath and all semblance of logic. He tilted his head slightly and deepened the kiss. She moaned, and when her lips parted, he eased his tongue inside.

He tasted as wild as the sea and slightly salty. She'd always been the kind of girl who liked salty more than sweet. He groaned, and the sound vibrated all the way to her toes, making them curl.

He pulled back and stared down at her, both of them panting for breath. "If you want me to stop, say so now."

This was the moment of truth. It was her decision. What

did she want?

Sam knew if she told Ezra to go, she'd regret it for the rest of her life, no matter how long or short that might be. She raised her arms and wrapped them around his neck. "Stay," she whispered.

His eyes seemed to blaze like turquoise fire. He had the thickest lashes she'd ever seen on a man, but they in no way detracted from the fierceness of his face. If anything, they emphasized the harsh planes and angles of his cheeks and the hardness of his jaw.

"You're sure?"

She nodded. "I'm sure."

. . .

Ezra had never heard such beautiful words in his life. So simple, but they made his heart race and every muscle in his body tightened in anticipation. Sam wanted him.

She was here in his bed with her arms wrapped around his neck.

Maybe he was crazy. Maybe this was all some elaborate scheme of the Knights, but he just didn't see how that was even possible. Inside him, his dragon half roared with displeasure that he was even questioning what they were about to do. His more primitive half wanted him to claim Sam.

Her taste was on his lips, slightly sweet and salty from the food she'd eaten. That gave him pause. She hadn't eaten nearly enough. Neither of them had. The food was still on the kitchen counter, growing colder by the second.

He would make her something else when they were done. Because nothing short of a nuclear blast could make him leave this bed.

He kissed her, groaning when she slid her hands down his broad shoulders and dug her fingernails into his shirt.

He wanted her hands on his bare skin. He pulled back and yanked his shirt over his head. Her eyes widened and then narrowed as she visually traced his tattoos.

"These are so beautiful. So wild and primitive." She ran her fingers over the curve of one of the symbols and on to the next one. His dick was as hard as bedrock. Having her hands on his chest was making him crazy, but also content in a way he'd never been.

That's the way it had been for both his brothers. Their dragon sides had *known* the right woman when they met her. Ezra had given up hoping it would happen for him. Never had he expected to pluck his woman from the sea, but it was fitting.

"I've never seen anything like them before." He could hear the wonder in her voice, but that was all. There was nothing to suggest she understood what it was she was seeing.

"They go all the way down your arm, too." Her fingers followed, flowing down his arm to his wrist.

He had to get her naked. He started to reach for her and remembered her injury at the last second. That stopped him cold. What in the hell was he doing? Not only was Sam still healing from her wound, only minutes ago, she'd been crying over the death of a friend. He was taking advantage of her.

"What's wrong?" she asked.

"You're injured." It was hard to get the words out when every cell in his body was screaming at him to just shut the fuck up. Sam was here, warm and willing. He could smell the faintest hint of arousal. It made the fine hairs on the back of his neck stand on end. He wanted to bathe in her scent until it covered his entire body.

She frowned and glanced down at her arm. "It doesn't feel that bad."

"The bullet grazed you. Took out a layer of skin. You lost some blood."

The corners of her mouth lifted. He'd found her beautiful when she was wet and bedraggled. Clean and warm and smiling, she was radiant. "You can do all the work. I'll just lie here."

She was teasing him. He couldn't remember the last time a woman had teased him like this. It made the weight of the years he'd lived and survived slip away. He felt younger, more alive than he had in centuries. Usually, only the ocean made him feel this way.

"I can, can I?"

She nodded. "Uh-huh."

"Well then, I should get busy removing your clothes." He waited to see if she would protest. When she didn't, he levered himself off her and knelt beside her. He pulled off her socks, which were really his and way too big for her, and then skimmed the oversize pants down her legs. She was bare beneath them.

He stared at her long legs and slightly rounded hips. Sam was strong and lean and all woman. He wanted to crawl between her legs, but he wanted her totally naked first. He reached for the first button on the flannel shirt and slipped it through the hole. He wanted to rip the garment open, but that might harm or frighten her. He didn't want that. She was a gift, and like any present, she was meant to be unwrapped slowly, to be appreciated.

The pulse in her neck was fluttering wildly by the time he undid the last button. He eased the edges back and stared down at her breasts. They weren't overly large, but they were well formed and tipped with tight pink nipples.

Ezra groaned and lowered his head. He had to taste her. He trailed his tongue around the outer edge of her nipple before dragging it over the very tip. Sam cried out and pushed closer. He opened his mouth and covered her. She tangled her fingers in his hair and held him close.

He wanted to roar with satisfaction. Something inside him clicked into place like a bank vault slamming shut. He'd bring ruin to the world before he'd let anyone take her from him.

He'd thought he understood what his brothers felt for their women, but he hadn't. There was no explaining what was happening between them. Sam was his, just as surely as the ocean was.

It was that simple and that complex.

She completed him in a way he couldn't even begin to speculate. Right now, he had to claim her. He needed to hear her cries of pleasure, hear his name spill from her lips.

He kissed his way over to her other breast.

"Ezra." His name was little more than a breath of air, but the savage satisfaction it brought him was unparalleled. He sucked her taut nipple into his mouth, savoring the cries of her pleasure.

It wasn't enough.

His pants were annoying him. He left her long enough to strip them off. Her eyes widened when she got her first good look at him totally naked. "Wow, your tattoo goes all the way to your ankle." She lifted up slightly, supporting herself with her good arm.

He didn't want to talk about his tattoo. Not now. He wrapped his hands around her ankles and slid her legs apart. She licked her lips and his cock seemed to swell even larger. What would it feel like to have her mouth wrapped around his shaft? He'd find out, just not today. She was still healing. He'd take care of her, take care of them both.

He knelt between her spread thighs and lowered his head. He inhaled first, taking in the musky scent of her arousal. She wanted him. She was pink and damp and all his.

But he wasn't ready to take her. Not yet. Not until she found satisfaction. He wanted to watch her come, to see what she looked like when she orgasmed.

He ignored the throbbing of his cock and the way his balls squeezed up close to his body. He would make Sam come first. And then he would claim her as his own.

. . .

Sam held her breath as Ezra lowered his head. Her breasts felt swollen and her nipples ached for his touch. She'd never found her breasts to be all that sensitive before. Obviously, Ezra was a whole other class of lover. His touch ignited flames of desire deep within her. It was like dropping a match on dry tinder. Maybe she was reacting so quickly because she'd been in a dry spell. She hadn't had a lover in over two years. Or maybe it was Ezra himself. There was something compelling about the man.

When he touched his clever tongue to her most sensitive part, she sucked in a breath. He lapped at her like he couldn't get enough of her. He stroked up one side of her labia and down the other.

Whimpers of need broke from her lips. She gripped the covers beneath her. Her left arm pained her slightly, but not enough for her to ask him to stop.

Then he stroked the flat of his tongue over her clit. Her lower half jerked upward. "Oh God," she cried. Ezra growled, he honest to God growled, and the vibration shot through the tiny kernel of nerves making her shudder.

He pushed one thick finger inside her, not stopping until it was inserted all the way. She'd never gotten this hot, this fast. She was so close to coming she could almost taste it. "Ezra." She didn't want to wait. She wanted the glorious release that only he could give her.

He pulled his finger back to the edge of her slick channel and slowly pushed it back in. She was panting hard now. She reached down with her good arm and gripped a handful of his thick hair. She wanted more, needed more.

Ezra sucked her clit and pulled his finger out once again, this time curling it so he hit the sweet spot inside her. Sam's entire body bucked, her thighs trembled, and she called his name.

He did it again, and her cries echoed around them as she came. Everything inside her clenched hard before releasing with a sigh of relief. Tears stung her eyes, and her heart raced. She was exhausted yet exhilarated. Never had an orgasm taken over her in this way.

Ezra raised his head and watched her. Then, like a great predator, he prowled up her body until he was hovering over her. He kissed her, and she tasted herself on his lips.

She felt the nudge of his cock against her inner thigh. Like the rest of him, it was big. She wasn't sure she could take him, but she was more than willing to try. She parted her thighs and he broke off the kiss to stare down at her.

• • •

Ezra licked his lips, tasting Sam. She was beautiful when she came, so open, so raw. He hadn't even had her yet, but he was already more satisfied than he'd ever been in his long years.

She was watching him, her cheeks flushed, her green eyes slightly glassy. He frowned. Had she shed more tears? He didn't like that. He wanted only pleasure for her.

She lifted her lower body slightly, pressing against his cock. Liquid seeped from the tip, and he gritted his teeth. He had to get inside her. "I'll take my time," he promised. At least he hoped he would. He'd never been this on-edge before.

He positioned the head of his shaft at her opening and pressed inward. Her body was naturally resistant to the invasion, but he kept a steady inward movement until it stretched to accommodate him. He was breathing as though he'd swum a hundred miles at top speed.

He forced himself to stop and breathe. Sam was panting, too, her eyes wide open.

"Does it hurt?" He didn't know what he'd do if she said it did. Then he corrected himself. If it hurt, he'd stop. It was that simple.

She shook her head. "Feels full." She took several breaths. "Feels good."

He flexed his hips and drove in another two inches. His eyes almost rolled back in his head it felt so damn good. Having Sam under him, having her hot channel cling to his dick, was the most unbelievable thing he'd ever experienced. And he was barely inside her.

Sam lifted her legs, and he slid deeper. She hooked her ankles around the backs of his thighs and pulled him toward her. The muscles in his arms ached as he pushed his clenched fists into the mattress and held his weight off her. He had to be careful not to put too much pressure on them, or he could drive them right through the bed. And wouldn't that kill the mood.

He gritted his teeth and thrust, not stopping until he was seated to the very hilt, every inch of his cock inside her.

"Oh God. Oh God," she repeated over and over.

Ezra captured her lips, stealing the words from her. His cock was pulsing heavily, beating in time with his heart. Her inner muscles clamped down around him suddenly and unexpectedly.

Ezra tipped his head back and yelled, just managing to swallow back the roar of satisfaction that wanted to escape. He began to rock his hips back and forth, only pulling back a couple of inches before thrusting in again.

"Ezra," Sam moaned his name. Her sheath sealed around him, squeezing.

He rocked faster. "Come for me." He wanted her to find release once again. "Sam."

As soon as he said her name, her entire body convulsed. Ezra let go. His orgasm shot from the base of his shaft and out the tip. It was never-ending. He shook and shuddered, gripped handfuls of her glorious red hair and held on.

She dug her fingernails into his back, sending him off on another spasm of release.

He lost all track of time. When he finally collapsed, he had enough presence of mind to ease to the side so he didn't crush Sam.

He wrapped his arm around her and threw one of his thighs over her legs. He was totally spent and relaxed. He closed his eyes and savored the moment. Sam snuggled closer to his warmth. He managed to snag one end of the comforter and flip it over her so she was at least partly covered.

This was something worth fighting for. Sam was worth fighting for.

· · ·

Aaron Dexter was not in a good mood. It had taken them hours to reach the shore in the lifeboats. They hadn't contacted the coast guard. The only person he'd contacted was his employer. Or rather, his employer's watchdog. That's how he thought of Birch. The man had no other name that he knew of, and everyone in the Knights knew the man's loyalty was to one person—Karina Azarov.

In the hours since, he'd checked in at a local motel, showered, and changed into clean clothes that one of the crew had acquired for him. Now he was sitting at a local coffee shop getting his ass chewed out over the phone.

"Find the woman or her body," Birch ordered.

Aaron wanted to smash his cell phone on the table, but

that wouldn't change the reality of the situation. His ass was on the line, and all because some archaeologist had managed to take an important artifact.

"I'll need another boat."

"I'm contacting a local salvage company—Easton Salvage. They're not the biggest operation in the region, but they have the best reputation. You can contact Kent Osmond." Birch rattled off the phone number. Aaron didn't bother to write it down. He had a name and a company, he'd find the man. "Go with them if they'll let you. Ms. Azarov wants you on site."

"How can I do that and look for Sam's body at the same time?" He didn't want to spend long hours on some rusty salvage ship. He'd been cooped up long enough. It was his boredom that had led to his game of cat and mouse with Sam. He'd wanted her to think she was escaping before he captured her. And look where that had gotten him.

"Figure it out," Birch told him.

"What about the cell phone footage?" he asked before Birch hung up on him. "Was there anything on it?"

"Inconclusive. Not enough to say for sure, but it was most likely a whale. There were some in the area, and it's big enough to be one. It's rare, but not unheard of for a whale to ram a ship."

Birch hung up before Aaron could ask any more questions. The waitress walked over to his table, coffeepot in hand. "More coffee?"

"Yes." He waited until she'd filled his mug. "Where can I find Easton Salvage?" She was obviously a local, and it didn't hurt to cultivate some contacts. The fact that she was young, blonde, and pretty also didn't hurt.

"Down the road about two miles." She pointed to the right. "Can't miss it. They've got a big sign outside."

"Thanks." He gave her a wink. She blushed and hurried away. He took his time and drank his coffee while he made plans. Karina and her pit bull might think they owned him, but he wasn't about to fall in line for anyone. He had his own agenda.

He left enough money on the table to cover his bill and a big tip. She'd remember him if he came back. It was always good to have a few local sources for information, and he'd learned over the years that waitresses were the best.

He pulled on his coat, pocketed his phone, and headed out. He had a salvage company to find. And then, dead or alive, he'd find Sam Bellamy.

And if she still had that artifact on her, he was going to use it to buy his safety from Karina Azarov. She might be the leader of the Knights, but there were others who weren't happy with her leadership. And Aaron was a man who took advantage of opportunities where he found them.

Chapter Eight

With Ezra's arm around her waist and one of his thighs thrown over hers, Sam concentrated on getting her breath back. It wasn't easy. She'd had sex before, but she'd never had her mind blown like this, never felt such a connection to another human being.

She ran her fingers over the tattoo that covered his left arm. In fact, the swirling and stylized tattoo ran from his neck all the way to his feet, but only on the left side of his body. The design was intricate. It had to have hurt like hell to have it done and must have taken a very long time to complete.

Sam had never had an opinion about tattoos one way or another. She'd always figured a person was entitled to do whatever they wanted with their own body. On Ezra's massive body, the colorful design was downright sexy.

"What are you thinking?" He caught her fingers and brought them to his lips.

"How much it must have hurt to get these tattoos." He gave a bark of laughter and she twisted around so she was lying on her side facing him. "Seriously, your groin. That couldn't have been fun." She shuddered at the thought. Even the left half of his penis was inked.

"It didn't hurt," he assured her.

She didn't believe him. "Either you have the highest pain threshold imaginable, or you were asleep while you had that done."

"Neither." He lightly brushed his hand down her bandaged arm. "Speaking of pain, how does your arm feel?"

Now that he'd mentioned it, the darn thing was throbbing.

"It hurts, doesn't it?"

"A little." Not enough that she regretted what they'd done.

"Damn it." Ezra rolled out of bed and padded into the bathroom. Sam blinked and admired his broad shoulders, the musculature of his back, his firm behind, and his strong legs. The man had a swimmer's body, extremely wide shoulders and a narrow waist.

That amazing tattoo also covered the left half of the back and legs. It ran down the center of his spine, creating a delicious contrast between bare skin and incredible ink.

Sam stretched. She was only partially covered by the comforter, so she flipped the other end over so she was in the middle of the blanket with both sides covering her.

Ezra raised one dark brow when he returned. "Cozy?"

"Very." He set a glass and a small bottle of over-the-counter pain medicine on the bedside table and sat beside her.

The more she studied his tattoo, the less it seemed random. There was a flow, a pattern to his markings. He opened the bottle, shook out two pills, and held them out to her. "Take these."

Since the pain had amped up, she wasn't about to be stupid and refuse. She popped both pills into her mouth and followed them with the water he handed her. When she was done, he set the empty glass aside and pulled down the comforter.

"Hey. I was using that." Now that they weren't having sex, she was a little uncomfortable being naked around him. He, on the other hand, was totally relaxed. Not having any clothes on didn't bother him in the least.

"I need to look at your arm." He unwound the gauze and gently pulled back the thick padding. It was stained with a small amount of blood but actually looked better than she'd thought it would. He grunted and wrapped it back up again.

"Well?" she prodded when he didn't say anything.

"You'll live."

Ezra was turning out to be the most frustrating, sexiest man she'd ever laid eyes on. "Thank you, Dr. Easton." Sex obviously hadn't put him in a good mood, and he was quickly ruining hers. She knew her problems weren't going away, but she'd hoped for a little longer respite from them. She sat up, making sure to keep the comforter around her.

"Where are you going?" he asked.

"To get cleaned up and dressed. I need to make plans. And I want to see that book I stole. I risked my life for it. I at least deserve to get a good look at it."

Ezra scowled, and his entire demeanor became dark and angry. "The book is dangerous."

Really. He was going to say that to her. "I know that. I was shot because of it." She scooted off the bed and began to shuffle to the bathroom. "I'm hungry, too. I didn't finish breakfast."

Behind her, Ezra swore. She didn't hear him move, but his large hands descended on her shoulders and held her in place. "I'm worried."

It wasn't an apology, but it seemed like it was the closest she was going to get. She sighed and rubbed her forehead. "I'm worried, too, but knowledge is power."

Ezra snorted. She swiveled and looked up at him. "What?"

"You remind me of someone. He also thinks knowledge is the key to running the world."

"He'd be right. Money can only do so much, but if used properly, knowledge can get you just about everything you want or need."

Ezra trailed his fingertips down her bare shoulder. "We could conserve water and shower together."

He was something else. "I'm all for conservation," she began. He started to grin. "But," she added, and his grin disappeared. "If you join me, we'll probably end up wasting twice as much water, because we won't be just showering." She hated to admit to weakness, but it was best to be truthful. "And I'm not up to another round."

He scooped her right off her feet. He did it so quickly, she gasped. Damn, the man could move. He carried her into the bathroom and set her down on the vanity. "A bath would be better. That way you can sit down. And you're less likely to get your bandage wet."

Without waiting for her to agree or disagree, Ezra started the water running in the tub. Since she agreed with him, she didn't say anything. If she was going to be around longer, she'd be more insistent about him taking charge of her life. But since she was leaving soon, she figured she'd save her energy for the bigger problems, like the book.

She wanted a better look at the thing. She hadn't cracked the cover of it on the *Integrity*, concerned that someone might see her reading it. She hadn't wanted to bring any more attention to the artifact than necessary. It was the hum of power the book emitted that had told her it was special and extremely dangerous. Definitely something the Knights of the Dragon would want.

Ezra lifted her off the counter and set her on her feet. She was still clutching the comforter, and they played a short game of tug-of-war, which she lost. He dumped the blanket onto the floor and deposited her into the tub.

The man carted her around like she weighed nothing at all. It was not something she was used to since she was five-eight. But around Ezra, she felt positively small. He had at least a foot on her, and probably a hundred pounds, maybe more, all of it solid muscle.

The hot water felt good, and she sank deeper. "I'm going to grab a quick shower and then see if I can rescue any of our breakfast. If not, I'll make something else." He turned off the taps in the tub and walked over to the shower stall.

She shouldn't be watching him, she really shouldn't. But it was impossible to turn away, not when she had a perfect view. Ezra was quick and efficient. Water slid over sculpted muscles, caressing his massive body. Sam's entire body surged to life. Her breasts ached and the water, which had soothed only moments before, now aroused her.

As if sensing her gaze, he turned and stared right at her. She wanted to look away, but couldn't tear herself away from his molten turquoise eyes. The outline of the blue tattoo was the same color. It had to be intentional, and it was stunning.

He looked like an ancient warrior, ready to battle any foe, slay any enemy.

He was also very aroused. His shaft was long and thick and while she watched, he eased his hand down and gripped it.

Sam forgot how to breathe.

• • •

Ezra knew he should turn away from Sam. Her arm was hurting and she needed to rest. She didn't need to watch him jerk off in the shower. Of course, the only reason he had his fist wrapped around his dick in the first place was because she was watching him.

How could he not be aroused?

Her amazing red hair curled around her shoulders, the tips damp. With her green eyes and sultry smile, she could be a siren, sent to lure him to his doom.

And he'd go willingly.

That made Sam Bellamy a very dangerous woman.

Swearing, Ezra turned his back on her and began to wash. He needed to get away from her before he did something stupid, like drag her out of the tub, slam her against the wall, and fuck her until they both exploded with pleasure.

She wasn't up to that. Yet.

His cock jerked, and he swore again, thankful the rush of water kept her from hearing. He gripped his cock once again and pumped. He wasn't human and could go for hours without needing to rest. Right now, his balls were so full they hurt.

He told himself he wasn't going to turn back toward her, but he did. Sure enough, she was still watching him, her eyes wide and her lips parted. Her skin was flushed from the heat of the bathwater and a rush of arousal.

She lowered her gaze and licked her lips. That was all he needed. He stroked his cock faster. He slapped his free hand against the tiled wall for support and kept their eyes locked together. He wanted her with him, even if it was only having her watch him.

He'd like to do that someday. Watch her pleasure herself. The idea of seeing her touching her breasts, stroking her slender fingers in and out of her tight core sent him over the edge.

He roared, and the glass wall that partially enclosed the shower stall vibrated as the spray of the shower washed away his release. Sam was leaning against the edge of the tub with both arms resting on the rim, as though she wanted to get closer. He closed his eyes and sucked in a deep breath. The orgasm might have slightly eased the physical ache in his body, but it did nothing to calm the turmoil swirling inside him.

He gave his chest and groin a fast wash and turned off the water. In the silence, he could hear Sam's heavy breathing. "You almost done?" He grabbed a towel and wrapped it around his waist.

"What? Ah no." She grabbed the bar of soap from the holder and ran it over her legs. "I'll be another few minutes."

He left her there soaking in his bathtub. Possessiveness swirled inside him. She was his siren. He liked the idea of her in his tub, in his bed, in his house. He wanted to see to all her needs, provide her with whatever she needed, as long as that didn't include her wanting to leave him.

That he would not do.

He removed the towel and ran it over his hair and body, all the while listening to the sounds of water splashing as Sam washed. The creature that lived inside him, his dragon half, also listened intently. He'd never seen the beast so focused on a woman. That was a good thing, because Sam was staying.

He still wasn't certain about her connection to the Knights. Whatever it was, he'd have to find a way to deal with it. Because there was no fighting his primal instincts. Sam belonged to him. Besides, it was too dangerous out there for her to be on her own. Now all he had to do was convince her of that.

He tossed the towel aside and yanked on the jeans and shirt he'd been wearing earlier. He grabbed the damp towel and stalked back into the bathroom. Sam was just standing but sat back down when he entered.

"No need to be shy." He dumped his towel on the counter and reached for her.

"I'm not shy. Not really." She stood, accepted the hand he held out, and stepped over the side of the tub.

He couldn't get enough of her. He devoured her with his gaze, loving the way several droplets clung to her breasts. One trailed down to the tip, and he bent and swiped the errant bead of water away with his tongue. It tasted almost sweet, like Sam. He particularly enjoyed the way her nipple puckered even tighter at his touch.

Sam groaned and swayed toward him.

She needed tending, he reminded himself. Food and rest. He grabbed a large towel and wrapped it around her. "I'll be down in the kitchen. Call if you need me."

"I need to see that book, Ezra."

He paused in the doorway but didn't turn back. "I know." While he understood the necessity, that didn't mean he liked it.

• • •

Sam pulled the plug in the tub and then sat on the edge, still wrapped in a towel. Now that Ezra was no longer in the room, she could breathe a little easier. He was so big, such a large, vibrant presence, he seemed to suck the air right out of her lungs.

Watching him jerk himself off in the shower had left her feeling hot and horny. She'd never seen anything quite so sexy, especially since she knew the show had been all for her.

Well, maybe not all of it. She grinned and shook her head. He'd certainly enjoyed himself.

He'd caught her watching him and had showed her just how much she affected him, made himself vulnerable to her. That was almost as sexy as the water cascading over his naked body.

She rubbed her hand over her face. "Focus." The pain medication had dulled the ache in her arm, and the bath had soothed any soreness from their lovemaking. She dried off and padded back to the bedroom. The flannel shirt she'd worn earlier was still on the floor, along with the sweatpants so she pulled them back on. By the time she added socks, she had her wayward thoughts mostly under control.

She took a few more minutes to tidy the bathroom and hang the damp towels to dry. Since Ezra's comb was sitting on the vanity, she dragged it through her curls before tossing it back down. There wasn't much else she could do with her hair.

She studied her reflection. She didn't look as pale as she had. Of course, thinking about Ezra naked in the shower was enough to bring color to any woman's cheeks.

Her stomach growled, so she left the bathroom and headed downstairs. Ezra was standing at the stove. "I'll warm the pancakes and bacon in the microwave, but I'm scrambling more eggs. Nothing worse than cold eggs."

She took her seat back at the counter, content to just watch him. Before long, he had everything done and was taking his seat. She started in on the pancakes and bacon, not speaking until she'd eaten a good chunk of what she'd piled on her plate.

"Do you want more?" Ezra indicated the still half full platters.

She shook her head. "I'm stuffed." Even though she'd been hungry, she could only eat so much.

Ezra dragged each platter in front of him and proceeded to devour every remaining scrap of food.

"Wow, you must have been hungry." He was a big man and probably needed to eat a lot more than she did.

"You have no idea." His hot gaze stroked over her. Sam almost picked up her napkin and fanned her face but caught herself in the nick of time. He already knew he was hot stuff, best not to add to his ego.

"So what now?" There was no putting off this conversation any longer. They were both sated from their lovemaking and the meal, both clean and dressed. There was nothing left to delay them.

Ezra rose from his stool, put the dishes in the dishwasher, and poured them each a mug of fresh-brewed coffee. Sam knew she should help, but she also knew if she tried, he'd tell her to sit. In any case, there wasn't a whole lot to clean up. "Let's go into my office," he said.

She took the mug he offered. "Sugar?"

He got a small container from the cupboard and dug a spoon out of the cutlery drawer. "Do you want milk?"

She shook her head and added two teaspoons of sugar. "No. This is fine." Finally, there was nothing left to delay them. "Lead on." Now that the time was at hand, she was reluctant. It meant her time with Ezra was almost over. She barely knew him, but she'd miss him.

The living, dining, and kitchen areas were an open L-shape, but his office had walls and a door. It also had big glass patio doors that opened up to the outside and let in the sunlight. Shelves filled three walls of the room. Each was filled with glass jars and cases.

Drawn to them, Sam walked to the nearest one. Beach glass filled several tall crystal vases. It was an explosion of color. She didn't know much about beach glass, other than that it was pretty, but she did know that certain kinds were much rarer than others and that red and orange were the Holy Grail to those who collected.

It made sense since colored glass would have been a luxury item years ago. The ocean took broken shards of glass and lovingly polished them until they were something else entirely, but still works of art.

The vases on the shelves were filled with red, orange, yellow, blue, green, and more. And there was a lot of it. "This is incredible." He must spend hours and hours on the beach to collect so many specimens. He also had to have travelled.

"How long have you been collecting?"

"All my life." She moved on to a case filled with coins. Silver and gold, ancient and more modern, from all different cultures.

"You're a beachcomber?"

He laughed. "You could say that. A salvager, too."

She hated to pull herself away. Ezra liked to collect old things, too. He got the value of their history. It was something they had in common, even if what they collected was slightly different. She understood his passion.

Another shelf was filled with shells of different kinds. Some she'd never seen. "Do you dive?" He had to in order to have such amazing specimens.

"You could say that." At his dry tone, she forced herself to turn away from his collection.

"I'm sorry. I could spend hours in here. This is amazing." She could tell he was pleased by her reaction. And why wouldn't he be? Any collector liked when someone appreciated their collection.

He motioned her to a large leather chair in front of a massive wooden desk. The desk itself looked as though it had come off a ship from the seventeen hundreds. Instead of sitting behind it, Ezra took the other brown leather chair next to hers. He set his mug down on the desk. She took a sip of her coffee and almost moaned at the delicious flavor.

He reached out, took her mug, and set it next to his. Then he angled both chairs so they were facing one another. He took his hands in hers. "What do you know about the Knights of the Dragon?"

Chapter Nine

Sam's hands were cold in his, and Ezra frowned. The house was chilly. That was something he rarely thought about since it didn't matter to him. He'd have to start thinking differently now that Sam was here.

He stood and went to crank up the thermostat. He was glad Tarrant had talked him into having heat put in even though he didn't need it for himself. He had a fireplace in the living room, but that was more for ambiance than for warmth.

"You should have told me you were cold." He sat back down and took her hands once again.

She appeared slightly bemused. "I hadn't really noticed. I'm always cold."

He'd have to be extra careful in the future. "Now, about these Knights of the Dragon you mentioned earlier." He needed to know everything she did.

What he really wanted to do was show her his collection. He could tell her where every piece came from. Not many people appreciated beach glass, shells, and odd coins, but Sam did. As an archaeologist, she saw beyond the monetary value of the object to the intrinsic value it had as a piece of history. She hadn't even gotten to his pottery shelf. And this was only a small fraction of his collection.

But once again, the Knights intruded.

"It's too crazy to be believed." She dragged her fingers through her hair and sighed.

"You mentioned they're a secret society. That they believe dragons are real." He hated lying to Sam, pretending he didn't know anything, but that was the best way to find out what she knew.

Sam leaned her head back against the seat of the chair and briefly closed her eyes. She still looked pale and tired. It had been less than twenty-four hours since she'd been shot and he'd dragged her home. Yes, it was only a graze, but the adrenaline dump and the blood loss, plus the ride back here in an open dinghy, all added up and took their toll. Add on top of it their lovemaking, and it was no wonder Sam was tired.

"We can talk about this later." Tarrant would kill him for not interrogating Sam, but he couldn't make himself do it. It just felt wrong.

She shook her head and opened her eyes. "No. I can't stay here much longer. As I told you earlier, these people have a very long reach. They seem to have people everywhere, in law enforcement and in government. Rich people, powerful people." She drew her feet up onto the edge of the chair and wrapped her arms around her knees.

"How did you find out about them? Was it because of the book your friend discovered?" That didn't seem like enough to send her down this path.

"No." She turned and stared out the window at the sea. The wind was brisk today, creating whitecaps on the waves. The water wasn't blue. No, it was stormy gray. It was a hum in his blood, calling to him. But even the lure of the sea couldn't drag him away from Sam.

"I was approached after Brian's funeral by a man named Gervais Rames." She gave a small laugh. "I thought he was out of his mind when he claimed a secret society had killed Brian. I mean, who in their right mind would believe such a thing?"

She looked so small and fragile curled up in the big leather chair. He knew she was strong, had a backbone of steel, or she wouldn't have accomplished what she had. But he was bigger and stronger and longed to shelter her from harm.

He reached out, scooped her into his arms, and settled back in his chair with her on his lap. "You do that a lot," she informed him.

He shrugged, totally unrepentant. "I like you here." The fact that she didn't argue told him just how worn out she truly was. "What did this Gervais Rames want?"

She leaned her head on his shoulder. "He told me about the Knights and what they did. I mean, the idea of drinking dragon blood when the creatures don't even exist is really out there. He told me how they killed people like Brian all the time in their quest for power and eternal life." She tipped back her head and peered up at him. "I gotta tell you, I almost called the cops right then and there. I mean, there's no such thing as dragons and eternal life. That's all fantasy. Right?"

"Right," Ezra agreed. No need to upset her by informing her she was sitting in the arms of a water drakon who'd lived for thousands of years. And by the way, if she drank his blood on a regular basis, she'd be cured of any disease and live indefinitely. Nope, best to keep his mouth shut. His dragon grumbled inside him but didn't give him too much grief.

"But the fact remains that these people think it's real. It's like the alchemists centuries ago trying to turn base metal into gold. People do kill in the pursuit of arcane and forbidden knowledge. I've made it my life's work to study such things. I know what different cultures have done since the dawn of time, the atrocities they've committed in pursuit of their cause."

Ezra was well aware of the lengths humans would go to in order to try to live forever or appease their gods, whichever ones they happened to be worshipping at the time in history.

"So you believe the society is real, but not the creatures they're searching for?"

"Exactly."

"So how did this Rames know about them?"

She rubbed her hands up and down her arms. Ezra reached out and snagged her coffee. She gave him a grateful smile and took a large swallow. "Thanks."

"Rames?" he reminded her, eager to finish this conversation so she could rest.

"This is where the story takes an even crazier turn."

He flashed a quick grin. "I think I'm past being surprised."

"It seems that Rames was part of another secret society, only this one works to oppose the Knights of the Dragon. Their mandate is to protect all dragons. They call themselves the Dragon Guard."

He'd told her he was past being surprised, but he'd lied. She'd managed to totally stun him.

• • •

Sam knew she'd finally shocked Ezra. He'd been surprisingly calm about the whole secret society thing up until now. She guessed it had just taken one step too far into crazy land, even for a man as level-headed as Ezra.

He was staring at her like she'd finally lost her mind. She knew where he was coming from. She'd thought the same thing a year ago. "I'm not lying, and I'm not crazy." She felt it important to point both those things out.

"The Dragon Guard?"

She nodded. Why he seemed more stunned by the news about them and not the Knights of the Dragon, she had no idea. "Rames told me they'd existed as long as the Knights had, formed to oppose them. They're all about protecting the innocent and saving dragons where they can."

"Where is this Rames now?"

"I don't know." This is where things got dicey. "He disappeared not long after he introduced himself and gave me the information on the Knights. Said he had a lead on some book and would be working toward getting it away from them."

"What book?" Ezra radiated an intensity that was downright scary. She tried to push out of his arms, but he simply tightened his hold. He wasn't hurting her, but she wasn't getting away unless he let her. She'd never met a man as strong as Ezra. And she had a feeling he wasn't even exerting himself.

"I don't know. He never said."

"Think, Sam. This could be important." Ezra lifted her, positioning her so she was facing him, her thighs resting on the outside of his. It was a very intimate position. Of course, she couldn't really complain considering how intimate they'd been earlier. Somehow, this was different. It was one thing to be naked and having sex, quite another to be emotionally vulnerable, and that's how she felt.

"Ah." She rubbed her head and tried to remember the couple of conversations she'd had with Rames. "I only spoke with him at the funeral and twice after, once in person and once over the phone."

Ezra swore.

"What?"

"Phone records. If Rames called you, the Knights could access your phone records."

She was surprised Ezra had thought of that. She hadn't at

the time. "He slipped me a phone at the funeral. It was one of those prepaid ones. I dumped it after he was out of contact for a couple of months. By then I was too scared to keep it any longer."

Ezra rubbed his big hands up and down her spine. "Think, Sam. Did he say anything else?"

"Why do you want to know?" she demanded. Her exhaustion was making her way too complacent, and that wasn't like her. She was usually the one asking the questions and digging for answers. This was beginning to feel more like an interrogation than a conversation.

Why was he focusing on the book and not the Knights of the Dragon? Suspicion was an ugly thing, but it began to rise inside her. What did she really know about Ezra, other than the fact he'd probably saved her life?

His gaze narrowed. "Because it's important to know as much about your enemy as you can."

It sounded like he spoke from experience, and that piqued her interest. He was also right. And at this point, he already knew most of it. She might as well tell him the rest. She closed her eyes, since having Ezra so close was distracting. She went over their conversations in her head. "At Brian's funeral, he gave me a brief overview of the Knights and insisted I take the phone. I called him a week later, once I realized the book Brian told me he'd found was missing and the police had all but filed his case away." That had been a rough time in her life.

"We agreed to meet, and he told me about the Knights and the Dragon Guard and what they did. I didn't believe half of what he told me. Honestly, I was convinced he was out of his mind."

"Understandable." Ezra kept up the even pressure, his touch warming and stealing some of the tension from her body.

"He told me about a woman named Karina Azarov. Said

she was the one who put out the hit on Brian. That it was her people who'd retrieved the book he'd found." She opened her eyes and peered up at Ezra. "The woman's a socialite and a prominent businesswoman. I researched her. She's a member of the board on a large pharmaceutical company and other businesses as well."

The whole idea of the Knights was crazy, but she kept up her explanation. "I saw pictures of her in newspaper articles. She's a beautiful woman, always dressed impeccably, and always attending charity functions. It's hard to picture her ordering a murder."

"I can imagine." Ezra let her take her time and order her thoughts. She was grateful for that.

"Rames gave me some links to check out online. There were references to the Knights of the Dragon out there in modern times. That made his story about them killing Brian more believable, especially since the book he'd discovered was missing."

Sam was getting warmer. Being near Ezra and having him touch her was driving away the chill. She wanted to melt against him and sleep. She hadn't slept well the past year. Her eyelids grew heavy and started to close. But she needed to get the whole story out.

She shifted upright. "Temple. He mentioned something about someone named Temple."

Ezra was as still as a statue, every muscle in his body taut. "You say this Rames was trying to get a book away from this Temple person."

"Yeah." She stifled a yawn. She needed more coffee if she was going to stay awake.

"And that was the last you heard from Rames? How long ago was that?"

"Ah, let me think. At least six months. No, closer to eight." She studied the intense expression on Ezra's face. "Why?

Why does that matter?"

• • •

Ezra's brothers wouldn't believe it. If he was understanding her correctly, the person who managed to infiltrate the Knights, steal a valuable book, and hide it in the midst of Herman Temple's vast library was Gervais Rames. That was the same book Darius and Sarah had found and destroyed.

Was this a coincidence or something more sinister? He wanted to believe Sam, he truly did, but her story was almost too perfect. "How did you get to be on board the *Integrity*?"

Sam reached out and retrieved her coffee mug. She drank and then made a face. "Cold." She set it back down.

"Sam?" Impatience was eating at him.

"I researched Karina Azarov and discovered she liked to fund expeditions, so I applied to her foundation for a grant. I was turned down for the grant but was contacted about a position on the *Integrity*. I knew if Rames was telling the truth, the Knights would know about me.

"The whole thing sounds like something out of a movie. Certainly nothing any sane, normal person would participate in." She sighed and rubbed her forehead. "My plan was if I found anything pertaining to the Knights, I'd steal or destroy it. It was the only justice I could get for Brian."

Ezra's blood ran cold at the thought of Sam in the midst of those vipers. There was no loyalty among the Knights. "So you're what? Part of this Dragon Guard?"

She shrugged. "I guess, even though Rames was the only person I had contact with."

"I need to make a call." Tarrant would be able to discover if such a society existed. He might have seen references to it before and passed it over since it sounded like some role-playing group.

She fisted her hands in the front of his shirt. "You can't. The more people who know about this, the more chance of the Knights finding out. That would put you in danger."

There was no faking the sincerity flowing from Sam. Ezra was a creature of instinct, relying both on the intellect of his human side and the primal instincts of his dragon side, and both were screaming that Sam was telling him the truth. No matter how farfetched and convenient her story was.

"Don't worry. My friend can get to places without leaving a trace."

"How is that possible?" She looked skeptical, and rightfully so.

Ezra grinned as he stood and set Sam on her feet. "He's the best hacker in the world. Just ask him."

"I hope you're right." She looked more resigned and sad than scared. "Or we're all dead."

"Come with me." He grabbed both their mugs and headed to the kitchen. He noticed Sam glance longingly at his bookshelves as she followed him. "You can explore later if you'd like."

She bit her lower lip. "I need to see the book I took from the *Integrity*. It might be able to tell us something. I can read different languages, ancient ones."

He poured the cold coffee down the sink and poured fresh into their mugs. "And it might be dangerous." Especially to him if it contained any kind of information on how to trap a drakon. He pushed her mug toward her.

His phone rang. His business line. That rarely happened as he had competent people in place to handle things for him. "I have to take this." He plucked the phone out of its charger on the counter. "Yeah."

"Hey, boss, it's Kent." Kent Osmond was the manager of Easton Salvage and one of his top divers. "Hate to call you at home, but we've got a big job."

Ezra started to smile. "The *Integrity*."

Kent went silent for a second. "You really do know everything, don't you?" Ezra chuckled at the longstanding joke. Kent liked to complain that Ezra knew everything when it came to salvaging, the weather, even the history of artifacts they stumbled across. Of course, he'd never told them it was because he'd lived four thousand years and was part dragon.

"Not everything, just most things," he shot back his usual answer. "When do you start?"

"I've got the first team heading out in the *Easton*." The *Peter Easton* was the official name of his salvage ship, but they all called it the *Easton*. "I'm taking one of the speedboats out later. I had a few things to take care of here."

"Who is our contact?"

Kent shuffled some papers in the background. "Aaron Dexter. He's the representative for Ms. Azarov, who owns the *Integrity*."

"Aaron Dexter." Beside him, Sam froze. The hunted expression on her face tore at his heart. "Get started. I'll be out later tonight or tomorrow morning at the latest to check in with you."

"Will do."

Ezra ended the call and tossed the phone aside. Sam backed away from him. "Are you working for Aaron?"

Ezra nodded. "I run one of the best salvage companies around. It's not surprising they called on us to see if we can refloat their vessel. And if not, salvage what we can."

"Right." She clung to the counter and nodded. "You told me that." Her green eyes were blazing in her pale face. "You need to turn them down. Let them hire someone else."

"Why?" Why would she want to keep him away from the ship? Was there something else on board, something she hadn't told him about?

"Why?" She looked at him like he was a total idiot.

"Haven't you listened to anything I've been telling you? The Knights are dangerous. You do not want to be on their radar. What happens if one of your crew stumbles across another artifact?"

"We give it to the owner of the *Integrity*."

Sam shook her head. "If they believe for one second your people might talk about what they've found, they'll kill them. Just like they did Brian."

"I can handle things to make sure that doesn't happen." He was already planning a late-night foray to the original sunken vessel to check things out. If there was anything else to be found, he'd make sure he uncovered it first.

"You can handle things, can you?" She stalked around the counter, hands on her hips. "Just like Brian could handle things." She drilled her index finger into his chest. "Just like Gervais Rames could handle things. Just like I could handle things." With each statement, she drove her finger a little deeper. "I'm trying to keep you out of this."

He pulled her hand away and wrapped his arms around her and held her close when she stumbled against him. "I'm already involved." Then he kissed her.

Chapter Ten

Sam lost her train of thought when Ezra kissed her. She was mad at him for something, but darned if she could remember what it was with his tongue sliding against hers. He surrounded her with his big body, making her feel cherished and safe.

Safe. That was it. Ezra wasn't safe if his company took this salvage job. She put her palms against his chest and pushed. It was like trying to move a small mountain. It took everything she had not to sink into the kiss. Her entire body pulsed with need. He was addictive.

With a cry, she wrenched her head away. "Stop."

He immediately released her, a deep frown on his face. "What's wrong?"

The man was as stubborn as a goat. "You have to listen to me. The Knights are dangerous." Why couldn't she get him to understand that?

He cupped her face with his large hands. "Baby, I am, too."

Frustration ate at her. "They're a large, ruthless group that will stop at nothing to get what they want."

"Trust me." He ran his fingers through her curls, stopping

when several of them snagged.

Sam sighed. "Why can't I make you see that this is too dangerous?"

When he stepped away, he looked remote and alone. It tore at her heart. "I believe in you," she assured him. And she did. She might not have known him long, but there was something about him that made her believe he could do anything he set his mind to. But everyone had limits. "You're just one man, and they're legion."

"We need information." He picked up a cell phone. Not the one he'd taken the business call on, but another one. He didn't waste any time and the phone was soon ringing. She was grateful he'd put it on speaker so she could hear.

"What?" a deep male voice rumbled.

"You're on speaker," Ezra told him. It sounded to Sam like he was warning the other man to watch his words, but why?

"Just got a call to salvage the *Integrity*."

"Did you now?" Sam wished she had a face to put to the deep voice. She could hear the light tapping of keys in the background and assumed he was working on a computer.

"Yup. My people are on it. I thought I'd make a late-night run to the site." That was the first she'd heard of it. She didn't like the idea of Ezra going off on his own, wasn't going to stand for it. If he went, he was taking her with him.

"Is that wise?" the stranger asked.

"Thank you," she piped up. "I'm glad someone is the voice of reason."

Ezra chuckled. "If you think he's the voice of reason, then we have a problem."

"Fuck off," the man shot back. "Now why are you calling me?"

Ezra was all business. "I need to know about a man named Gervais Rames. He's the man who approached Sam after her mentor was killed."

"Brian," she muttered.

"After Brian was killed," he corrected.

"You think he's with the Knights?"

She glared at Ezra. Just how much had he told his computer-hacking friend? Ezra shrugged, looking totally unrepentant and unaffected by her glare.

"According to Sam, he was going to try to steal a book from a man named Herman Temple."

"Is that so?" The stranger's voice held speculation and, worse, familiarity.

"You know who Herman Temple is, don't you?" How was that even possible? Sam backed away from the phone and Ezra. Maybe it was more than coincidence that Ezra had plucked her from the water.

He was watching her, looking slightly concerned but not overly upset. And why would he be? Not like she could run away. She was on a freaking island.

"This is too coincidental," the unknown male pointed out.

"Exactly my thought," she countered. Maybe she should keep her mouth shut and play stupid, but all her emotions were raw. She'd slept with Ezra, had feelings for him. "Did you sleep with me to get information?" she demanded.

The stranger swore, but she didn't care about the voice on the phone, only about Ezra. He shook his head. "I slept with you because I had to." He reached out and stroked the side of her face. She didn't flinch away, nor did she react. "I plucked you out of the sea," he continued. "You're mine now."

And what the hell did he mean by that? "I'm not salvage."

He loomed over her, closing the gap between them. "No, you're not salvage. You're treasure. My treasure."

Sam looked into his clear turquoise eyes and was lost. If he was lying to her, he was the best liar on the planet, because she believed him. "Ezra," she whispered his name.

"Still here." Impatience bled from the stranger's voice. She could almost imagine him sitting somewhere glaring at the phone.

"What do you know about the Dragon Guard?" Ezra's change of subject startled her.

"Who?" More tapping in the background. "Sounds like something from a computer game."

"According to Sam, they're a secret group that tries to fight the Knights of the Dragon. Gervais Rames was one of them, and he was trying to get a book from Temple's library."

There was a lot of muttering over the open phone line. Something about coincidence and circles. Sam couldn't quite hear it all.

"Gervais Rames owned a used and antiquarian bookstore. If he's dead, the store is vacant and might even be gone by now, depending on how long he's been deceased."

Sam shivered. All this talk of death unsettled her. Ezra wrapped his arm around her and pulled her against him. She rested her cheek against his broad chest and took comfort in the heavy, steady beat of his heart.

"I'm not finding much on this Dragon Guard. I'll have to do more in-depth research and get back to you."

"Be careful," she warned the man. "The Knights have people everywhere. They probably have hackers as skilled as you."

"Sweetheart, no one is as good as me."

Ezra grabbed the phone. "And we're done. Call if you find out anything."

"And you be careful," the man on the other end demanded. "If something happens to you, I'm going to be pissed."

"I'll be cautious." He ended the call and tossed the phone onto the counter. He cupped her jaw and raised it so she was looking at him. He stared down at her for a long time before finally giving her a decisive nod. "Let's go look at the book."

· · ·

Ezra might be making a colossal mistake. Even if Sam didn't want to hurt him, the book could still be dangerous. His brother Darius had firsthand knowledge of just how dangerous such items could be. One such book, most likely the one Gervais Rames had stolen and hidden, had almost killed Sarah when she and Darius tried to destroy it.

Tarrant would discover anything there was to know about Rames and the Dragon Guard. He'd also be digging into the lives of Brian Guest, Aaron Dexter, and Sam, of course. Anyone associated with the *Integrity* and the book in his safe would be thoroughly investigated. By the time Tarrant was done, he'd know what size and style of underwear they wore and what they'd eaten for breakfast. His brother was downright scary when it came to discovering secrets and information.

He'd also make sure both Darius and Nic were kept up-to-date on the situation. He hadn't wanted to raise Sam's suspicions by telling Tarrant to inform the others about the latest developments. He knew he didn't have to. His brother would be on top of all that and more.

Sam was quiet. He glanced her way to find her watching him. "What?"

She shrugged. "I wasn't sure I'd actually see the book again."

In other words, she'd expected him to keep it from her. She wasn't far off. "Thought about it, but it is best we know what we're dealing with. But," he warned, "if I think it's too dangerous, it goes back into the safe."

"How will you know if it's too dangerous?" She fixed the cuff on one of the sleeves of her shirt that had come unrolled.

"I just will." If they were going to do this, it was best to get it done.

He kicked back a corner of the area rug to expose the wide-plank hardwood floor, went down on his knees, and spread his arms wide, hitting hidden pressure points. A small section of the floor sank down and slid aside.

"That's so cool." Sam came down on the floor beside him and peered into the opening. Then she scrambled back. "I'm sorry. I probably shouldn't be seeing this."

His brothers would probably agree with her. "It's fine." He leaned down until his eye was over the retinal scanner. It made a low beep and the green light came on. He had sixty seconds to input the twenty-four-digit security code. After that time, a small charge inside the safe would be armed and would explode, destroying whatever was inside. Tarrant was nothing if not thorough.

Ezra quickly punched in the security code and another light flashed green. He turned the small handle and the safe opened. The only thing inside was the plastic bag containing the book. He lifted it out.

Sam was sitting in the chair she'd occupied earlier, leaning forward and watching him intently. "I feel like I'm in some action adventure movie. That's some safe."

He caught himself before he blurted out that it was his brother's idea. He left the safe open, as he intended to put the book back as soon as they examined it. He walked over to his desk and removed the book from the plastic bag. The leather and pages were slightly damp. He hoped they weren't too damaged, or maybe that would be for the best. Maybe he should just destroy it.

Sam was out of the chair in a heartbeat, hovering beside him. "We should be wearing latex gloves." She chewed on her bottom lip. "Although, I suppose after everything the book had been through, it won't matter too much as long as we're careful."

"Can you feel the book?" Sam had told him she sensed

the power of certain artifacts, and he believed her. He placed it on his desk and took a step back.

"Yes." She started to reach toward the book and then pulled her hand back. "It was muted in the safe."

"Titanium."

"Hmm. That's interesting." She bent forward and examined the cover. "No title. Good leather binding." She glanced up at him. "May I?"

Ezra opened the top desk drawer and pulled out a seventeenth century dagger he used as a letter opener. He flipped the small weapon into the air and caught it by the blade. He heard Sam's breath catch as he offered her the handle. "This way you don't have to touch it to turn the pages."

"Right. Smart thinking." She slowly took the dagger. She raised it into the air and studied it in the sunlight pouring in through the door and windows. "This is fine steel. The ruby in the pommel is genuine. Looks Spanish."

"You have a good eye." It pleased him that she was knowledgeable about such things.

"Salvage?"

He shot her a grin. "Treasure hunt."

"You do that kind of thing?" He could sense her excitement.

"Occasionally."

They grinned at one another, and then Sam cleared her throat. "Right. I should open the book." She slipped the tip of the blade beneath the edge of the leather cover and pushed it back.

Ezra stood beside her, ready to grab the book if it seemed like it might be a danger to either him or Sam. "It's a private journal. The handwriting is quite good. It's amazing the ink isn't more faded than it is. It was protected in several containers and not exposed to sunlight or air, so that probably helped." She ran the tip of the blade over the title page. "Herein are the observations and thoughts of Frederick Bazal, member of the Knights of the Dragon."

The ink was crisp, but Ezra didn't think it was drakon blood. The Knights had a nasty tendency of using that instead of ink to write their treatises as it protected the book and the writing from virtually everything, including drakon fire. Only a drakon's own fire could destroy his blood. It was an evolutionary trait, probably developed to keep drakons and dragons from destroying one another. It was only recently they'd discovered another way to destroy such books, and it had come at a steep price.

The fine hair on the back of his neck rose when Sam pushed back the next page.

She frowned and moved closer. "This is a combination of Latin, French, Spanish, and Ancient Greek. Some of the symbols are Egyptian and others Etruscan. Whoever this Frederick Bazal was, he was a scholar. He changes languages randomly and frequently.

Ezra peered over her shoulder. "The contents of this ledger are for the Knights of the Dragon. Death to those who are not ordained in the blood of their great mission."

Sam jerked back and stared up at him. "You can read this?"

"Told you I was good at languages."

"You're not good. You're exceptional if you can decipher it so quickly." Sam was practically vibrating with excitement. "What do you think he means about death to those who aren't, what was it?"

"Ordained in the blood of their great mission," he repeated. "In other words, if you aren't a member and haven't drunk of dragon blood." He studied the writing on the page. "Why would it matter if they've drunk dragon blood or not?"

"Do you think there's a basis to the curse, or is it just to scare anyone who might stumble across it?" She inserted the tip of the dagger under the next page and flipped it.

It was something to consider. "I don't think the Knights are the type to do something without it having meaning." Which meant the book was dangerous and could possibly be booby trapped in some way. "Blood of their great mission," he repeated.

"They probably mean dragon blood, but since they couldn't have found any, maybe they used some other sort of blood in their rites."

"What makes you think they didn't have dragon blood?"

Sam stopped looking at the book long enough to stare at him. "What makes you think they did?"

He pointed to the book. "This man could speak many languages fluently. He was educated, probably rich. Why would he use those exact words if they weren't true?" He was playing devil's advocate, but he really wanted to know Sam's thoughts on the matter. Did she believe in dragons or not?

"People believe"—she pointed the dagger at him—"in fairies and mermaids, sea monsters and gods. Even the smartest, most intelligent people believe in the unbelievable. They're able to see past the boundaries of reality. Without such people, we'd probably still be living in caves. But even great minds get things wrong sometimes."

She honestly believed that. Sam didn't think dragons were real. There was no way she was a member of the Knights. The last shred of doubt disappeared, but his tension remained. The book could still be deadly to them both.

"They thought the blood of a dragon could heal them of all illness, make them immortal." He could practically see her mind working as she mulled his words.

"Poison."

"What? Is there a recipe there for poison? Or maybe it's one of the formulas they used to trap and enslave a dragon?"

Sam was shaking her head. "No. The paper might be

infused with poison. It isn't common, but some alchemists did such things. That way anyone who stole their journals and tried to read them would die."

Ezra grabbed Sam and swung her away from the book. "You didn't touch it, did you?" He knew she hadn't, but that didn't stop him from running his hands over her shoulders and down her arms.

"I'm fine," she insisted. She held up her right hand, which still held the dagger. "See. Only the tip of the blade touched it. Besides, I might be totally off base. It might simply be words to scare an unwary reader away, much like the Egyptians carved such curses into the sides of sarcophagi."

He knew Sam was right, but he was growing warier of the damn journal with each passing second. Sam patted his arm. "Let's look at the next page."

He didn't like this book one damn bit. Everything the Knights touched was tainted and perverted in some way. It was their nature to do so. "Fine."

He frowned as a thought occurred to him. "Did you handle the book when you first discovered it?" Maybe it wasn't laced with poison. If it was, she'd have absorbed some of it. She might have gotten sick, maybe even died.

She shook her head. "No. I was too concerned about damaging it." She patted his arm and positioned herself in front of the book once again. She held the tip of the blade just above the writing. "This seems to be some kind of spell or incantation." She started to read the Latin words and the air in the room began to shimmer.

"Stop." Ezra slammed the book shut.

Sam grabbed his hand and yanked it away. "What did you do? You're not supposed to touch it. What if the leather has been poisoned?"

"Didn't you feel that?" he demanded.

· · ·

Sam was worried about Ezra. Not only had he touched the book with his bare skin, there was a wild fury in his eyes. But she couldn't deny he was right. She tossed the dagger onto the desk and dragged her fingers through her hair, trying to dispel the uneasy feeling running through her. "I did feel something."

It was best to be honest with him. "It was almost as though something was compelling me to read the words on the page, but why?" And how was it even possible?

"Because you can." He grabbed the dagger and used it to flip the book back into the bag before sealing it tight. "Because you're one in probably a handful of people alive who could simply pick up this book and read the contents."

"I don't understand. You're making it sound as though the book has a will of its own." And didn't that just give her the willies. She'd been around ancient artifacts all her adult life, and she couldn't deny that some items held unexplainable power.

"It does. It wants to trap a dragon."

"But that's crazy. There's no such thing." There was something in Ezra's demeanor that was frightening her. He was more intense, more focused, more angry than he'd been in the short time she'd known him. That was it. He wasn't just angry, he was furious.

"The book is dangerous and needs to be destroyed." He made to grab it, but she wrapped her hands around his powerful forearm. It was like gripping steel.

"Why? It's just a book." But she didn't believe that for one second. There was something about it, something compelling.

"Is it?" He glared at the small object. "And what would have happened if you'd finished speaking the words?"

"I don't know."

"You don't know. And I don't know, either, but I'm not willing to take a chance whatever you do will unleash something neither one of us can control."

"This is crazy. You know that, don't you?" She wanted reassurance when she suspected there was none to be had. "There's no such thing as magic and curses." She desperately wanted that to be true, but she had a sinking feeling in the pit of her stomach she was wrong.

"No such things as magic and curses," he repeated. She wanted the old Ezra back, the one that smiled and kissed her. This Ezra scared the crap out of her.

Right now, he was humming louder than any artifact ever had. That gave her pause. She only responded to ancient, dangerous artifacts, the kind that revolved around the mystical. She'd always believed the aura and power she picked up on were imbued by the belief and worship of the people using the artifact for decades, sometimes hundreds or thousands of years. This was the first time she'd ever had to face the fact that the artifacts themselves might be the source of the power. It was also the first time a person had ever given her that sensation.

"Just as there are no such things as dragons?"

She nodded slowly, afraid to do anything that might set Ezra off. As frightening as he was, she wasn't afraid for her safety but for his. There was no telling what he might do if she set him off. Was the power from the book affecting him? Maybe some poison was leaching into his system from where he'd touched it.

That had to be it. "We should wash your hand and get you to a hospital."

Ezra shook his head. "What?"

Sam nodded. "The binding of the book. There could be poison pumping through your body right now."

The look he gave her was incredulous. "You think I'm out

of my mind because of poison?"

"Yes." She had to believe it, because the alternative was too scary.

He put his hands on her shoulders and yanked her close. He was big and scary, yet all she wanted to do was burrow closer. She had to help him.

"I'm not crazy," he told her. "The power of the book is real."

"How can you know?" she demanded. She was walking on unsteady ground, as though her view of reality was about to be pulled from beneath her.

"Because, sweet Sam, I'm a drakon."

Chapter Eleven

Sam was falling into the turquoise depths of Ezra's eyes. He believed what he was saying. But he hadn't called himself a dragon, had he? No, he'd said something different. "A drakon? You mean a dragon?" Was he confused? Was the binding on the book indeed poisoned?

"No. I mean a drakon."

Maybe it was best to humor him, keep him talking until she could figure out what to do. "Okay, what's the difference?"

Ezra grabbed the baggie and tossed it back into the open floor safe. When he slammed the thick metal door shut, the floorboards automatically shifted back into place. As much as she wanted to keep reading it, to know what it contained, there was no denying the thing was incredibly dangerous. She'd felt something as she read the words on the page. Something that left a queasy sensation in her stomach and her palms sweating.

He prowled toward her, reminding her of a predator on the hunt. She should be scared to death but was more fascinated than anything. Worried, too, but not about herself.

"A dragon is a mythical creature that came through a portal from another dimension over four thousand years ago. They're cold-blooded, cold-hearted, immensely powerful creatures."

He took her hand and began to pull her from the room. "Where are we going?"

Ezra ignored her and kept on talking. "Using their great power, they were able to temporarily take the shape of men and mated with human females." They reached the front door and he opened it. "They had sons."

She was getting confused. "Who had sons? The dragons and the human women?" It felt crazy to be saying such things, like something out of a fantasy novel.

"Yes."

The cold bit at her hands and face and breezed up the hem of the oversize flannel shirt she wore. Ezra didn't even seem to notice the temperature.

"So what happened to the children?" She had to hurry to keep up with his long, powerful stride. She only had socks on her feet and walked gingerly along the path.

He stopped abruptly, and she almost plowed into his back before she managed to stop herself. He whirled around. "Not children. Sons."

Intensity rolled off him in waves. She was getting very worried the book had done something to him. "Why don't we go back inside and talk about it?" She kept her voice calm and low.

The look he gave her was incredulous. "I'm not out of my mind or poisoned." He started back down the path to the dock. "The children were always sons. When they became teenagers, it was evident something wasn't right with them. They weren't human. But they weren't dragon, either."

Sam managed to yank her hand from his when they reached the first wooden plank of the dock, but only because

Ezra released her. "What were they, then? Drakons?"

She didn't know if she should humor him or make him face the truth. This entire situation was spiraling out of control. And why did Ezra believe he was such a creature?

"Dragons could hold a human form for a short time. But the base form of a drakon is that of a human." Ezra yanked off his shirt and tossed it aside. Sam was immediately mesmerized by the breadth of his chest and the swirls of his tattoos.

What was he doing? "Please." She held out her hand. "Let's go inside." She needed to get him out of the cold and away from the dock. The Atlantic Ocean was unforgiving in November. The water temperature was frigid and she was afraid he was going to jump in.

He unbuttoned his jeans and shoved them down his muscular thighs. He wasn't wearing any underwear. He looked like an ancient god standing there on the dock totally naked, with the wind whipping his brown hair back and his turquoise eyes flashing like jewels.

"Drakons are cunning and strong, with the instincts of a dragon and the intellect and emotions of a human." He raised his arms to the sky. "Look at me, Sam."

She couldn't look away if she wanted to. She took a step toward him, wanting to help him in whatever way she could. "Let's go back inside. We can have some coffee or hot chocolate and discuss this."

There was no boat around, no people, no one but her to help him.

Ezra smiled at her. "Watch me," he whispered. Then he dove off the side of the dock.

"No!" She raced to the edge and peered into the water. Where was he? Where did he go? "Ezra!" She screamed his name. He was going to die of hypothermia if she didn't get him out of there quickly.

She almost collapsed onto the dock when his head

popped out of the water. "Come here. Please."

"Watch me, Sam."

"Ezra." She fell to her knees and extended her arm over the water. "Take my hand. Please."

The air around him seemed to shimmer. His tattoo began to pulse, turning the water around him a deep blue. His features began to blur. She blinked and yanked her hand back. His skin was no longer skin, but a series of shimmery blue scales, outlined in the same deep turquoise shade as his eyes. His head flattened on top and became wedge-shaped. His entire body seemed to explode, becoming something else entirely. Something massive.

Sam fell back on her ass. She'd obviously been poisoned somehow and was hallucinating. "Ezra," she whispered. The creature whipped its head around and stared at her.

It rose up slightly, and she caught a glimpse of wings. *Wings?* Powerful ones that flapped once, sending a huge wave crashing over the dock before he disappeared beneath the water.

The salt spray soaked her to the skin, but she didn't care. What had she just seen? "It's not real," she reminded herself. She scrambled back to the edge of the dock and peered into the depths.

He was still in there. She got to her feet and ran along the edge all the way to the end. She was about twenty feet from shore with the driving wind chilling her wet body. "Ezra," she called again.

She caught a glimpse of something to her right and whirled around. The creature, the drakon, rose like a phantom from the inky depths and plummeted deep again. Sam was shaking so hard she couldn't stand any longer. Her knees gave out and she fell to the hard planks.

Then determination settled in. If she was hallucinating, that meant the dragon-like creature was really Ezra, and he was really in the water. "Come on," she muttered. When he surfaced again, she didn't hesitate. She dove headfirst into the ocean. The frigid water closed over her, sucking the air from her lungs. God, she'd never been this cold in her life.

Ezra had been in the water even longer.

She struck out, swimming toward where she'd last seen him. After about a dozen strokes, it became harder to move her arms and legs in a coordinated manner. The flannel shirt and sweatpants she was wearing weighed her down and impeded her motions. She kicked her legs and arms, searching frantically for him. She lost track of time as she began to get weaker and colder.

She couldn't find him. She had no idea how long he'd been in the water, but it was far too long for safety's sake.

Water churned around her, and Ezra suddenly popped up in front of her. He was no longer a creature. Maybe the cold water had washed away whatever poison she'd been exposed to, or maybe the cold had shocked her.

"What the hell are you doing?" he demanded.

"Rescuing you." Her teeth were chattering and thinking wasn't easy. She reached out her hand, or at least tried to. "Get to shore."

He yanked her against his surprisingly warm body and swam straight to the dock, reaching it quickly and easily. He surged out of the water, taking her with him. Why wasn't he as exhausted as she was? He wasn't acting at all like a man who'd been in the frigid water for an extended period.

He began to strip her wet clothes off her. She slapped at his hands, but there was no stopping him. The water on her skin seemed to turn to ice when the wind hit her bare flesh. Tears rolled down her cheeks. Talking was too much of an effort.

Ezra grabbed her and bolted toward the house, leaving their clothing behind. He was swearing a blue streak, but at least he was alive.

She was tired and let her eyes drift shut.

"Wake up, Sam." She tried, but it was too much of a bother.

"Sleep." She managed to slur the one word.

Then she was standing, leaning against Ezra. When she started to fall, he supported her, keeping her upright. Where were they?

Water began to beat at her flesh. She cried out. It hurt. "Burns."

He kissed the top of her head but wouldn't let her move away from the painful sensation. "It's only warm water, but you're so cold."

But he wasn't. He was toasty warm. She burrowed closer, trying to get away from the hot spray. They were in the shower. How had they gotten here? Oh yes, he'd carried her.

He'd jumped into the ocean.

She reared back, her heart pounding. "Are you okay?" She ran her hands over his muscular chest and abs.

"I'm fine. Why did you jump into the sea?"

She cocked her head to one side and stared at him. "You were there. You were hallucinating, and so was I."

He sighed and reached around her to turn off the taps. The water stopped and the sudden quiet was deafening. He grabbed a towel and wrapped it around her before lifting her once again.

"It wasn't a hallucination," he informed her.

"Of course it was." She was a scientist, one who studied the arcane and the mystical beliefs of cultures long gone, but a scientist nonetheless. She believed in what she could see and touch.

She also knew there were some things in life that couldn't be explained, but that hadn't stopped her from searching for an explanation.

He tossed aside the damp towel and bundled her into bed before he crawled in beside her. With the covers over her and Ezra's body wrapped around her, Sam began to shiver.

• • •

Ezra had never been as scared in his life as he'd been when Sam had jumped into the ocean, not even when she was shot. He hadn't known her as well then. Now, even though he'd known her an incredibly short time, she was a part of him. Whether she wanted it or not, whether she believed him or not, she owned a piece of his heart.

Maybe all of it.

Her skin was still icy, but she was shivering. That was a very good sign. He dragged her on top of him, ignoring the way his erection nestled against her stomach. He didn't know if he wanted to shake her for daring to put her life at risk or fuck her senseless until she screamed his name. He did neither. He was shaking, but not because of the cold. He didn't feel it the way she did.

"What did you think you were going to do?"

Sam yawned. "Rescue you." She nuzzled her nose against his neck and kissed his chin.

"Rescue me?" He was a water drakon and she'd planned to rescue him.

"Uh-huh." She ran her hand down his side all the way to his thigh.

It was getting more difficult to think with her touching him. "I'm a water drakon, sweetheart. I don't need rescuing when I'm in the water."

She heaved a deep sigh. "Hallucination."

It both frustrated and amused him that she didn't trust her own eyes even after seeing him. That damn book was giving her the perfect excuse. "I'll just have to shift again once you're well." It was his fault for taking her down to the dock. He'd wanted her to see him in his natural environment. Figured it would be more dramatic that way.

It had been dramatic all right. She could have drowned. At the very least, she had mild hypothermia.

"Sleep. I'll watch over you," he promised.

"Okay." Seconds later, her entire body went boneless, and he knew she was sleeping. There were so many other things he should be doing, including getting out to the site of the *Integrity*. His crew would be out there now, assessing the situation. He should contact Tarrant again and see if he'd discovered anything, and bring him up to date on the book.

But he made no effort to move. There was nothing as important as making sure Sam was safe and well. He'd done a piss poor job of it so far, but he'd learn from his mistakes and do better.

This was the second time he'd plucked her from the sea. He hoped it wasn't going to become a regular occurrence.

The sun shifted, sinking low, and night arrived. He stayed where he was, content as he'd never been in his life. It was rare for both sides of his nature—man and beast—to be at peace. Sam gave him that.

When she finally stirred, he brushed her now dry and very curly hair away from her face. "Hey."

She tilted back her head and peered at him, blinking several times before she smiled. "Hey. How are you feeling?"

"I'm fine. How about you?" He was starving, but nothing could make him leave her.

She yawned and sighed. "I'm good. My arm is throbbing again."

He'd forgotten all about her injured arm, hadn't bothered to change the wet bandage. "I should have a look at it, and you need to take more pain medication."

"Good idea. I have to go to the bathroom first." A rosy

color bloomed on her cheeks. She was embarrassed.

Ezra managed not to grin until he'd eased away from her and was looking in the closet. He grabbed a pair of jeans and yanked them on. Then he selected a blue flannel shirt and carried it back to the bed. "Here you go." He held it open.

Sam kept the sheet in front of her as she sat up, dropping it only at the last second and slipping her arms into the sleeves. "Thank you." She wrapped it around her and scurried to the bathroom.

Ezra dragged the covers up on the bed and straightened them. The damp towel was still on the floor, so he grabbed it. "I'm heading down to the dock to retrieve our clothing." If it was still there.

The bathroom door was jerked open. "You shouldn't go down there by yourself."

The fear on her face just about felled him. "I'm okay. I'm just going to get our clothes and come straight back." He went to her and dropped a kissed on her sweet mouth. That seemed to momentarily startle her. Then she went up on her toes, threaded her fingers through his hair, and guided him down to her.

The kiss was volcanic. Heat rose from the depths of his soul like drakon fire, threatening to consume everything in its path. He pulled himself away from her when all he wanted to do was take her back to bed.

She needed medical care, food, and rest. It was time to put her welfare above his selfish needs. It was his need to have her see and accept him for what he was that had gotten them into this latest mess.

"I'll be back," he promised. He left, but it wasn't easy to make himself leave her side. He went straight to the dock, letting the November breeze cool his heated skin. Darkness had fallen, but he didn't need light in order to see. With his preternatural vision, the moonlight was more than enough.

It took him a couple of minutes, but he found everything. His shirt had blown a ways down the shore, but everything else was where it had been tossed.

He hurried back, not wanting to be away from Sam for longer than necessary.

. . .

Sam was no longer cold by the time Ezra left her alone in the bedroom. His kiss had left her quite toasty. She shook her head and padded to his dresser, helping herself to a pair of thick wool socks. Further searching netted her yet another pair of sweatpants. She was glad he had such an extensive collection, but this was the last pair. She needed clothing of her own. She was tired of wearing oversize male attire.

Ezra returned empty handed. "Did you find our clothes?"

"It's all in the laundry room." He motioned to her to go into the bathroom. "I want to look at your arm."

She wanted a look at it, too. There was always the possibility of infection, and she couldn't exactly go to the local emergency room or clinic for treatment. She had no idea where Aaron Dexter was, or who the Knights had looking for her.

Sam tried not to look in the mirror as she passed. She was pale and her skin appeared bruised beneath her eyes, brought on from fatigue.

She slipped her arm out of the sleeve of the borrowed shirt while Ezra pulled out the first-aid kit. He removed the bandage and gently pressed the skin around the wound. "Doesn't look swollen or infected."

The skin around the wound was bruised and red, but considering her dip in the ocean, it looked pretty good.

He spread an antibiotic cream all around and bandaged it once again.

"Thank you." She slid the shirt back on and buttoned it to the neck.

"You hungry?" As though that was the cue her stomach had been waiting for, it growled. Ezra grinned. "I take it that's a yes."

"I could eat." They could both use the fuel after their unexpected ocean swim.

They started down the stairs, with Ezra keeping an eye on her the entire way down.

"You're okay now, right?"

She nodded. "Yes. I'm still tired and I'm hungry, but I'm okay." A few days rest would have her back to her normal self. But time was a factor. The Knights were not going to sit around waiting for her to recover. Aaron Dexter would be on the move, searching for her and the book.

"And I'm also okay."

She paused at the base of the stairs, wondering where he was going with this.

"You agree that if there was any poison in the book, and I'm not sure there was, that it's gone from our systems?"

"Yes." She felt normal, just tired. And if she'd gotten any of the poison into her system, it would have been from Ezra, transferring from his skin to hers when he'd taken her hand and dragged her outside.

"Good." He walked to the door and opened it.

"Not again," she muttered. He heard her and chuckled.

"No water. I promise." He stepped outside, leaving her in the open doorway. She shivered and wrapped her arms around herself. Ezra quickly shucked his jeans. He was very aroused, his shaft thick and full.

"What are you doing?" She'd had enough insanity for one day, especially coming on the heels of the day before.

"Showing you what I really am."

Like before, the air around him began to shimmer. Power

pulsed, and his body changed form, growing larger. Wings burst from his back. Thick plate-like armor slammed down on his skin. His head became wedge-shaped with an elongated jaw. He no longer had fingernails but wicked eight-inch claws.

Sam knew she was breathing way too fast. This couldn't be true, but it was.

She shuffled forward, needing to touch him but half afraid to. The beast was massive. Around fifteen feet long, and that was not including thick tail that was as long as his body.

"Ezra?" The only thing she recognized was the eyes. They were the same.

"It's me." His voice was rough and so very deep.

She swallowed hard and pinched herself, not sure she wasn't dreaming. But the pain in her arm and the chill of the wind were very real. She noted her hand was shaking as she touched one thick scale. It was warm to the touch, almost hot. Not in the least cold as she'd expected.

"What are you?"

He shook his massive head. "I told you. I'm a drakon."

It was all true. What the Knights of the Dragon were doing was all too real. That meant that everything Gervais Rames had told her was true. There were people who would stop at nothing to capture Ezra and use him for their own gains.

"Change back." She looked around, terrified someone might be watching through the darkness. "Shift, or whatever it is you do."

The air shimmered, and in seconds, he was a man once again. He pulled on his jeans. His expression was grim. She ignored him and grabbed his arm. "Get inside. Are you crazy? You can't let anyone see you do that." She dragged him inside and slammed the door shut. She couldn't stop herself from glancing out the window.

When she turned back around, Ezra was watching her, a quizzical expression on his face. "What?" she asked.

"You're not afraid of me?"

Sam had to stop and think about it. Her heart was racing, and she was in awe of what she'd just seen. She was face-to-face with a creature from myth. A legend.

He was the find of a lifetime. His discovery would change the way mankind viewed the world and would guarantee her name in the history books alongside the greats in her field.

And she didn't care. Because when she looked at him, all she saw was Ezra, the man who'd saved her life and stolen her heart. If that meant she was crazy, then she embraced it.

Being a member of the Dragon Guard took on a whole new meaning. Before it had just been the title of a group, one she'd never truly been a part of. She'd stayed on their fringes in order to get the information she needed to avenge her friend and mentor. Now she knew she'd protect Ezra with her life. Not because he was a drakon, but because he was hers.

Chapter Twelve

Pure, unadulterated relief slammed into Ezra. Sam didn't seem to be afraid of him. He wasn't certain she was convinced he was a drakon, either, but that was okay. It was a lot for anyone to take in, especially a scientist like Sam. But his Sam also believed in magic, whether she admitted it or not, why else would she study the legends and myths of ancient cultures.

He captured her lips, taking the gift she was freely offering him. He lifted her off her feet so it was easier to kiss her. He could taste her sweetness, hear the frantic beat of her heart, feel her hands against his bare chest.

Whatever was between them was real and incredibly powerful.

She wrapped her legs around his waist and clung to him as though she would never let him go. The beast inside him roared with pleasure, and he groaned. He never wanted to let Sam go. She'd been made for him, was his match sexually and intellectually. She was his. His dragon side had known from the beginning that she belonged to him. Now that he knew what it was like to kiss her, to make love to her, he knew he could never let her go.

He kissed a path from her lips down her jawline. He should take her to bed. No, he should feed her. But that would mean he'd have to stop kissing her. He didn't want to do that.

"Ezra." She gasped his name and tangled her fingers in his hair.

"Mmm." He didn't want to talk. He nibbled on her neck. He wanted to map every inch of her skin with his tongue.

"We should…" She sighed and rested her head against his shoulder. "We should talk about this." She shivered. It was a stark reminder of what she'd been through.

In the past twenty-four hours, she'd been shot and dragged across the open ocean in a dinghy. She'd also made love with him, taken a plunge into the icy waters off his dock, and had to come to grips with a new reality. It was far more than anyone should have to deal with. The fact that she was still on her feet and thinking was a testament to her strength.

He carried her toward the kitchen and deposited her onto one of the stools. "We should turn on the lights," she said.

Once again, he'd forgotten she couldn't see as well as him. Night had fallen, leaving the room in shadows.

"I'm sorry." He flicked on several switches, and Sam blinked. Her lips were full and slightly damp from his kiss. Her cheeks held a tinge of color, and her eyes were luminous. And her hair. He loved her hair. It was wild and vibrant.

"You can see, can't you?" She rested her elbows on the counter and propped her chin on her hands. "In the dark?"

"Yes." His stomach growled. They might as well eat if they were going to talk. He opened the freezer and pulled out three large pizzas.

"Are you sure that's enough?" The dry humor in her question surprised a laugh from him.

"It's not nearly enough, but it's a start." He turned on the double ovens, ripped open the boxes and wrapping, and placed all three pizzas inside. Then he set the timer.

"You're serious, aren't you?"

He folded the boxes and tossed them into his garbage bin. He didn't worry about recycling. He had an old metal barrel not far from the house and used his drakon fire to disintegrate all trace of his trash.

"Very." He retrieved two bottles of water from the fridge and set them on the counter. Sam reached for one, opened it, and drank. "I burn a lot more calories than a human. I need at least three times the calories to function normally."

"Wow." She licked a droplet of water off her bottom lip. He swallowed a groan. She was not making this easy on him. His dick was straining against his jeans, practically begging him to grab Sam and take her upstairs.

Oblivious to his predicament, she continued. "So you have enhanced vision. What else?" She was watching him, her expression rapt. It made him slightly uncomfortable. He didn't like feeling as though he was a relic she was examining. On the other hand, he liked that she was interested in him enough to ask.

It was better than her reaction might have been, maybe should have been. "Why aren't you screaming or crying or in shock? You just discovered I'm a drakon, something that's not supposed to exist." That bothered him more than it should. She was taking this all too calmly.

She rubbed her forehead. "I am shocked, but I'm fascinated, too."

"I'm not a damn artifact," he snapped.

She straightened and sat back on her stool. "I'm well aware of that." She tilted her head to one side and frowned. "Did you want me to be scared of you? To cringe and cry?"

The thought of her doing just that made his stomach ache and his chest hurt. "No. No, of course not." He dragged his fingers through his hair. "You just seem to be accepting this all too easily."

She laughed, and this time he heard a tinge of hysteria. "You think I'm accepting this too easily. I've had a year of coming to realize there's more to the world than I could ever imagine." She pointed out the window into the darkness. "How many people on the mainland sitting in their living rooms watching television know that the Knights of the Dragon or the Dragon Guard exists?"

She wrapped her arms around herself. "How many of them have had a friend murdered for a book? A damn book." She blinked hard. He hated the sheen of tears in her eyes.

"Sam."

She shook her head, making her curls dance. "No. You think this is easy. Well, it's not. But what other choice do I have? The Knights are out there looking for me. When they find me, they'll kill me. Then there's you."

He held his breath when she pointed her finger accusingly at him.

"You've exploded into my life like a tsunami, sweeping away every preconceived notion of reality I had. You made love to me and made me feel things I never have before."

"Really?" He liked the sound of that. He liked it a lot.

"Oh, shut up," she muttered. "I don't want to feel an attachment to you." She pressed her hand against her heart. "I have to leave in order to protect you. I felt that way when I thought you were just a man. Now that I know who you are, what you are, I have to leave immediately. The Knights can't find out about you."

She swiped at an errant tear. "I swore after Brian died and I discovered what I was facing that I wouldn't get close to anyone. I knew getting justice for him might come at a high cost. Then I met you."

Her laugh was sad and made his heart hurt for her. "I haven't known you for very long, but it feels like I've known you forever." She turned pleading eyes toward him. "How can that happen? It can't be real, can it?"

Ezra walked around the counter and pulled her into his arms. "I feel the same." He pressed a kiss against her temple. "I wasn't looking for you, but I found you when I least expected." He met her open gaze, moved by the raw emotion swirling there. "I can't explain it any better than you can. I only know I can't let you go. You belong to me."

She caught her breath. "You can't mean that." He could tell she wanted to believe but was still fighting to be logical.

The emotions he felt for her defied all logic, but that didn't make them any less real. "I'm four thousand years old, and I've never had this reaction to a woman before. Drakons use intellect and reason, but we're also instinctual creatures. I always knew that when I found the right woman, I'd feel it. And you, Sam Bellamy, were made for me."

Four thousand years old. As unbelievable as it was, she knew he was telling the truth. She couldn't fathom living that long, all the things he'd done, the places and civilizations he'd seen. It made her head swim. He'd probably met kings and queens. Been with some of the most beautiful and cultured women in the world. She was a twenty-nine-year-old archaeologist. How could she compete with that?

"Ezra," she began, but he pressed his lips against hers, smothering her denial in a kiss. When she was pliant in his arms, he pulled away and continued.

"No. Whatever is between us is real. You're the treasure I've been searching for all my life."

The oven timer chimed, and he set Sam back down on her stool. He didn't want to let her go but knew they both needed time to deal with his confession. He hoped he hadn't scared her off but figured if his being a drakon didn't send her screaming, this shouldn't, either.

He didn't bother with oven mitts since the heat couldn't

hurt him. Best she start to know the real him and everything that meant.

. . .

Sam helped herself to a piece of the pizza. She had no idea what was on it and didn't care. Because she knew he'd nag her until she ate, she bit off a small corner. Spices exploded in her mouth. Her stomach rumbled. It seemed the body demanded its due even when emotions were in turmoil.

She took a larger bite. Pepperoni and cheese tempted her taste buds.

Ezra had already inhaled two pieces and was on a third. He really was different. She knew he needed a lot of extra calories and also that he had exceptional night vision. Oh, and he could change into an extremely large dragon-like creature.

"So do I call you a drakon or a dragon?" How did he think of himself? It was easier to focus on such things rather than face the myriad emotions swirling inside her.

He licked a string of cheese from his fingers. "Technically, I'm a drakon. But I have a human form and a dragon form. It doesn't matter to me one way or another what you call me."

She sensed she'd somehow hurt him with her question. She took another bite of pizza and pondered. "I see you as Ezra," she assured him. He was all man, but more than a man. "I see you," she repeated.

He sighed and went back to the oven for the second pizza. He didn't speak again until he had it on the wooden slab of a cutting board and was running the pizza cutter over it. "I worry that I'm now nothing but an anomaly for you, a legend to be studied and maybe written up in a paper."

She dropped the crust of her pizza onto the edge of the board. "No, you're so much more than that. You're the man who wormed his way into my heart without trying." It was important he knew he was special, and not just because of what he was. "You're the man I'd die to save," she reminded him.

She'd jumped into the frigid waters knowing it could mean her death, and she'd do it again. In that moment, she knew the amount of time they'd known one another didn't make a damn bit of difference. He mattered to her in a way no other man ever had.

He set the pizza cutter down. "Don't ever do that again." His big body shuddered. "I couldn't bear it if anything happened to you."

She gave a small laugh. "Where does that leave us? You want to protect me. I want to protect you. But we have a bunch of crazy people searching for me, people who would love nothing more than to capture you and drink your blood."

Just saying it aloud made her lose her appetite. She pressed her hand against her belly. "I can't stay." There, she'd said the words she didn't want to. A part of her knew the faster she got away from Ezra, the better it was for both of them. Another part cautioned that what they had was special and should be guarded at all costs.

To say she was conflicted was a huge understatement.

"You have to stay." He pressed his hands into the stone countertop and stared directly into her eyes. "I can't protect you if you don't stay."

"And I can't protect you if I do." It was all so mixed up. "They can't find out about you. And unless they find my body, they'll never believe I'm dead."

The Knights were nothing if not thorough.

"How did you find me?" It occurred to her with everything else going on, she'd taken what he'd told her at face value, but that was before she'd known exactly who and what he was.

He lowered his head and blew out a breath. "I was in the water watching the *Integrity*. I'd planned to sneak on board and see what you'd found."

Sam knew her mouth was hanging open and closed it. "That's what your friend meant earlier when he said you should have left me there. Why were you even there? How could you know what the *Integrity* was searching for?" It was time she found out exactly what Ezra's involvement in all of this was.

He grinned. "Told you the guy I was talking with earlier could find out anything."

"Just who is he?"

Ezra shook his head. "I can't tell you. Not yet."

It hurt her more than she expected even though she understood. "You're right. It's best I don't know." What she didn't know couldn't be tortured out of her if the Knights caught her.

"Sam." He reached across the counter, but she ignored his outstretched hand and grabbed another slice of pizza, even though she was no longer the least bit hungry. "I can't tell you someone else's secrets. Not without their permission."

Now she felt petty and small. "You're right. I shouldn't have asked you to do that. I'm sorry."

Ezra watched her intently. His appetite wasn't suffering. He chowed down on several more slices. "So," she continued. "You were there in the water." It all made perfect sense. "You rammed the boat."

"Yeah, I did. I'm sorry Dexter shot you."

She waved aside his apology. "You had to suspect I was with the Knights."

"I did." He polished off the last piece of the second pizza and went back to the oven for the third. He wasn't kidding about his appetite. She'd hate to have his grocery bill.

"But you still brought me back here. You could have taken the book and left me adrift."

He shook his head. "I couldn't. There was something about you." He rubbed the back of his neck. "I can't explain it any better than that. I found you. You were mine."

"Like salvage?"

"Treasure," he corrected. Maybe she was being naïve and stupid, but she couldn't help liking the idea of being someone's treasure. Of being Ezra's treasure.

Ezra licked his lips, sending a river of molten heat flowing through her. She cleared her throat. Now was not the time for sex. There were too many other things at stake, things that needed to be discussed and decided on.

"Okay, you know I'm not with the Knights. I know you're a drakon. Where do we go from here?" And it sounded crazy to say those things.

For a split second, Sam was outside herself, watching and listening to the conversation. It was all surreal. She began to shiver and clutched at the edge of the counter.

"What is it? What's wrong?" Ezra abandoned the last of his pizza and hurried to her side.

"You're a drakon," she said, as if it were news to him.

His expression was grave. "I know."

"Dragons are real. I mean drakons are real." It was all so confusing.

"You can call me a dragon, if it's easier for you. A part of me is just that." Now he looked downright concerned. "Maybe you should lie down."

Like some damsel in distress. Not happening. Still, she did feel a little lightheaded. "I'm fine." She wasn't, but she would be.

Ezra started to lift her, but she scooted off her stool. "I can walk." It was important he not feel as though she was weak, as if he always had to be the one rescuing her. That wasn't at all a balanced relationship.

Oh God. They had a relationship. She was in a relationship with a drakon.

A large shudder worked its way through her body.

Ezra ignored her efforts to keep him at bay. He scooped

her into his arms and carried her into his office. It was his favorite room in the house. Plus, it held all his treasures, of which she was the greatest. He once again sat in one of the large chairs, swiveling it so it gave them an unimpeded view out the patio doors.

"What is wrong with me?" she muttered.

"Delayed reaction." He rubbed his big hand over her arm. "I should have suspected. You were a little too calm about things."

"Well crap." Sam began to tremble from head to toe, and no amount of effort on her part could stop it. All she could do was cling to Ezra and ride out the wave.

· · ·

Herman Temple studied his recently promoted head of security. Luther was a big man, physically intimidating. But unlike many in Herman's employ, he didn't run around in black combat gear. No, the man wore suits. He was smart enough to follow orders, but not so smart as to start thinking for himself and cause problems.

A flawed character trait his last security head had possessed. He'd been loyal and dedicated until he'd met Karina Azarov and become the woman's lover and spy. Temple had no idea what had happened to the man. He'd gone on some mission for Karina and never returned. Temple figured Karina had either gotten tired of him or he'd fulfilled his purpose. Either way, he was gone and no longer a problem.

"You're sure?" he asked Henderson.

"Yes, sir." He didn't nod, didn't fidget. "Ms. Azarov has hired a local Maine company to do some salvage work."

This could work in his favor. Yet another mistake by their leader. He was tired of taking orders from a woman, especially one who was years younger than him.

And time was running out. He was aging at a normal rate once again. He needed dragon blood, and he needed it now. If not for his son's monumental stupidity, he'd have been able to discover if Darius Varkas was indeed a dragon and trap him. But the book with the potion was lost and Varkas was in the wind.

He sat back in his large office chair and contemplated his next move. He needed to be the leader of the Knights. He suspected that Russian bastard, Anton Bruno, had a dragon on tap. He was looking young and healthy when Temple knew he was much older.

If Temple was leader, he could visit Bruno from time to time and partake of the dragon's blood. Bruno wouldn't be able to refuse him if he was in possession of all the secrets of the Knights. To get those, he needed to get into Karina's records and find out what she knew.

The best way to do that would be to kill her, but she was much too cautious for that. His only other way in was to undermine her authority. From there, it would be a small matter to push her out and take over.

"Find out what's going on. If they unearthed an artifact, I want it."

"Yes, sir. I'll leave immediately and send word as soon as I know something." Henderson left him alone, leaving as quietly as he'd arrived. For such a large man, he moved quickly and quietly. Another reason why he was good at what he did.

Temple rose from his chair and headed to the door. He'd go upstairs to his living quarters and think about the situation a bit more before he went to bed. He paused in the doorway, surprised to discover his assistant was still at her desk. He hadn't realized she was still here.

"Victoria?"

She paused in her typing. "Yes, sir. Is there anything you

need?" Victoria was young, beautiful, and incredibly efficient. She knew nothing about the Knights of the Dragon, only his legitimate businesses.

"Why are you still here?" he demanded. His regular staff always left on time. His security teams were always on site since he ran both his business and had his home in the same downtown Manhattan building. Only Victoria came to work early or stayed late.

"You said you needed the sales report for your meeting tomorrow morning." She tapped several more buttons and nodded. "I just sent it to your computer." She pushed away from her desk and unplugged her laptop. It would go into the safe for protection.

Nothing ever left the premises unless he approved it first.

"That's fine. Go home."

Victoria went through the procedure of unlocking the safe and deposited the laptop. She was relaxed and acting normal. She must not have overheard anything from his office, even though the door hadn't been closed securely. Or had it? Maybe Henderson hadn't closed it all the way on his way out.

Yes, that had to be it.

Victoria gathered her coat. Her purse would be waiting for her at the security desk out front. "Good night, Mr. Temple."

He waved her away but followed, watching as she made her way to the checkout area at the front door. The security guard on duty handed her purse to her and tried to engage her in conversation. Victoria was polite but didn't go beyond that. Just the way he liked things. He didn't encourage his employees to fraternize.

He put all thoughts of her out of his head and went to the elevator. Usually, he took the stairs, but he was finding he was tired at the end of a day lately.

He needed dragon blood.

Chapter Thirteen

Ezra was worried about Sam. Her entire body was trembling, and the expression in her eyes concerned him. It was a combination of disbelief and fear. Was she afraid of him? Or was it her own reaction she was afraid of? Either way, it wasn't good.

Even a strong person had a breaking point.

She took one deep breath and then another, and before his very eyes, she pulled herself together. She amazed him with her physical and mental strength. He'd known many human men who hadn't possessed half of her stamina or depth of character.

Was it any wonder he was crazy about her?

"Sorry about that."

He lifted and positioned her so she was straddling his lap. He ran his hands up and down her back, wanting to soothe and comfort her. "It's totally understandable."

She gave a small laugh and rubbed her forehead. "It's been a crazy—" She broke off and shuddered. "Has it only been twenty-four hours? It seems longer."

"It feels like I've known you forever." He didn't know what else to say to help her. He and his brothers were more doers than talkers. Except maybe for Nic.

Sam planted her hands on his chest. "It's strange, but it does feel that way. I'm more connected to you than I've ever been to another person."

The way she said that gave him pause. "That worries you, doesn't it?" His beast stirred inside him.

She closed her eyes and lowered her head. "It does." She sounded tired. "Everyone I've cared about has died. My parents. Brian." She shook her head and raised it, meeting his gaze. "I've never dated much, either. In case you hadn't noticed, I'm a little odd." She laughed again, but it was filled with sadness, not happiness.

"You're perfect." He needed her to understand that.

"Far from it." She rubbed her hands across his chest. "But I appreciate the sentiment."

He growled, the deep sound rising in tone until the entire room vibrated. "You are perfect for me," he corrected.

She blinked and then swallowed. "Thank you." She ran her hands up to his shoulders. "I wish I could see you better."

Ezra swore under his breath. Once again, he'd forgotten to adjust to the fact Sam was human. "I'm sorry." He reached out and turned on the small desk lamp on the corner of his desk. It was a recent edition, something Darius had purchased while he and Sarah had been visiting so she could work at the desk in the evenings.

The ambient glow wasn't overly bright, but it cast the room in a dim light. "Better?"

"Much." She leaned down until their noses were almost touching. "I like being able to see you. All animals use visual cues in communication."

He imagined she sounded like this when she was instructing her students at the university. It was hot as hell.

Then he frowned. All those horny male college guys probably spent a lot of time ogling their professor.

Sam shivered. "What are you thinking about? It can't be pleasant. Not with that ferocious scowl on your face."

He caught her hips in his big hands and pulled her closer. The bulge in the front of his jeans pressed against her mound. "You don't seem scared."

She affected a serious mien. "I have it on great authority that I'm perfect."

Her teasing delighted him. It also turned him on. "That so?" He lifted her slightly, rubbing her against his straining erection.

She gasped and gave a tiny moan. "That's so." She dug her fingers into his shoulders. "What are we doing, Ezra?"

He shuddered, his entire body vibrating with pleasure. He loved it when she said his name. "If you have to ask, I must not be doing it correctly."

As he'd hoped, she laughed. "You have a one-track mind."

"When you're around," he agreed. "I've been alone for so long." He hadn't meant to say that. It made him sound weak. Desperate, too.

Sam threaded her fingers through his hair, the tips massaging his scalp. He almost purred with pleasure. "You're not alone any longer," she said.

He stilled. Barely daring to breathe or to move. "Do you mean it?" If she didn't, it might break him.

"I can't stay and put you in danger, but for as long as I am here, you're not alone."

Ezra didn't bother correcting her assumption that she was going anywhere. No way could he let her leave him. She'd have no protection from the Knights out in the world on her own.

"I can protect myself, protect us." He nuzzled her temple and then her ear. "Promise me you'll stay." He slipped his hands under the oversize flannel shirt she wore and cupped her bare breasts.

She jerked and then groaned. "You don't play fair."

"I'm a drakon," he reminded her. "A drakon never gives up its treasure."

. . .

Sam meant to stay firm on her decision to leave, but she faltered when he once again called her his treasure. He was lonely, but she didn't get the sense he would ask just anyone to stay. Women would flock to him wherever he went. No, he wasn't lacking for female companionship if he wanted it.

And wow, thinking about all those unnamed women touching him, tempting him, made her feel more than a little violent.

"What's wrong? Maybe I shouldn't have said what I did, but I meant it."

She loved her blunt drakon. Oh shit. She couldn't love him. They'd only known one another for a day. But the heart didn't always think, and it definitely didn't abide by any rules of conduct.

She was in love with Ezra.

"Sam?"

"I hate the idea of you being with other women."

He tilted his head to one side and studied her. "I can't tell you I've never been with other women. That would be a lie."

She knew that. She felt stupid for bringing up the whole subject.

He brushed his lips across hers. "I can guarantee from this moment forward, you're the only woman in my life."

She wanted to believe him, she truly did. Her own insecurities were creeping in. She'd only had two serious relationships in her life, and both had ended with the man complaining she loved her work more than she did him. The sad part was they'd both been right.

"I don't do well at relationships," she warned him.

"Me, either." He smiled slowly, and her bones almost melted. "We can learn together."

"I get obsessed by my work," she cautioned. Was she seriously considering staying here and having a real relationship with Ezra? And why not? There was nothing waiting for her. She'd taken leave from her job and had no close friends, no family.

There was the tiny problem of the Knights of the Dragon searching for her because she'd stolen a precious artifact from them. There was no way they were ever going to stop.

He nipped at her chin before running his tongue over her bottom lip. "I get obsessed, too. We can get obsessed together." He slid his tongue past her lips. She groaned and kissed him back. They could worry about the details later. She'd do whatever she thought was best for him. If he wouldn't protect himself, she would.

"You're thinking entirely too much." He started undoing the shirt she wore, opening one button at a time. He gave a hum of pleasure and brushed the fabric down her shoulders, leaving her bare from the waist up. "Look at you." He placed his palms over her breasts. "Lovely." He winked at her. "And perfect."

She laughed, unable to help herself. Ezra was stern and serious, but he could also be playful. She liked that. Considering his age and the vast amount of knowledge he must possess, he didn't treat her as though she were inferior to him.

The light from the desk played across his chest, highlighting his tattoos. She placed her index finger on one and followed the curving design from the top of his shoulder to the waistband of his jeans. "Where did you get this?" It fascinated her.

"I was born with it."

"Really?" No wonder the design was completely symmetrical. It was a birthmark of sorts. She wanted to ask him if all drakons had them, but this wasn't the time. "It's incredible. The outline color matches your eyes, but the main color is…" She paused and thought about it. "Blue, like the ocean."

He circled his palms on her breasts, teasing the nipples into hard nubs. "I'm a water drakon."

Sam no longer cared what he was as long as he didn't stop what he was doing. It wasn't until he chuckled that she realized she'd spoken her thoughts aloud. "I have no plans to stop," he assured her.

He removed one of his hands, lowered his head, and closed his lips over her taut nipple. Sam's head fell back as she moaned. God, that felt good. He flicked the tip with his tongue, sending pulses of sensation rocketing through her. Her entire body was alive as though his touch had electrified it.

She almost cried when he pulled his other hand away. She loved his hands. They were so big and strong, rough with calluses in places. He stroked them down her back and under the waistband of her pants. He found her bare bottom and squeezed.

Sam lurched upward and moaned, on fire with a need that kept growing and growing with each stroke of his fingers, each lick and suckle of his tongue and mouth.

His skin was almost hot beneath her palms. The muscles of his chest jumped beneath her touch. She marveled at the bands that delineated his abs.

Then she reached the button on his jeans blocking her from her ultimate destination. She undid it and slid down the zipper. Ezra groaned. "Careful, sweetheart," he cautioned, but she was past all caution.

She reached into the opening and wrapped her fingers around his thick, warm shaft. It pulsed with life and started an answering throb deep inside her.

Ezra gripped the waistband of her track pants and ripped. The material gave beneath his immense strength. Then he was touching her, stroking her damp folds, lightly rubbing her clit.

She panted, her heart racing. Ezra shoved the tattered remains of her pants down to her knees. "I can't wait," he told her.

Neither could she. She had to have him. "Now."

"Fuck," he muttered. He yanked her close and lifted her until the tip of his shaft nudged her opening. "You sure?"

He needed to stop torturing her. "Yes," she almost yelled. She tried to move, but there was no getting around his strength. He wasn't going to allow her to move until he was good and ready. "Ezra."

He swore again, driving his hips up at the same time he pulled her down onto his cock. Stars exploded and she cried out. He stretched her, filling her completely. They were joined as intimately as two people could be, and it still wasn't enough.

She gripped his head and kissed him, needing to feel the heat of his mouth against hers. He tilted his head and deepened the exchanged. He stroked her tongue with his, ratcheting up the heat level to nuclear explosion.

He worked her up and down his shaft until they were both gasping and moaning. There was little finesse, only raw need on both their parts. She managed to open her eyes so she could watch his face. The intensity of need etched there made her heart ache.

He growled and banded one arm around her waist, urging her on. Placing her hands on his shoulders, she moved with him. Each time he left her, she felt bereft. And each time his shaft slid back inside, it stimulated every sensitive inch of her core in the most delicious way.

He slid his hand between them, stroked the tip of his thumb over her clit, and she cried out her release. The delicious constriction of every cell in her body was followed by an explosion of pleasure. It ripped through her until she didn't think she could take any more. But she was mistaken. The pleasure went on and on.

Sam heard a great roar that shook everything in the room, felt the heat from Ezra's body and the flood of his release. She fell against him, pillowing her head against his shoulder. When she placed her hand on his chest she felt the thundering of his heart. Her own was racing a mile a minute. She clung to him and concentrated on simply drawing one breath into her starving lungs and then another.

Ezra tilted his head back and closed his eyes, but his arms were still locked around her. She kissed his chin and sighed.

• • •

That was not what he'd meant to do. Talk about a quickie. He was still wearing his jeans, her pants were in tatters around her knees, and she was still wearing socks. At least he'd managed to get the damn shirt off.

He'd meant to talk and comfort her before taking her upstairs to bed, not nail her in a chair. It was a comfortable leather chair, but a chair nonetheless. For a man who had thousands of years' experience at lovemaking, he was acting like a youth who'd just discovered the wonders of sex.

Still, he couldn't argue with the outcome. Sam was all warm and snuggled against him, and he was relaxed and content. Maybe that wasn't a word most people would use with exceptional lovemaking, but content was the right one for him.

Sam brought a sense of peace to both his human and

dragon sides. He ran his fingers through her hair, loving the way the fiery locks tried to wrap around them. He adored her hair.

He mentally began to compose a list of things he needed to order. Clothes and grooming products were at the top. If he wanted Sam to stay with him, he had to provide for her.

His chest expanded at the thought of giving Sam whatever she needed to make her happy. It fed the primal male inside him.

She shifted her position slightly, and he groaned. He was still hard inside her. One of the benefits of being a drakon was that he didn't need the same recovery time as a human.

Sam eased upright and smiled at him. "You look pleased with yourself."

He wasn't exactly sure how he should answer that. He was pleased, very pleased, but that might not be what she wanted to hear. Yup, he'd definitely learned a few things about women over the years.

She laughed. "Now you look worried." She leaned forward and rubbed her nose against his. "You can be pleased. You knocked my socks off." She glanced over her shoulder at her feet. "At least figuratively."

Ezra threw back his head and laughed. Joy bubbled up inside him. He couldn't remember the last time he'd experienced joy at this level. Maybe never. He hugged her tightly and just held her. She was indeed his treasure.

Sam kissed his cheek and then shivered.

"Are you cold?" Stupid question, of course she was cold. The air had a slight chill. He spied the discarded flannel shirt on the floor, leaned over, and snagged it.

"A little." She tried to make light of it, but he knew she could be worried about being human when he was much more.

He held the shirt so she could slide her arms inside and

then pulled it closed. He hated not being able to see all of her. What he needed to do was turn on the heat in his bedroom and take her upstairs, lay her out on the bed, and make love to her all night long. Or maybe he could drag a mattress downstairs in front of the fireplace. That might be more romantic.

A fireplace in the bedroom wasn't something he'd wanted or needed when he built his home. Now it was a necessity. Maybe an electric one would do. It would give off heat and provide ambiance.

But that would all come later. Right now, he had to leave Sam, something he wasn't looking forward to.

"What are you thinking?" She fastened two of the buttons on the shirt but didn't bother with the rest.

"I need to go out to the site."

• • •

Sam's body might still be vibrating from her orgasm, but none of her relaxed feelings remained. Tension invaded her body. "It's too dangerous." She gripped his shoulders and tried to shake him. It was like trying to move a small mountain.

"It's necessary, and they'll never know I was there. I want to take a look around. I'm a water drakon," he reminded her. "I want to scout both the *Integrity* and the *Reliant*."

"Why?" Even as she asked the question she knew the answer. "You're looking for artifacts."

"We can't assume the book is the only one. If there was one artifact on the sunken vessel, there might be more."

She knew he was right, but that didn't mean she had to like it. "You're not going alone." On that point, she was adamant.

"You're sure as hell not going with me." Whatever it was he saw in her face, he immediately began to backpedal. "It's not safe. I don't have a boat for you to go in."

"What happened to the dinghy?"

"I scuttled it and stashed it in a crevice deep in the ocean." He gave an unapologetic shrug. "I didn't want any evidence leading the Knights to you."

It made sense, but— "We might have been able to use the dinghy to fake my death."

Ezra lifted her, and she sucked in a breath as his shaft left her. He was still hard, but the mood had dramatically changed. He carefully zipped his jeans and dragged his fingers through his hair. "I didn't think about that."

"You did what you thought best. And maybe you were right." She stood and tried to pull up her pants, but the waistband was shredded beyond repair and the garment fell around her knees.

Ezra gave a snort of laugher, but when she glared at him, his expression was stern. She knew he was trying not to let her see he was laughing. "I need my clothes. Was any of it salvageable?"

"Your jeans and underwear are in the laundry room. Your coat is, too. Your thermal shirt and sweater were a loss."

"I need clothes. At this rate you won't have any left." She kicked aside the remains of the pants, thankful the shirt was long and covered her. She padded over to the patio door and stared out into the night. There was a click and the desk lamp was turned off, plunging them into darkness. There was no other sound, but she knew Ezra had joined her, could feel the heat from his body, sense the sheer power that surrounded him.

She had no idea how she'd missed the deadly aura he emoted when she'd first opened her eyes and found him watching her. He made her senses hum harder than any artifact ever had. She'd put it down to the trauma she'd been through. Now that she was on the mend, it was constant. But it wasn't unpleasant. In fact, it made her skin tingle whenever he was around.

"It's too dangerous." She heard the finality in his voice, but she was adamant.

She shook her head. "I can't let you go alone. I can't." She turned her back on the night and faced him. "Can't you understand that?"

"Having you there will only endanger us both. I can dive deep if I'm spotted. No one on the salvage ship will even know I'm there."

"The salvage ship. It's your crew out there, not the Knights." There was no reason she couldn't go with him. They'd need a boat, of course, but Ezra had to have one somewhere.

Ezra snorted. "If you think for one second there aren't Knights on board the *Easton*, you're mistaken. I'd wager anything that the guy who shot you is on board."

He was probably right. Aaron Dexter was nothing if not determined. She knew that firsthand. Maybe it was stupid, but something in her gut was screaming at her not to let him go alone.

"I'll stay in the boat far away from the wreck site, but I'll be close by in case you need me." He started to shake his head. "I need to do this, Ezra. For myself and for Brian."

He growled at the mention of another man's name.

"Brian was my mentor. He was like a father to me," she reminded him. Ezra rubbed his hand over his jaw. She knew he was weakening. "It's important to me to be there for you. What happens if the Knights have some kind of artifact and use it on you? What if they have a book with some spell that can trap you?"

She didn't believe in magic, but she hadn't believed in dragons, either. And here she was with the son of one. So maybe magic was real. Maybe there were artifacts imbued with some kind of energy that could hurt Ezra. Maybe there were words that when spoken aloud could enslave him.

When she'd read from the book she'd stolen earlier, something had definitely happened. The air had stirred, and she'd almost been able to taste the power.

"And what will you do if they try to trap me?" She knew he was concerned about her. She understood that. But she wasn't helpless just because she was human.

"I'll shoot the bastards."

Ezra shook his head. "You're not going with me, and that's final."

Chapter Fourteen

Ezra glanced back at the small dinghy he was dragging behind him. Sam waved and settled back in the boat. How had she talked him into this? Oh yeah, by asking him. He was a pushover when it came to her. And to think that he'd teased his brothers about being twisted around their women's little fingers. Oh, how the mighty had fallen.

At her insistence, he'd outfitted her with a rifle. He and his brothers all had guns in their homes in case they had to fight. It was much easier to explain gunshots to the authorities than drakon fire. The modern age was hard on an immortal drakon. Everyone had a cell phone and recorded everything. Information went around the world almost instantaneously. There were few places to hide. They did exist, but most of them were already home to a drakon or paranormal creature of some kind. The world had already had a fair share of such creatures long before the dragons ever arrived from their own world.

He wondered if he should mention that to Sam and decided it was probably better he didn't. At least for now.

She'd drag him around the world searching for them. And some of them were downright hostile. Not that he blamed them. Most just wanted to be left alone.

In spite of the danger facing them, excitement stirred inside Ezra. He loved being out on the water. This was where he felt most at home, cutting through the waves and sometimes diving deep. The wind was up slightly tonight, but nothing he couldn't handle. He did worry about Sam.

He never had to concern himself about the wind speed or temperature before. It was all the same to him. But now it was a constant concern. Sam was wearing jeans and her sneakers. She'd borrowed a pair of thick socks to add a layer of warmth. She was also wearing a T-shirt and sweater, both of which belonged to him, under her coat. The black wool hat was back on her head and she'd stuffed her hands into her pockets.

At his insistence. He'd loaded several blankets on board the boat. Sam hadn't looked around sufficiently to realize there was a cave on his island, reachable only from the sea, where he kept several small boats. He had a speedboat, but it sat too high in the water and would be easily seen. The dingy had been the best choice.

He'd been thinking about what she'd said earlier. Maybe she was right about the dingy he'd scuttled. He could always retrieve it and have it *conveniently* wash up on shore somewhere. It would be found and word would get back to the Knights. It might be enough for them to write Sam off as dead. Then she could stay with him.

He dropped the towline and circled back to the boat. He was in his dragon form and placed his head carefully across the bow of the tiny vessel.

"Are we close?" she whispered. "I have no sense of how far the *Integrity* is from your home."

"Another ten minutes." They'd already been travelling for quite some time. "Are you warm enough?"

She held up the insulated mug she'd filled with coffee before they'd left. "Still have some left." She tugged at one of the blankets. "I'm warm enough." She was also low in the boat so the edges gave her some protection from the wind.

"I don't like this." His voice was deeper than usual. When he sighed, smoke poured from his nostrils.

"I can tell." She reached out and stroked the side of his wedge-shaped head. That tiny touch stoked the fires inside him. "Everything will be fine."

He wasn't as confident as she was. He'd lived a very long time, and it was his experience that when you expected something to be fine, it was usually a shit storm.

He dove deep into the ocean, letting it soothe some of the restless energy that swirled inside him. As much as he loved having Sam with him, sharing his beloved ocean with her, he wished she was home waiting on the dock for him to return.

He rocketed back to the surface, hating to leave her alone even for a short time. His dragon wanted her in sight at all times. He snagged the towline in his mouth and started out again. He didn't need a compass or GPS to know where he was. He had a built-in radar and map system. There wasn't an inch of the world's oceans he hadn't explored.

On land, he'd probably get lost without directions. But the ocean was his home, his playground, where he loved to be. He had excellent navigational skills within its depths.

It was taking him longer than it had the night before. Mostly because he wasn't going at top speed, and he was occasionally checking on Sam to make sure she was doing okay. He had no trouble aborting the mission and heading home if Sam got too cold or frightened.

He snorted, sending a spray of water showering out in front of him. Yeah, like that was going to happen. She most likely wouldn't even tell him if she was cold. And she was too courageous to turn back, even if she was scared.

No, the quicker they did this and he got her back to his island, the happier he'd be. He dropped the line and let the current gently carry it. His company boat, the *Peter Easton*, was just ahead and to the right.

When the dingy drifted alongside, he went over his plan with Sam once again. "You stay in the boat."

"Don't worry. I have no intentions of going in the ocean." That reassurance relaxed him some, but it did nothing to dispel the low-level tension thrumming inside him. That wouldn't dissipate until he had her back on dry land, as far away from the Knights as he could get her.

"I'm going to dive down and check out both wrecks. Can you feel anything?" He believed Sam when she told him she could sense objects of power, artifacts used by people in their arcane rituals. Scientists might scoff at such things, but Ezra had lived long enough to know the truth. Such things did exist, had always existed, and would be here long after mankind was nothing but a memory.

Sam shut her eyes and concentrated. "I think so," she told him after about a minute. "It's difficult with you so near." When he stared at her, she shrugged. "You emit a constant hum in my blood."

He couldn't help but smile. He liked the idea of her always being aware of him, of him being—how had she phrased it— in her blood.

She made a shooing gesture with her hands. "Maybe you could swim off for a few minutes. That would clear the area so I could get a better idea."

"One minute." He wasn't going any farther away than he could swim in one minute. He didn't like the idea of her being alone. It would be different when he explored the wrecks. At least he'd be between her and the salvage boat. She was asking him to leave her alone with it and head in the opposite direction.

"Fine." She shut her eyes again, and he dove deep, rocketing off in the opposite direction. He counted from one to sixty. As soon as he was done, he made a sharp turn and swam back, using his wings and tail to propel him even faster.

When he popped his head out of the water, Sam gasped and then slapped her hand over her mouth. Sound carried over water. They had to keep as quiet as possible.

"Well?" He was growing more impatient with each passing second.

"There's something else down there. The *Integrity* only recovered one artifact that sent my senses humming, so there has to be something else down there on the older wreck."

That's what he'd been afraid of. Neither of them knew what it was or what harm it might bring him, but they both knew they couldn't leave it there for the Knights to discover.

Sam chewed on her bottom lip. "I'm not sure you should do this," she began. There was fear in her beautiful eyes, but it wasn't for herself. It was for him.

"Remember what I told you." He wanted to shift from his dragon form so he could kiss her one more time, but he couldn't risk bringing any attention to them. "If something happens and I don't return—"

"Call your friend." She patted her left pocket and the phone she'd secured there. "Got it."

Ezra swore and dove deep. When he got down around forty feet, he thought it was safe enough to shift. His scales shimmered with a luminous glow as his big body shrunk and the man returned. Most people would die without diving equipment. Ezra simply shot back to the top, not pausing at intervals to allow his body to adjust. It wasn't necessary for him.

Sam was whispering his name when he shot out of the water and into the boat. She fell back and knocked her coffee mug over and struck the rifle by her side. Ezra grabbed the rifle and righted the mug. "I'm sorry," he whispered.

"What is it? What's wrong?" Her face was pale in spite of the chill and the brisk wind buffeting the dinghy.

"This." He caught her face in his hands and kissed her. It was really too tame a word for what he was doing. He inhaled her essence, claimed her lips, and branded her with his touch.

Everything inside him settled. He would protect Sam with his last breath. He'd lay waste to kingdoms for her. She was his strength and his Achilles' heel. If the Knights ever discovered how important she was to a drakon, they would not stop their relentless search so they could exploit her. They might believe her dead, but unless a body turned up, they'd continue to search for years to come.

He forced himself to end the kiss. The quicker they did what they'd come to do, the quicker he could get her back to his home.

She was staring at him, wide-eyed, her chest heaving. "What was that?"

"A promise to return as fast as possible. Stay safe. And shoot only to protect yourself." He patted his skin. "Once the scales are on, no gun or weapon can harm me."

"Only potions and magical items," she reminded him. It was why they were here.

"I'll be as fast as I can," he promised. "The current will take you beyond the *Easton*, but you won't drift any closer to it. Stay low."

"Be careful." She brushed her cold fingers along his jaw.

He gave a brusque nod. "I will."

Turning his back on her, he dove, shifting as he went. He could see and function better in the depths in his dragon form. The *Integrity* was on its side with two large holes puncturing its side. He ignored it and went to the older wreck. The *Reliant* had gone down years before. The sea had consumed the human remains and much of the wood, but there was still enough there to know it had been a sailing ship.

Plants and small sea creatures had made it their home, covering it and obscuring much. That didn't matter to Ezra. He'd been salvaging sunken vessels and exploring the deep long before humans had found their way to the depths. He knew what to look for and how to find it.

• • •

Sam studied the black waters until the ripple disappeared and only the ocean waves remained. Ezra was gone, vanished in the depths. Her heart was still racing from the kiss he'd given her. It had tasted too much like good-bye for her peace of mind.

He was worried, and rightfully so. Whatever was down there had the potential to harm him. Why else would the Knights spend so much money to retrieve it? "Maybe it's not as dangerous as the book," she whispered just to hear herself speak.

The ocean had never seemed as vast, as lonely, or as dangerous as it did at this moment. Usually when she was part of an ocean excavation, she was a member of a team on a large vessel. Drifting at the mercy of the current in a tiny dingy was unnerving.

Ezra is down there, she reminded herself. He wouldn't let anything happen to her. And it was her job to make certain nothing happened to him.

The salvage ship was a decent size, probably forty feet or so. It looked well cared for, but she wouldn't expect anything less from Ezra. He'd do everything in his power to protect the people working for him.

There was no movement on the deck, at least none she could see from this distance. Not surprising since it was the middle of the night and they had no reason to set a watch.

There was probably someone camped out at the helm, keeping an eye out on the weather and for other vessels on the radar. The dingy was probably small enough not to register. Or maybe the radar couldn't tell such things. She really had no idea how it worked. Her area of expertise was the artifacts.

The phone seemed heavy in her pocket. She'd urged Ezra to call his hacker friend before they left. She had no idea who the guy was, but if he knew Ezra, maybe he knew what he was. Why else would Ezra insist she call him if he got into trouble?

Maybe he was another drakon.

Sam glanced at the dive watch Ezra had given her to wear. When she'd questioned it, he'd laughingly told her he used scuba gear when he dived with his team from the *Easton*. She could only imagine how strange it must feel for him to suit up in all that gear before diving when all he had to do was jump in the water. Did it make it more difficult for him to dive?

She had so many questions to ask him.

He'd been gone twenty minutes. Not surprising, since finding whatever they were searching for was like looking for a needle in a haystack.

She reached into her pocket and touched the phone, needing the reassurance. The dinghy was drifting farther away from the *Easton*, away from Ezra, and moving in the direction of the shore. It was getting more difficult to see the deck of the boat.

From this distance, the rifle Ezra had given her would be useless. She knew how to fire it, but she was no sniper.

She shivered and huddled beneath the blankets. Her coffee wasn't gone, but what was left was cold. She drank it anyway, needing the caffeine boost. The roll of the waves and the adrenaline crash were making her sleepy.

She leaned her head against the curved edge of the dinghy and stared up at the stars. They were so much brighter away from land. She'd always loved the stars. She wanted to sit out on Ezra's deck with him on a warm summer's night and share them with him. Would that happen, or would she be long gone from his life by then?

Another five minutes passed. She had no idea how long he could stay underwater or if he was coming up at intervals for air. This far away, she was running blind.

She reached into the pocket and touched the phone again. Ezra was not going to be happy with her. Swearing under her breath, she yanked it out and hit the only number in his contacts.

It rang once. Twice. She began to worry no one would answer. It was answered on the third ring. "You better have a good reason for calling, Ezra. I was otherwise occupied."

The voice was deep and gruff. She shouldn't have called.

"Ezra? Talk to me, man."

She almost hung up, but the concern in the man's voice stopped her. Whoever he was, he cared about Ezra. "This is Sam."

"If you've hurt Ezra, I'll gut you while you're still alive and watch you bleed." As threats went, it was an effective one. Sam believed him. Sweat broke out on her already clammy skin, and her heart pounded so hard her chest hurt.

"Sam? Are you there? Is Ezra okay?"

There was no point in hanging up now. She'd called him and the situation hadn't changed any. She glanced toward the boat and kept her voice low. "Ezra is diving down to the original wreck site, to the *Reliant.*"

"Why would he do a fool thing like that? No, let me guess, he thinks there might be more artifacts?"

Sam nodded and then sighed. Whoever was on the other end couldn't see her. The wind and cold were beginning to muddle her senses. "Yes," she whispered. "He's been down there a long time. How long can he stay down before something happens to him?"

"How much air does he have in his tank?"

She closed her eyes and said a prayer for strength. This person was protecting Ezra, which meant she could trust him. "He's not wearing a tank."

The stranger on the other end began to curse. "You know."

It wasn't a question. "I know. That's why I'm so worried." She briefly debated how much to tell him, but Ezra had said to call him in case of an emergency. "The book we found is dangerous."

"He looked at it?" The roar had her holding the phone away from her ear. She looked toward the *Easton*, surprised they hadn't heard it.

"Keep your voice down," she whispered. "I'm in a dingy not far from the *Easton*. And we took precautions, turning the pages with the tip of a knife." No need to tell him that Ezra had touched the damn book. He was upset enough as it was.

"What did it say?" he demanded.

"It was a journal belonging to a man named Frederick Bazal. He was a member of the Knights of the Dragon. A scholar. The writing is a combination of many languages. He changes them frequently in the writing. If something happens to us, it's in Ezra's safe."

"I can get to it," he assured her.

"It's dangerous. I started to read a few words and could sense the power." She hurried on, not knowing if he'd believe her or think she was crazy. "You'll need a scholar, maybe two—people who can decipher the languages. But you have to be careful. It's dangerous to people like Ezra." She didn't want to come right out and say what he was. The phone lines were never secure.

"I can read whatever languages are written in the journal."

"You can?" Of course he could. If he was like Ezra, he probably spoke many ancient languages. Maybe it was a stretch, but she believed she was talking with another drakon.

"I can. And to answer your earlier question, Ezra can stay underwater as long as he needs to."

"I should go. It's not safe for me to be talking out here." Although the sound of the wind and waves, coupled with the distance she'd drifted made it safer than it would have been only fifteen minutes ago. The current was really starting to carry her.

"Any sign of Ezra?"

She peered out over the inky surface. It was difficult to see anything past the hand in front of her face. Only the stars and the moon gave her any light. She couldn't risk a flashlight. She did check the luminous face of the watch, careful to make sure it was facing away from the *Easton*. Not that anyone could see it from this distance, but better to be safe than sorry.

"Nothing."

"Listen to me. If he's in the water, he'll be okay." Sam wasn't sure who he was trying to convince, her or himself. "Call me back in an hour if he hasn't returned."

"I will." It was a promise she could keep. "If I don't, it's because something has happened." She didn't want to think about what could happen. The ocean was a vast and dangerous place. She hung up, wanting to conserve power even though the phone had been fully charged when they'd left. She made sure it was on vibrate before she tucked it back into her pocket and zipped it shut. The last thing she needed was for it to ring.

She tugged the blankets over the bottom half of her face to block the wind, stared out over the waves, and waited.

· · ·

Aaron Dexter walked on the deck with a bottle of whiskey in hand. He'd planned on staying in his room, but the space was tiny, barely enough room for a bunk.

The air was frigid, and he knew it was late, but he wasn't going to be able to sleep, not without something to help him along the way. Which was where the bottle of whiskey came in.

He knew his days were numbered if he didn't complete his mission. They might be numbered even if he did. The Knights were not known for leniency when it came to mistakes.

And losing a multi-million-dollar research vessel and letting Sam Bellamy escape with a priceless artifact were huge mistakes. It was all Sam's fault. If she hadn't taken the damn thing and tried to run with it, they wouldn't have been focused on her. Maybe the whale, or whatever the hell hit them, would have been spotted on radar and they could've avoided it.

Or maybe he was grasping at straws.

All he knew was that he needed whatever else was down there. It was his only hope. He needed something to take to another member of the Knights to try to get some leverage. He needed someone who hated Karina Azarov. That shouldn't be difficult to find. The Knights were all power hungry, and they all wanted to be leader.

And if there was nothing left in the wreckage? That was why he wasn't sleeping. He leaned against the railing of the *Easton* and looked out over the water. He had divers of his own on the way, men loyal to him to join the crew of the *Easton*. He wasn't risking any new artifacts slipping through his fingers.

Something splashed in the distance. He narrowed his gaze and peered out over the water. He reached into his pocket and drew out a small pair of binoculars. "Shit." He scanned the water, but it was too damn dark to see much of anything. Who would be out there?

He panned back and forth and squinted. Was that the edge of a boat? Then it was gone. Probably a figment of his imagination caused by the cresting of the waves. He jammed the binoculars back into his pocket, cracked open the whiskey bottle, and took a swallow. It was mellow and warmed his stomach.

He continued to stare out over the water, not able to shake the sensation someone had been out there watching. Had Karina sent another team to keep an eye on him? Well, fuck them. If he found anything in the wreck below, he was keeping it.

And then there was Sam Bellamy. It was logical to assume she was dead, the dinghy swamped and sunk or drifting out at sea. He'd shot her. Problem was, he didn't have any idea how badly he'd hurt her.

She could still be out there. In fact, his gut was telling him she was.

Just then, something jumped in front of him and disappeared back into the water. A fish of some kind. Damned if he knew what it was. He hated the water. Much preferred to be on dry land.

If he found his way free and clear from this situation, he was never setting foot back on the ocean again.

He tilted the bottle back and took another swig. Tomorrow, he was starting his search for her. He'd rent a boat and cruise up and down the shoreline. There had to be a sign of her somewhere. She couldn't have gone far.

He kept drinking and watching the ocean.

He couldn't wait to get back on dry land.

Chapter Fifteen

Ezra turned his back on the *Easton*. The urge to lunge up, grab Dexter, and drag him down to the depths was almost overwhelming. He'd shot Sam. In Ezra's mind, he deserved to pay for his crime. And only death would stop a man like him. He was a Knight to his core.

The only thing that could override the urge to extract his own brand of justice was that the Knights would double their efforts if one of their men disappeared from the deck of the *Easton*. That would possibly put his crew in jeopardy. Even more importantly, Sam was out there on her own, and he'd been gone much longer than he'd anticipated.

But it had been worth it. After a lot of searching, he'd finally unearthed a small metal box. Whatever was inside was potent. Even he could sense the muted power humming inside. He hoped this was the last of the Knights' treasures from this wreckage. Likely was. They wouldn't have risked sending too many priceless artifacts on the same sailing ship all those years ago. The danger of shipwreck had been a very real concern, as was evidenced by the *Reliant*. They hadn't had radar, forecasts, and the coast guard to depend on. It wasn't like today, where you could fly precious cargo around the world in a matter of hours instead of weeks or months aboard a ship.

He turned his back on the *Easton*, knowing he'd have to go out there later today and meet with his client and crew. Sam would be staying home on that trip. No way could he risk Dexter seeing her. And there was no way of knowing how many men or women the Knights had on shore.

Each passing hour meant the danger to Sam grew exponentially.

With the box secured in his claws, he swam toward the dinghy. It had drifted quite a bit farther than he'd expected. It had taken him much longer to uncover the hidden treasure, but he hadn't given up. Finding treasure was what he did. It was in his blood, part of his soul. That Sam shared such a passion was a huge bonus.

She was awake, even though her eyes drooped. She was shivering, too. Her body wasn't meant to handle these colder temperatures for this long.

She startled, then gave a small cry and flung herself at him, wrapping her arms as far around his snout as they would go. "I was so worried," she whispered the words, and he could hear the fatigue in her voice. She was slightly hoarse, too. Not good.

He waited until she released him and then tossed the metal box into the boat. "Don't touch it until we're home." He had no idea what it was, but he respected the power it possessed.

Sam nodded. "I won't." She picked up one of the wooden paddles and shoved the box against the side of the boat. Then she left the paddle against it, using it to keep the box in place.

She stared at it and shuddered. "It's powerful." He could tell she was worried. "Maybe even more than the book."

And wasn't that just a happy thought. "Don't touch it," he repeated. With that, he grabbed the towline in his mouth and set out for home. The quicker he got Sam there, the better he'd feel.

• • •

Sam heaved a tired sigh when Ezra's island came into view. He had to be exhausted. She was, and all she'd done was sit in the boat. Hours of tension had taken their toll. She yawned and forced her eyes to stay open. No way could she let herself fall asleep with that box sharing the dingy with her.

She still had the wooden paddle jammed against it, keeping it up against the side of the boat. The metal box was small. What could be inside that would give off such a hum of power? Sam wasn't sure she wanted to know.

She'd have to tell Ezra she'd called his friend, as he'd be sure to mention it when they were in contact again. She knew he wouldn't be pleased, but he'd have to get over it.

As if seeing his home had given Ezra a boost of energy, he sped up. The dingy bounced across the waves. She slid sideways and gave a small yelp. He slowed almost immediately and was there, poking his big dragon head over the side.

"You okay?" It was still odd to hear Ezra's voice coming from the large creature, albeit a much deeper version.

"Yeah. I just wasn't expecting the burst of speed."

If a dragon could look sheepish, he did. "Sorry about that."

She shook her head. "No, that's okay. I get it. I want to get home, too." Both of them froze when she realized what she'd said. She'd called Ezra's house her home. "We should keep going." Her fingers were numb because she couldn't put them in her pocket to keep them warm and hold the paddle securely at the same time.

Ezra ducked beneath the waves, and the boat began to move once again, only this time at a much slower pace. Even so, the dock came up swiftly on the right.

There was a flash of light beneath the waves, and then Ezra jumped onto the dock and secured the rope. Water dripped down his chest. He raked his fingers through his hair, sending rivulets of water down his shoulders and back.

There was something so solid, so enduring about him. He was also completely naked. She might be cold and wet and miserable, but she was also human. There wasn't a woman alive who wouldn't be moved by the sight of him.

"Sam?" He held out his hand. She tried to release the paddle, really she did, but she'd been holding it for so long her fingers had cramped.

She licked her lips, tasting the salty sea. "I'm not sure I can."

Ezra swore and jumped into the boat. It dipped to one side, coming perilously close to capsizing, but he immediately adjusted his position and it settled. He crouched beside her. "What's wrong?"

"Ah, my hands are cold."

"You should have told me sooner." He wrapped his big hands around hers. In spite of being in the water for hours, he was still warm.

"What could you have done?" She hadn't told him because there'd been no point. It's not like he'd had a pair of gloves in his back pocket or anything, because he'd been totally naked and, more importantly, a dragon.

"This." He leaned close and took a deep breath. When he released it, the warm air flowed over her skin. He did it again. This time his breath was even warmer, almost hot. It felt wonderful against her chilled flesh.

"Oh, that's so good."

"Try moving your fingers," he instructed. She did, and he

blew once again. This time, the breath he released was much larger. It circulated around her entire body. She shuddered and began to shiver. It was only when warmth hit her that she understood just how cold she was.

"You should have kept your hands under the blanket."

She shrugged. "It kept sliding off. I couldn't hold the blanket in place and keep the paddle steady on that box you found." Not at the speed they'd been clipping over the water, but she didn't tell him that. He'd only feel bad.

Ezra pried the paddle from her thawing fingers and tossed it aside. His big hands enveloped hers until she could move them normally once again. "Let's get you inside." He helped her stand. She was grateful for the assistance. After so many hours of sitting, she was a little shaky.

He lifted her and deposited her on the dock. Then he looked at the metal box. It was next to the edge of the boat, looking completely innocuous. They both knew that to be a lie.

Ezra retrieved the blanket and tossed it over the box, putting a layer between him and the artifact.

"Maybe you should drag it out to sea and dump it." Might be safer for both of them.

"I need to see what's inside first. Once we know what we're dealing with, I might just do that. The book, too."

As much as it hurt her archaeologist soul to destroy precious artifacts, she was more than ready to take the boat out herself and dump both if need be. Some things were never meant to be found.

He climbed back onto the dock and took her hand. "Come on."

"What about the rifle?" It felt wrong to just leave it there.

"I'll get it later."

They hadn't left any lights on in the house. Of course, Ezra didn't need them, but she was all but blind except for the moon and stars. She stayed close. The last thing she needed was to take a tumble.

She was stiff, like some old lady, shuffling along.

As soon as they were inside, Ezra dumped the blanket on the floor just inside the door and kept going toward the stairs. He turned on the light at the bottom. Sam blinked and held her free hand in front of her eyes. It seemed overly bright after being in the dark for so long.

"What are you doing?" Securing the artifact was the most important thing.

"Getting you into the shower." Her teeth were chattering by the time she reached the top. "Letting you come with me was a mistake."

She yanked her hand from his as soon as they entered the bedroom, walked over to the bedside lamp, and turned it on. "It's not like you had a choice."

He snorted. "I could have just left you here. Not like you were going anywhere without a boat." He was right. She didn't like it, but he was right.

She tried not to stare at his muscled back and tight butt bisected by his amazing tattoo as he went into the attached bath. But it did help drive away some of the chill. She rubbed her hand over her face. The cold had obviously hampered her brain cells if she was justifying leering at him.

Her entire life had entered the twilight zone. Or maybe she was Alice falling down the rabbit hole. She was involved with a drakon, and they were being hunted by a secret society, or at least she was. They didn't know about Ezra.

She looked longingly at the bed but didn't dare sit. If she did, she might never get back up. And she desperately needed to use the bathroom and get a shower.

Water began to run in the shower. As if some force was pulling her, she moved toward the open door and peered in. Ezra was setting out fresh towels on the vanity.

"Get your damp clothes off."

He was right. They were damp. The boat had protected her somewhat, but it hadn't held back the spray from the water as he'd tugged her along or the occasional larger wave while she'd been drifting.

She blinked several times and toed her wet sneakers off. Ezra grew impatient and came to help her. He tugged off her coat, the sweater and shirt beneath, leaving her in her bra.

"I can do it." She wasn't some damsel in distress who needed rescuing. Except that's exactly how they'd met. He'd rescued her from death at the hands of Aaron.

He dropped his hands back to his sides instead of reaching for her bra. She wasn't sure if that was a good thing or a bad thing. "I'm going to get the rifle and hide the dinghy. I'll be back."

"Don't touch the box." She wanted to be there when they opened it, just in case.

He briefly touched the side of her face. "I won't."

She nodded and went up on her toes and kissed him. Ezra groaned and dragged her against him. The kiss was hot and deep and much shorter than she wanted.

"Boat," he reminded her. "And shower." He urged her toward the stall and left her alone.

Chapter Sixteen

Ezra placed both hands against the tile and leaned forward, letting the shower spray fall over him. The boat was anchored back in the cove, and the rifle was stowed in its proper place. The shower was to rinse the salt water from his skin and also to try to cool his ardor. His dick was so hard he was hurting. He'd wanted to go to Sam, sweep her into his arms, and carry her up to his bed.

But she was exhausted. Being in the small, open boat for hours, worrying about him, had taken its toll. She needed care, not him climbing on top of her so he could slake his lust. He shook his head and grabbed his shampoo. Sam had used his shampoo. Her hair and her skin would smell like him. It was ridiculous just how much that pleased him.

He wanted to be the one who provided everything she needed. Not exactly politically correct, but he'd never claimed to be that enlightened.

He rinsed and stood there another minute, letting the water beat down on him. Salt water or fresh, it never failed to revive him.

Only his hunger to be near Sam and his physical hunger for food hurried him along. She was already in the kitchen putting together a meal, and he didn't want to be away from her any longer.

He dried off and pulled on a pair of jeans, doing his best to ignore his hard-on. He knew damn well a man couldn't die from arousal. It only felt like it.

He could hear her humming when he silently padded down the stairs. After a quick glance toward the front door to make sure the blanket and the treasure it contained was still there, he went to the kitchen. Sam was standing in front of the stove stirring something in a pot. He inhaled deeply and the fragrance of tomatoes, basil, oregano, onion, and other spices hit his nose.

Sensing his presence, she glanced over her shoulder. "I figured pasta was quick and filling. Hope it's okay?"

"It's better than okay." He couldn't resist her lure any longer. Her gaze never left him as he walked over to her and took the spoon from her unresisting fingers. "I should have cooked something." After everything she'd been through, she had to be exhausted.

Yet a part of him was thrilled by the idea of eating something she'd prepared, even if was pasta from a box and sauce from a jar. She'd made it. For him.

His dragon preened inside him, the creature smitten. He was no better. He wanted to kiss her but knew if he did, they'd never eat. "Let me get this." He drained the water and poured the large pot of sauce all over it. Lifting the pasta pot, he gave it a shake.

Sam laughed and shook her head. "That's one way of doing it."

He loved the sound of her laughter. That he was the one who'd caused it was a bonus. "It's the right way. The only way," he teased back. "Now have a seat so I can serve."

She made her way around to where she'd set two places with large plates and cutlery. He grabbed a fork and used it to scoop several mounds of pasta onto Sam's plate.

He eyed his plate and thought about eating straight out of the pot, but he decided that might be a little bit much. He was about to plate some up when Sam stopped him. "You can eat out of the pot if you'd like. I don't mind."

"You sure?" He didn't want her to think he was an animal.

"One less dish to wash." She dug into her own pasta, swirling the long noodles around the tines of her fork. Then she winked at him.

Ezra shoved aside the plate, set the pot on the counter, and began to eat. As soon as the first bite hit his stomach, he was ravenous. He devoured every last bite. It took the edge off, but he was still hungry.

Sam was about a third of the way through her meal and watching him with wide eyes. He shrugged. "Told you I need a lot more food." He didn't feel embarrassed, not exactly. At least that's the lie he told himself. He'd never cared what anyone thought of him before Sam.

"If you're still hungry, you should get something else to eat."

He hesitated for a moment.

She carefully set her fork on the edge of her plate. "Ezra, you are who you are. And you expended a lot of energy tonight. You're amazing." She reached out and touched the side of his face. His chest puffed out. She thought he was amazing. And his brothers would laugh their asses off if they ever heard about this. "You should eat."

He gave a curt nod, practically jumping off his stool and shooting back into the kitchen. He wanted to touch her so badly his hands shook. He'd faced entire armies in centuries past without batting an eye, but this one woman's touch made him tremble.

He went into the utility room that housed the laundry and two large freezers. He grabbed a package with three flank steaks out of the largest of the two and went back to the kitchen.

Sam was glancing out the window but turned her attention back to him. "Does it feel odd to be eating pasta as the sun is rising?" Sure enough, there was the slightest tinge of color on the horizon.

He shrugged and pulled out his large grill pan. "I eat when I'm hungry. Doesn't matter to me what time of day it is." He tore open the package and slapped the frozen steaks onto the grill pan.

"Shouldn't you thaw them first?" She pointed her fork toward the microwave.

"My way is faster." He leaned down, concentrated the fire within him, the fire that every dragon and drakon possessed. Controlling the flow, he blew softly. He wanted to thaw the steaks, not burn them to a crisp.

The air around the meat heated and the ice crystals melted. He flipped them over and did the same to the other side. When he was satisfied the meat was no longer frozen, he set the pan on the stove on medium heat.

"That is a handy skill." Sam set her utensils down and pushed her plate away. It was still half full.

"Have you eaten enough?"

"Any more and I'll burst," she assured him. He wasn't convinced, but he remembered a conversation he'd overheard between his brothers. Tarrant had called Darius asking about what he'd termed *girl food*. Apparently, women ate a lot differently from drakons. He'd have to look into that.

"If there are other foods you prefer, just write them on the list." He pointed to a magnetic notepad on the side of the refrigerator. "I call in for groceries twice a week and someone delivers them to the dock."

"Now that's what I call service."

He shrugged and flipped the steaks. "I pay for it, but it's worth it."

"Because you don't have to leave your island to grocery shop?" Sam was coming to know him well.

"Yes."

Sam put her dirty plate and utensils in the dishwasher and rinsed the pots while he finished cooking his steaks. She wandered over to peer out the window while he forked the meat onto a plate and then sat to eat. The mood was getting more pensive with each passing second. He was about to ask her what was wrong when she finally turned to face him.

"I called your friend." She looked as though she was confessing a great crime. He chewed the last bite of his steak and shoved his plate aside.

"When? And where is my phone?"

"While I was waiting. You were gone for so long I got worried. Ah, it's still in my coat pocket." She caught her bottom between her teeth. "I know I probably shouldn't have done it."

"It's okay," he assured her. Tarrant was probably losing his mind right about now, but his brother would just have to deal. "I should have come up more often to check on you." Her frown indicated she didn't like that, but it was true. "You didn't know how long I can stay under."

"And just how long can you stay under?"

He got up from the counter and shoved all his dirty dishes into the dishwasher. "I don't know. I've never run out of air in all the years I've been swimming the oceans." He shrugged and wiped down the counter. "I'm not sure I need to come up for air at all."

"Wow." She rubbed her hands up and down her arms. She looked small and lost, which wasn't right. He knew her to be brave and courageous. He tossed the dishcloth aside and went to her.

"What about your friend?" she asked before he could touch her.

He lowered his head and blew out a breath. She was right. The faster he called Tarrant, the better. "Wait here." He turned and sprinted for the stairs. The blanket was heaped by the door. Waiting. Just waiting.

It was time to see what he'd rescued from the sea.

. . .

Sam rubbed her full stomach. She'd eaten way too much, but not nearly as much as Ezra. He could really pack away the food. Must be great to be able to eat that much and not gain a pound. He was all solid muscle. Not an ounce of fat on him.

She'd started a load of laundry earlier, so while she was waiting, she went to the laundry room and transferred the washed clothing to the dryer. If nothing else, she'd have clean underwear and jeans that actually fit her.

Ezra's footsteps sounded on the stairs. He held his phone in his hand. "You might as well hear what he says." He pressed the one contact number in the phone and waited. It rang once before it was answered.

"Where the hell have you been?"

Sam jerked back. Ezra's friend was furious. Not that she blamed him. They should have called him right away.

"Sorry." Ezra dragged his fingers through his long, brown locks. "I had to get Sam warmed up and get something to eat."

"I'll just bet you warmed her up."

Sam stiffened, and Ezra growled. "Careful what you say. You're on speaker. And I was more concerned about hypothermia than about getting Sam into bed."

"How is she?"

"She's fine," Sam snapped back. She was getting tired of

them talking about her like she wasn't even here. The stranger simply laughed.

"What did you find?"

Ezra glanced at the mound by the front door. "I don't know. It's a metal box, possibly silver, but it's not the box we're interested in, but what's inside."

"Don't open it."

"Tarrant."

"No, you don't know what's inside."

Now Sam had a name for the stranger. Tarrant. Whoever he was, he was worried about Ezra. "I can open it," she offered. "After all, the Knights are human. If it's safe for them to touch it, I should be fine." Or at least she hoped so.

"No offense, Sam," Tarrant shot back. "But I don't know you from Adam."

"You don't trust me." She didn't know why that should surprise her. It only made sense not to. Still, she was hurt.

"You're damn right I don't."

"That's enough, Tarrant."

"You're going to do it, aren't you?" There was a lot of swearing in the background. "Okay, let me set up a conference call with the others. I'll call you back in three minutes. Don't open the fucking box until I get back to you," he ordered.

"Done." Ezra ended the call and gave her a reassuring smile. "Looks like we're going to open the box."

She edged closer to the blanket covering their treasure. "Maybe Tarrant is right. Maybe we shouldn't open it."

Ezra tucked his phone in his back pocket and dropped his hands on her shoulders. "You don't really believe that, do you?"

She couldn't lie to Ezra. "Honestly, no. We need to know what we're dealing with."

He turned her until she was facing his chest, his bare chest. God, she'd done her best over their late-night snack or early breakfast, whatever you wanted to call it, not to stare at all that muscular exposed skin.

Right now, he was humming in her blood louder than the artifact. She placed her hand on his chest and stroked her index finger around an intricate swirl. He groaned and she glanced up.

"You shouldn't do that."

"Why not?"

In lieu of an answer, he slammed his mouth down on hers. The kiss was hot and consuming, burning every other thought from her brain. She'd been so worried about him while he'd been diving, and he'd been so aloof since they'd returned home. This was the Ezra she loved, the wild, untamed lover who'd rescued her body from the sea and stolen her heart.

His big hand cupped the back of her head, holding her in place while he deepened the kiss. Their tongues battled for supremacy. He stole her breath and then returned it to her. He pulled back, gasping for breath, groaned, and then kissed her again.

She ran her hands over his chest and shoulders, needing to touch him as much as she needed air to breathe. He slid his palms beneath the shirt she wore, cupping her bare bottom. He dragged her against him and his arousal pressed against her stomach.

The phone rang.

They both jerked apart, and Sam began to laugh. "Now you get passionate. When we're expecting Tarrant to call back."

"We can forget all about him." Ezra eyed the stairs to the bedroom.

Sam tugged at the hem of the shirt and tried to ignore the low-level arousal pulsing through her body. "Something tells me he isn't the kind of man you ignore. He might call out the national guard if you don't answer."

Ezra snorted. "Or worse, he might come here himself." He dragged the phone out of his pocket. "I'm here. Give me a sec."

"What the hell were you doing? No, wait, don't answer that."

"I won't." Ezra approached the blanket, but Sam stepped in front of him before he could touch it.

"Let me." When his brows lowered, she knew he was going to object. "We don't know how it might react to you. Let's be safe."

"Listen to the woman," Tarrant told him. "But I promise, you hurt Ezra, and I'll find you. There is nowhere on this planet you can hide from me."

She believed him. This was not a man who made idle threats. She ignored Ezra's warning growl and gingerly picked up the bundle. "Where are we doing this?"

"Office." Ezra led the way and she followed. "Are the others there?" he asked Tarrant. She wondered who the *others* were. Friends? Other drakons?

"Did you discover anything about the Dragon Guard?" she asked. Ezra indicated the center of the room. The sun was rising, but it was still dark enough that she needed some light. Ezra turned on the desk lamp before she asked.

"Who the hell are the Dragon Guard?" This new voice was even deeper than Tarrant's.

"According to Sam, they're a group set up to counter the Knights," Tarrant replied. Sam was beginning to feel superfluous to the conversation. Ezra was standing across from her, glaring at the phone. He tossed it onto the desk and crouched next to the blanket.

"Then why the hell haven't I heard about them?" the new voice demanded.

"Because contrary to your opinion, you don't know everything," Ezra shot back.

There was silence and then a snort of female laughter. There was a woman with one of the men. Sam's curiosity was piqued.

"He's got you there, big guy," the female replied. "Hi, Ezra."

"Hey, Sarah. Darius giving you trouble?"

"No more than usual, and nothing I can't handle."

"If you're through emasculating me, can we get on with this?" Sam found herself smiling at Darius's reply. He was trying to sound angry, but she could hear the wealth of love in his voice. Whoever these people were, they were very close to Ezra.

"Is Nic there?" Ezra asked.

"I'm here. I just can't get a word in edgewise with the other Chatty Cathys." All the men began to laugh. She knew it was some kind of joke, one they were all privy to, and one she didn't understand. It emphasized that she was on the outside of their group. Temporary.

Ezra rose and came to her side. He put his arm around her shoulders, leaned down, and whispered in her ear. "Darius and Tarrant rarely say two words when one will do. Nic is the chatty one."

"I heard that," Nic protested. "And you're… Well, you're right. What can I say? I'm a social butterfly, while the rest of you are hermits."

"Can we get on with this?" Tarrant groused. "I've been up all night."

"Translation, Valeriya has been up all night, and you want to take her to bed," Nic said.

"Shut up, Nic," Tarrant shot back. "And to answer your question, I'm still looking into the so-called Dragon Guard. With so many damn gaming sites and fantasy fiction, it's taking some time to weed through everything. Early indications are they might actually be real."

Of course they were real. They'd approached her, hadn't they? Okay, really only one man had approached her, but that had to mean something. Didn't it? It was giving her a headache just thinking about it.

"Can we just do this?" Sam was getting more nervous with each passing second. She carefully peeled away the blanket and studied the object. Going into clinical mode, she began to report. "The box is about eight by six and about four inches high." She knelt so she could get a better view. "It appears to be silver, or some silver alloy."

"Get some pictures," Tarrant ordered.

"You think you can trace it?" There were obviously benefits to having a skilled hacker around.

"If it's been referenced anywhere, I'll find it," he promised. "Any markings or writing on it?"

Tarrant thought like a scientist. "Give me your phone," she ordered Ezra. He handed it to her and she took several pictures from all angles. "Send these," she told him.

While he was doing that, she took a corner of the blanket and rubbed it over the metal. "There are markings, but they've been compromised." Worn down from years in the sea. "Where exactly did you find the box?" She hadn't thought to ask Ezra until now. She'd been excited by the fact he'd found something.

"Inside a pottery jar, but I smashed it open and took the box." Sam winced and Ezra shrugged. "I was more concerned with speed than preserving the jar."

Even thought it went against all her training, she knew he'd done the right thing. "Okay, so maybe whatever was etched on the box was worn off by years of use. I'm unable to determine when it was made at this point." She'd need more time and better equipment to do that. "The box has two clasps on the front. A skilled craftsman made this piece."

She glanced at Ezra. He looked worried, but not about

himself. "You don't have to do this," he told her.

She forgot there were other people listening to them. There was only Ezra. "I have to. If this is something that can hurt you, we need to find out so we can neutralize it."

He crouched beside her. "If something happens, I'm going to melt whatever is inside."

She blinked in surprise. "You can do that?" Then she shook her head. "Of course you can. That hot air is good for something more than thawing steaks."

Ezra had a pained expression on his face. Several male voices chuckled, but she could hear the underlying tension. It wasn't helping any of them to draw this out.

"Okay." She took a deep breath. "I'm opening the clasps on the box." Maybe because it had been stored in a jar for all these years, but the metal clasps opened easily.

Ezra was a large presence beside her, strong and steady. The others on the phone were silent. You could cut the tension with a knife. And speaking of knives. "Hand me that Spanish dagger we used on the book." It was better she didn't touch the box any more than she had to.

He retrieved it from the desk and handed it to her. "This is getting to be a habit."

"Let's hope this is the last time." She took the dagger and poked the tip under the edge of the lid and slowly lifted.

The velvet lining was faded, but what was inside glowed. Dark yellow gold shone. The thick chain was set with large rubies. She didn't need to be a jeweler to know they were exceptional. They glowed with an inner light that was breathtaking.

Beside her, Ezra stirred. "Son of a bitch."

Chapter Seventeen

Ezra was stunned by what he was seeing. This was the last thing he'd expected to find. Now that the box was no longer covering it, the object felt different.

"Can you sense the difference," he asked Sam.

She looked as dumbstruck as him by their discovery. "I can. The power coming from it, the energy isn't the same as the book. I'm not sure I can describe it." She held her hand about six inches from the stunning necklace. "It feels —"

"What? What does it feel like?" he demanded.

"It feels like you. Kind of, but not quite."

"What is it?" Tarrant demanded. "What's in the damn box?"

"A necklace," Sam offered.

"Drakon tears," Ezra told his brothers. "From a fire drakon."

"What are drakon tears?" Sam asked.

"Fuck," Tarrant swore. "Rubies?"

Sam was surprised that Tarrant knew what stones were in the necklace. Ezra knew he'd have to give her some answers once he was done talking with his brothers.

"Oh no." He heard Valeriya gasp. Both Sarah and Valeriya knew what it meant as they had necklaces of their own.

"What is it? What's wrong?" Sam demanded. "Is it safe to touch? Should I close it up again? Talk to me." Ezra took both her clenched hands in his and bowed his head. "Ezra, you're scaring me."

That was the last thing he wanted to do. "The only way the Knights could have that necklace was if they'd killed the person it belonged to or captured or killed the drakon who'd gifted her with it."

...

Ezra's explanation hit Sam like a ton of bricks. She'd made it her life's work to study the past. She knew people killed for artifacts. There'd never been a time in history when people hadn't killed one another and taken what they wanted, but somehow this brought it close to home.

"Was it someone you knew?" How much worse would that be? She might have studied history, but Ezra had lived it.

He shook his head. "I have no idea. Drakons keep to themselves, especially in the last three thousand years or so."

Geez, he said that like most people might refer to decades. If she hadn't already been sitting, she'd probably need to right about now. It was easy to forget he was as close to immortal as a person could get.

"Why? Why would they do that?"

A loud growl was emitted from the phone speaker. "Because it's what the Knights do. They enslave us for our blood so they can prolong their puny lives and cure their diseases."

Oh my God. Darius had said *our* blood. He was a drakon, too. She swiveled around to stare at Ezra. Everything Gervais

Rames had told her was true. She felt all the blood draining from her face. "It's true, isn't it? It can prolong their lives."

Before anyone could reply, she slammed the lid shut on the necklace. "We have to get rid of the book and the necklace. We can't let the Knights have anything that might hurt you."

Total silence. It might have something to do with the fact that she was acting like a crazy person, but that was fine with her. "How do we destroy the book?" she demanded. "Tarrant?" He seemed like he'd be the one to ask about such things.

"Is it written in drakon blood?"

The pasta in her stomach threatened to come racing back up. The Knights wrote their books in blood?

"I don't think so," Ezra replied. "I had a sense that it was just ink, but I could be wrong."

She tossed the blanket over the box and shoved Ezra, or tried to.

"What are you doing?" he asked.

"You need to stay as far away from these artifacts as possible." Why did he not understand that?

"But you knew I was a drakon. Why the sudden concern?"

Sam dragged her fingers through her curls, cursing when they got tangled in the thick mass. "Because it's real now. They want your blood." She sent him a fierce glare. "They can't have it." She grabbed his shoulders and shook him. Okay, she tried to shake him. He moved maybe an inch. "Do you hear me?"

"Ah, I think everyone heard you." He angled his head toward the phone.

His friends were still listening. Maybe she should be embarrassed, but she didn't care what they thought of her. Not as long as Ezra was safe. "Tell him I'm right. Tell him to get away from the box. And that damn book in the floor safe." She knew she was verging on hysterics, but the thought of someone trapping Ezra and keeping him locked up for his blood was unthinkable.

She couldn't, wouldn't let it happen. Not as long as there was breath in her body. "Tell him," she ordered.

"You've got a treasure." There was awe in Nic's voice.

"It's not treasure. It's dangerous. Haven't you been listening to anything I've been saying?" Honestly, the man was acting about as intelligent as a rock.

"I do indeed," Ezra whispered.

"What?" Sam felt as though she'd missed something. "What are you talking about?"

Ezra dragged her into his arms. "You. You're the real treasure." Before she could reply, he kissed her.

She tried to resist, there were more important matters to deal with than kissing. But when his lips touched hers, she couldn't quite remember what they were.

It was the sound of male laughter in the background that brought her back to her senses. She slapped her hands against his chest and pushed until she managed to get him to raise his head and stop kissing her. Even then, he kept her perched on his lap where he'd dragged her.

"There's no time for kissing." God, had she said that out loud? Totally mortified, she ignored the burning in her cheeks. "There are more important matters to attend to."

"There is nothing more important than kissing," Ezra solemnly informed her. The devil was enjoying her discomfort.

"I'm sure the others would disagree." Surely Tarrant and the others would back her up.

"He's right," Darius replied.

"I can't disagree," Nic quipped.

Tarrant was her last hope. "Tarrant?"

He cleared his throat. "Lock the damn necklace away and call back later." He gave a significant pause. "When you're done kissing." The bastard was laughing when he ended the call.

Ezra reached out one long arm and turned off his phone. Silence filled the space. He smiled down at her. "Now where were we?"

. . .

Ezra knew Sam was upset on his behalf. Maybe it was wrong, but it made him feel good inside. She obviously cared a great deal for him. Her reaction to the necklace hadn't been one of avarice or of scholarly interest. All she'd cared about was protecting him.

He tried to kiss her again, but she scrambled off his lap before he could stop her. "We need to deal with the necklace. The book, too." She began to pace around the room. Not even the artifacts lining the shelves in his office could distract her.

She really was upset.

Ezra pushed to his feet and gathered the necklace in his hand. The gold links ran through his fingers. There had to be more than a dozen perfect rubies set in the chain. At any time in history, it was worth a fortune.

"Put that down." Sam stalked toward him. "Haven't you been listening? That thing could be dangerous."

"It doesn't belong to the Knights. It belongs to the drakons."

Sam tried to take it from him, but he held it away from her. Her scowl deepened. "What if they put some spell on it? Did you think about that?"

Ezra closed his eyes and concentrated on the exquisite piece of jewelry. Whatever drakon had created the stones was dead. Otherwise, the Knights would never have obtained it. He tried to get a sense of something, anything from the piece. The only thing he got was the hum of power that seemed to emanate from the rubies themselves.

"What are you doing?" Sam's voice had lowered to a

whisper.

"Trying to get a sense of the piece." He opened his eyes, frustrated that he couldn't get anything. "Maybe Sarah can find out more."

"So you'll let this Sarah person handle it, but not me." She began pacing once again. "Great. That's just great. If I'm so unnecessary and untrustworthy, I might as well pack my bags and leave. Wait a minute, I don't have anything to pack. I might as well just leave."

Wow, his Sam had a temper. Ezra had to say he liked this latest discovery. He might have known, given the fiery color of her hair. "Sarah has the gift of psychometry." That got her attention. She stopped and placed both hands on her hips.

"Really?"

"Books are her specialty, but she can use it for other items, especially something as personal as this." Knowing he had to do this, for Sam and for their relationship, he held the necklace out to her.

She put her hands behind her back. "Why?"

Sexy and smart. She wanted to know why his sudden change of heart. "These are drakon tears." He ran the tip of his index finger over one of the rubies. The morning sun caught it and made it glow like fire.

"So you said, but what exactly are drakon tears?"

He ignored her question. "This was made by another drakon."

She tilted her head to one side and studied him. "Yes."

He knew she didn't understand. It felt stupid to say it aloud, but there was no changing how he felt. "I didn't want you touching something that was made by another drakon." He said it fast and then shut up.

• • •

Sam's mouth fell open. "You're jealous?" That didn't seem right. It was just a necklace.

"Possessive," he corrected. He dragged his free hand through his hair. She was beginning to recognize it as something he did when he got frustrated.

"Of the necklace?" She was still missing something.

"Not the damn necklace. Of you. Okay? I didn't want you touching something another drakon made."

Okay. Wow, that wasn't what she'd expected. And why did that warm her insides? She didn't need some guy to go all Neanderthal on her, but darned if she didn't like it.

She walked over to stand in front of him. He was wearing a pair of jeans and nothing else. The angle of the rising sun had him half in light and half in shadow. He was like a work of art with his broad shoulders, muscled biceps and chest, and carved abs. His face was too rugged to be pretty. No, Ezra was compelling, bold, and wholly masculine. The necklace, which was quite a substantial piece, appeared almost dainty dangling from his large hand.

The tattoo that bisected his body seemed more vibrant, almost as though it were alive. Was it glowing? She blinked, and the glow was gone. Must have been her imagination.

She reached out and ran her finger over the gold links. There was a definite pulse of energy coming from the piece.

Ezra swallowed and his grip on the necklace tightened. She made no comment and turned her attention to one of the rubies. It was multifaceted and almost seemed alive. She didn't try to take the necklace, but she turned Ezra's hand so it caught the light better.

The gemstone was better quality than anything she'd ever seen, and she'd seen treasure from many cultures, including the pharaohs of Egypt. These rubies were unrivaled. "I've never seen anything quite like it." She knew she'd been unable to keep the awe from her voice when Ezra growled.

When she glanced up, his eyes were glowing turquoise. She immediately took a step back and held up her hands. "I don't even like rubies, okay?"

He hung his head and huffed out a breath. "I know I'm acting like an ass."

She patted his arm. "That's okay. I forgive you."

He gave a snort of laugher and then went to his knees. She wasn't sure what he was doing until he pushed aside the blanket and the rug covering the floor. The safe.

"Do you think it's okay to put the book and necklace together?" She didn't like the idea.

Ezra paused. "I imagine they were together for years in someone's collection."

She twisted her hands together. "It just feels wrong to put something that belonged to a drakon next to a book that might have been used to hurt or enslave it." There was no logical reason for her reaction, but that didn't matter. All she knew was it felt wrong.

Ezra studied her face and then nodded. "What should we do with it?"

Sam was suddenly chilled. She rubbed her hands up and down her arms to try to warm herself. "Do you have another safe? It doesn't have to be Fort Knox like that one." She motioned to the floor safe.

He rose to his feet and nodded. "Come with me." He held out his hand, and she took it. Something had changed between them, and she wasn't sure what it was. There was an intensity about Ezra that hadn't been there before, and God knows, the man had been intense from the very beginning.

They went up to the bedroom, and Ezra went straight to the closet. Now she was totally confused. "You're going to store it with your shirts and jeans?"

"Watch." He shoved aside the hangers and pressed a hidden lever in the back of the closet. An area of the wall slid back to reveal a door. Like the safe below, there was a digital lock on it, but no retinal scanner. Unless you were looking for it, you probably would never suspect it was there.

"Jeez, you're like James Bond." No, that wasn't right. "More like Indiana Jones." She could see Ezra running around some jungle in search for treasure. Come to think of it, he and his friends probably knew where most of the world's treasures were located since they'd been around when it was buried.

He quickly input the code and the door opened. A light automatically came on, illuminating the small room. It was about six by six and filled with floor-to-ceiling shelves. Ezra had to duck to enter. There was barely enough room for the two of them to stand inside. Ezra took up a whole lot of what little floor space there was.

Sam was dumbstruck. Gold and silver coins from various civilizations filled chests on the floor. A vase from the Ming Dynasty sat beside a bronze sculpture and a gold bracelet. There was so much to see. Like his office downstairs, there was something curious and spectacular everywhere she looked.

"This is incredible." She had a feeling this might only be the tip of the iceberg. Ezra was a man with many secrets.

He carefully set the necklace on the lone empty shelf at the back of the room. "You collected all this."

"Yes."

"It must have taken you years." She couldn't imagine how many places he'd been and what he'd seen. Then it occurred to her that Ezra was a water drakon. "Is all this from the ocean? From shipwrecks?"

He walked toward her until she was forced to back out of the room. She would have liked to have a better look at everything, but now was not the time. He closed the door, locking the walk-in safe.

"Most of it came from ships I discovered at the bottom of

the ocean. Other items came from civilizations obliterated by natural disaster.''

And didn't that just give her the willies. Ezra closed the closet door and crossed his arms over his chest. Biceps bulging, he studied her.

"What?"

"You're not going to ask me if I sunk some of the ships myself so I could have the treasure?"

"Now you're really being an ass." Why would he even ask her such a thing?

He shrugged his massive shoulders. "I sank the *Integrity*."

"You were trying to save me." Wow, that was arrogant of her considering he hadn't even known who she was at the time. "Or rather, you were protecting yourself from the Knights. And considering what they want to do to you, I can't really fault you for that."

Sam walked to the window and stared out at the sea. The sun was a glowing ball on the horizon. She liked that Ezra had such large windows in every room of his home. There was something calming about the sea.

"I guess you'll be leaving soon, to check in with your crew on the *Easton* and see what the Knights are up to." She hated the idea of him being out there on his own, but there was nothing she could do to help him. She'd just be in the way.

"Maybe you could drop me at a department store so I could pick up some clothes." She chewed on her bottom lip as she tried to figure the logistics. "I need to get to Bangor. I've got a storage unit there with a new identity, money, and some clothes."

She'd known when she'd taken the job with the Knights that she'd never be going home again, which was why she'd ditched her apartment months ago and now lived in a weekly rental. If she didn't pay up by the end of the month, the landlord would simply get rid of her few belongings.

Everything of value was already in a storage unit in Vermont under the same name as her new identity. She hoped she'd be able to claim it at some point down the road.

Ezra's hands fell hard on her shoulders and he spun her around. "You're not going anywhere."

"Don't you see," she protested. "I'm a danger to you."

"Are you sure that's all it is? Or are you afraid of me?" He was positively glowering. His brows were lowered over his eyes, and he was emitting a low growl. She didn't think he was aware he was even doing it.

She did the only thing she could think of to convince him. She slapped her hands on either side of his face and dragged him down so she could kiss him.

Chapter Eighteen

Ezra was ready for a fight. No way was he going to let Sam leave. What he wasn't prepared for was for her to grab him by the face and plant her lips on his.

Inside, his dragon went from growling to practically purring like a kitten, the damn creature was so happy.

He didn't know what to think of Sam. She was unlike any other woman he'd ever met. He'd known his share of gorgeous, intelligent, and sexy women, but Sam eclipsed them all.

She'd shown the same enthusiasm for the cheap trinkets lining his office walls as she did for the gold, silver, and jewels in his larger safe. Come to think of it, she'd seemed more enthralled by what was down in his office.

Nor did she believe he'd destroyed the ships he'd gotten the treasure from, when it was a logical conclusion to reach. After all, he was a sea drakon. He could travel the ocean scuttling boats at will. And maybe some of his brethren had, although most drakons would not harm innocents. But if a boat filled with Knights of the Dragon happened to be crossing an ocean... Let's just say he wouldn't condemn any drakon for sinking the damn thing.

"Stop thinking and kiss me," Sam demanded. She was right. The rest could wait. He had her warm and willing in his arms. Nothing else mattered.

She was his. He didn't like the continued talk of her leaving. While it warmed him to know she was concerned about him, it made his blood run cold to imagine her out there in the world alone with the Knights searching for her.

He slid his tongue past her lips, claiming her sweet mouth as his own. Her moan of pleasure went straight to his dick, making the damn thing stand at attention and demand release from the confines of his jeans.

He knew he had to get out to the *Easton* and talk with his crew, check out the man representing the Knights. Dawn was long past, and he knew his crew would already be hard at work. The first thing they'd do is send down divers to assess the shape of the *Integrity*. They need to see if the holes could be patched or if there was too much damage to refloat her. They would have also contacted the proper authorities about dealing with the fuel on board the vessel. Last thing anyone wanted was a fuel leak polluting the area.

Sam went up on her toes and pressed her warm body against him. She was only wearing one of his shirts, but it was still too much. He needed to feel her skin against his.

He grabbed the front of the garment and ripped it open. Buttons bounced off the floor and one pinged against the windowpane.

She went back down on the soles of her feet and smiled. "You keep that up and you'll soon run out of shirts for me to borrow."

The rays of the morning sun caught the red in her hair, turning it into a fiery profusion of curls. There were shadows under her eyes, a reminder of just how trying the past couple of days had been, but there was a soft smile on her face.

He slid his hands under the cloth and slipped it down her arms. She let the shirt fall to the floor, leaving her naked in the sunshine.

Ezra fell to his knees in front of her and wrapped his arms around her waist. She left him speechless. He buried his face against her warm stomach, nuzzling her soft skin.

"Ezra?" She tunneled her fingers through his hair and tilted his head back. "What is it?"

He shook his head. He didn't want to talk, not now when she was naked in his arms like an offering. He didn't know what he'd done to deserve such a treasure, but he would do everything in his power to be worthy of her.

He wished it were summer. There was a field that filled with wildflowers not five minutes from the house. He wanted to lay her down on the sweet clover and make love to her while the hot breeze brushed her skin.

It was much too cold to do that in November, but with the sun reflecting in through the window, he could easily imagine how it would be.

He reached out and snagged the comforter from the top of the bed. Maybe it would be better to take her there, but the bed was still in shadows. The sun hadn't penetrated that far yet, and there was a sunbeam on the floor around them. He shook out the comforter, making a comfortable pallet for them to use.

"What are you doing?"

Would she understand, or would she think him odd for wanting to make love to her on the floor when there was a comfortable bed only feet away? "I want to love you in the sunshine."

Sam knelt in front of him. "I'd like that."

He slid one hand over the crown of her head. "I love your hair."

She laughed. "It's out of control. I need some products to

tame the curls."

He buried his head in the wild locks and inhaled the scent of his shampoo. It smelled even better when mingled with her unique perfume. "I love your curls."

He kissed her slowly, ignoring the lust gnawing at his guts and the hard throbbing of his cock. He wanted to take his time. She deserved no less. This woman was willing to risk everything to protect him. Other than his brothers, no one had ever been willing to sacrifice anything for him. Not even the woman who'd bore him. As soon as she'd discovered what he was, she'd tossed him out of her home. He knew she would have killed him if she'd known a way to do so.

It still made his heart ache all these millennia later.

Sam ran her hands over his chest and shoulders, returning his kiss, deepening the contact. She wanted him as much as he wanted her. He lifted her and eased her onto the comforter. It was thin, not nearly as soft as she deserved.

"Maybe we should use the bed." What was he thinking, taking her on the floor?

She shook her head. "No, I like it here."

The white bandage on her arm and the bruises marring her soft white skin were visual reminders he needed to be careful with her. He could cure her completely with his blood, but that wasn't something he was prepared to do unless it was absolutely necessary. She was already dealing with a lot. He wasn't sure how she'd react to the idea of drinking his blood. Best to wait until she'd had a lot more time to get used to what he was and what that meant.

"I'll be careful," he promised.

"I know you will." There it was. Trust. She offered it easily, but he knew it was a gift beyond price, and one he would work to make certain he never lost.

He knelt beside her and ran his hands over her shoulders. They were slender but strong. She'd carried much on them this past year, dealing with the death of her friend and her involvement with the Knights.

Her arms were sleekly muscled and her hands bore calluses. He rubbed one with his thumb. Sam chewed her bottom lip, something she did when she was nervous or thinking. "Occupational hazard," she apologized.

Sam worked digging and handling artifacts most people would never see outside of a museum. "I love your hands." He brought one of them to his mouth and kissed the rough skin. She sucked in a breath when he nipped at the pads at the base of her fingers.

He placed her palm against his heart, allowing her to feel the rapid beat, to know how much he wanted her. Sam's eyes widened and then lowered until they were only half open. A smile played at the corners of her lips.

He dragged her hand down his torso until he reached his erection. Without prompting, she wrapped her fingers around his hard length. He sucked in a breath, loving the feel of her hand stroking him in such an intimate way.

She was a pagan goddess, all fire and life, lying in the sunbeam. He stroked his hands over her soft stomach, smiling when she gave a sharp inhale. The firm mounds of her breasts were a temptation he could no longer ignore. He cupped them in his hands and ran his thumbs over the taut nipples. They were dark pink, like wild strawberries, not quite ripe on the vine.

Her grip tightened on his shaft, and he was forced to remove her hand. He kissed her palm and lowered it back to her side. "I plan to taste every sweet inch of you."

• • •

Sam had fallen into an erotic dream she had no desire to ever wake from. The sun was reflecting through the window, heating the small space around them. And what the sun didn't heat, Ezra did with his sheer presence. The way he was looking at her was making her blood simmer. Even though she was naked, she wasn't the least bit cold.

There was an unhurried quality that hadn't been present in their previous lovemaking. It was as though they had all the time in the world, even though she knew that wasn't true.

The world was waiting for them, and the Knights were searching.

But none of that mattered when Ezra was touching her with his large, capable hands. The way he was looking at her with his turquoise eyes stole her breath.

This massive, powerful man treated her like she was the most precious woman in the world. Tears stung her eyes, but she wouldn't allow them to fall. She didn't want him to think for one minute there was anything wrong, not when everything was finally right. It couldn't last, no matter how much she wished it would, but she'd take this time as the gift it was and cherish it forever.

Ezra ran his thumbs around the edges of her nipples before finally stroking them. Her breasts ached and a throbbing began low in her belly. If he touched her, he'd find she was already wet and ready for him.

But he seemed in no hurry. True to his word, he took his time. He lapped at her skin before drawing the taut bud of her breast into his mouth and sucking. She panted for breath, her skin tingled, and the ache between her legs grew exponentially every time he touched her.

Ezra truly was larger than life. He would tower over most men, but it was more than that. There was something intrinsically powerful about him, an aura of confidence and energy that would exist no matter what his physical size. Everything about him was unique, from the color of his eyes to the intricate tattoo that decorated the left side of him.

He stroked his hands over her arms, careful to avoid her injury. He traced the contours of her torso and hips. His hair brushed against her. It was soft and thick and added another sensual layer to her already overloaded senses.

He laved attention on her other breast before working his way lower, leaving a trail of kisses down the center of her stomach. He nipped at the curve of her waist and dipped his tongue into her navel.

Never had a man taken such time to arouse her. But he wasn't done. He ran his palms over her thighs, widening her legs before kissing the inside of her legs. Her entire body was electrified, her skin tingled and every cell quivered with anticipation. Heat rolled off Ezra in waves, cocooning the space around them so that no chill could touch her.

She reached out, needing to touch him, to reassure herself he was real and not a dream-induced fantasy. He took her hand in his much larger one and held it. His biceps bunched and his shoulders rippled with tension, but his touch was so gentle.

He kissed her palm and released her. Keeping his gaze locked on her, he lifted her thighs over his muscled forearms and leaned forward. She was wide open to him, all of her revealed to his view. He licked his lips and then her core.

She cried out, unable to hold back as sensual fire shot through her, bringing her close to finding release but not taking her over. "Ezra." She wanted him inside her, wanted to feel the pulse of his cock as it stretched and filled her.

"Not yet." His words were gruff, a sure sign he wasn't nearly as cool as he wanted her to believe. She fisted her hands in his hair and pulled him closer. If he wasn't going to fuck her, he had to put his mouth on her. She was strung so tight she knew it wouldn't take much to send her catapulting over the edge.

He lapped at her slick folds, teasing and stroking before

finally finding her clit. Her entire pelvis jerked when he sucked on the small nub. She shook her head and arched her neck. She wanted him to keep going. She wanted him to stop. She had no idea what she wanted.

As much as she needed to come, she didn't want to do it alone. Ezra had been alone for far too much of his life. She tugged on his hair until he looked up at her. "I want you," she told him. "Now." When he would have pulled away and gone back to what he was doing, she shook her head. "I don't want to come by myself. I want to be with you."

• • •

Ezra's heart swelled until his chest threatened to burst. His lips were coated in her sweet essence, the perfume of her arousal filled his nostrils, and her smooth skin was like velvet beneath his questing fingers. His plan had been to bring her to orgasm at least twice before he took her. He should have known better. Sam had been derailing his plans since the first moment he'd set eyes on her.

And he wouldn't have it any other way.

The lonely part of his soul yearned to be joined with her. The dragon part of his nature wanted to claim her, and the man just wanted her happy.

"Ezra." She opened her arms to him. "Come to me." He could no more deny her than he could stop the rising of the sun. He sat back on his heels and licked his bottom lip. That drew a low whimper from her. The sound vibrated through him, making his balls clench.

He stretched out over her, supporting his weight on his forearms. "Put me inside you." This was all about her. What she wanted. What she needed.

She didn't hesitate, reaching between their bodies and finding his cock. She brought him close and angled her pelvis so the broad head of his shaft was touching her opening. He swallowed, afraid he was going to lose it before he got inside her.

"I love you." She wrapped her legs around his thighs and dragged him toward her. He was so stunned by her words and her actions, he jerked forward, burying himself to the hilt. Her slick channel rippled around him, stretching to accommodate him. But even that pleasure was nothing compared to the explosion going on in his brain.

"You what?"

She shook her head and drew him down so she could meld their lips together. Physical need took over, roaring through him like an out of control locomotive. He began to thrust, slowly at first, but quickly gaining speed.

He swallowed her moans of pleasure, taking them inside him. Some primal part of him snapped the leash he used to keep it tethered, and he fucked her as though he could meld them together.

He shoved a hand under her bottom and tilted her hips so his pelvis brushed against her clit. He slammed into her again and again. He couldn't stop kissing her, unable to release her luscious lips. Sam was his.

His.

He wanted to stamp his possession on her body, mind, and very soul. She'd said she loved him. He didn't know if her confession had been brought on by their lovemaking or if she truly meant it.

At this point, he didn't care. She'd said it. That was all that mattered. Oh, he knew he should care, and probably would later, but right now, he wanted to revel in the sensation of belonging to and with someone for the first time in his life.

He knew he was being too rough, knew he should stop or at least ease up, but the dragon side of his nature had taken over. No, not taken over, but joined with his human half in an effort to tie Sam to him.

He pumped his hips, his lungs burning, his balls aching. Still, he didn't stop. He slid forward and caught her hands with his, twining their fingers together. Her nipples brushed against his chest. He wanted to roar, but that would mean he'd have to stop kissing her.

It happened so fast it took him by surprise. The slow burn started in his balls and shot through his cock. His orgasm slammed into him. He threw back his head and roared, managing to get enough control at the last second to temper the sound. Still, the windows rattled and furniture shook.

He ground his pelvis against Sam as he continued to pump in and out of her welcoming warmth. She cried out, and he felt the telltale squeezing of her core around his shaft and knew she'd found satisfaction. He couldn't stop thrusting, didn't want to ever stop. The unending pleasure finally cooled the heat of his lust to allow a moment of clarity. He had to stop before he hurt her. Like a bucket of cold water dumped over his head, that brought him back to his senses.

"Sam." He released his grip on her hands and cupped her face. Her eyes were closed, her lips parted. Perspiration dotted her forehead. "Look at me." Had he hurt her? He would never forgive himself if he had.

"Hmm." Her eyelids fluttered open, and she smiled.

The tension bled from him like air from a deflating balloon. If he'd hurt her, surely she wouldn't be smiling at him. "Did you mean it?" Maybe it wasn't fair of him to ask her that while she was still reeling from her orgasm, but screw fair.

"What?" She blinked, and her mouth turned down in a frown. "Did I mean what?"

"You love me." Talk about needy. God, he was losing his mind. He'd never wanted anything as much in his life. He'd give up every treasure he owed to hear her say those three words and mean them.

Sam glanced away and sighed. A weight settled over his heart, crushing the small bubble of hope he'd protected there. He shouldn't have asked her. It was far too soon for her to know her feelings. He should have kept his mouth shut and just enjoyed the feeling of having her come apart in his arms. "Sam?"

She turned back, and he could see her gathering herself like she was getting ready to deliver him a blow. She licked her lips. He wanted to kiss her so she wouldn't speak, but that wouldn't change a thing.

She gave a decisive nod. "Yes. Yes, I do love you."

Chapter Nineteen

Sam wanted to bask in the glow of their lovemaking but that wasn't to be. If only she'd kept her mouth shut. But she'd been filled with such love for Ezra she hadn't been able to contain it. Instead, she'd blurted out the words.

Now he wanted to know if she'd meant what she said. Maybe some people could have laughed it off or made a joke, but she'd never said the words before, not to a man. They were too important.

So she'd given him the truth and waited to see his reaction. Most men would run at the first sign a woman was getting serious so quickly. Even though she and Ezra hadn't known one another for a long period of time, it was the quality of that time that was most important. At least to her.

She wished she wasn't naked and sweaty and completely vulnerable right now. That only added to her unease. Would he try to find a way to brush her off or to convince her it was only sex? She honestly had no idea.

He was staring at her like he didn't recognize her. He looked...stunned. That was the word she was searching for.

The expression on his face was one of complete shock. Then he blinked and his eyes filled with what might be amazement. At this point, she couldn't be certain of anything.

His cock was still thick and pulsing inside her. Even though she'd come, she was edgy once again. "Ezra?" She wished he'd say something. Anything.

He kissed her. Completely taken off-guard, all she could do was surrender to the sweet caress until her body began to soften and some of her tension siphoned away.

When he slid his tongue between her lips, she welcomed him. When he began to pump his hips, she offered no objection. The earlier coming together had been passionate, bordering on rough. Both of them had been out of control, pushing toward the ultimate physical release.

This was different, but no less potent. Where the last time had been like racing down rapids, this time was more like drifting on a lake in a canoe. There was no rush, only the unhurried advance and retreat as Ezra filled her again and again. She rocked her hips against him in a sensual dance.

Her orgasm flowed through her in a soft wave, more twinkling lights than fireworks. Ezra moaned long and low, and she felt the warmth of his release fill her.

He lifted his head and their eyes locked and met. "Thank you."

She wasn't sure what he was thanking her for. For telling him she loved him, or for making love once again. "You're welcome." She wasn't sure what else to say.

She should be worried about unprotected sex, about a potential pregnancy, but that was the least of her worries. But still… "Should we be using condoms?"

"No." He stroked the side of her face and kissed the tip of her nose. "You won't get pregnant unless I want you to."

Now that was a useful skill. "You're sure?" Not that she didn't believe him, but that was one heck of a thing to take on faith. Then she laughed. Considering everything else she'd taken on faith since they met, this one was actually lower on the list of crazy.

"Positive." Ezra eased away and sprawled next to her, his arms stretched over his head and his eyes closed. He appeared totally relaxed. A part of her envied him that, and another part wanted to smack him. How dare he be relaxed when she was in inner turmoil?

She hated the separation even as she needed it. She had to get a grip on her emotions before she made her situation worse. She still had no idea what he thought of her confession, but he didn't seem upset. That was something.

Neither had he returned the sentiment, which she was doing her best not to dwell on. She was a big girl, a grown woman. She knew the score. People didn't always love you back. It wasn't the end of the world. In fact, it was probably for the best considering the impermanence of their situation.

"So what now?" She grabbed the shirt she'd been wearing earlier and drew it on. There were only two buttons still attached, and she did them up. It was better than nothing.

Ezra opened his eyes and rolled to his side. The sunlight made his tattoo shimmer, as though it were metallic. It was incredibly beautiful and another reminder he was more than a man. He was a rare and precious creature that had to be protected from those who wished to do him harm.

He was totally unconcerned with his nudity, but considering what he looked like, why would he be? He was also still aroused, which she tried not to notice. It seemed that along with enhanced senses, he also had other extra skills, like being able to make love all night or day.

Sam shoved thoughts of sex out of her head even as her nipples tingled. Now was not the time for more sex. She was going to be sore as it was.

"Now," he began. "Now I get dressed and go check on my

salvage crew and the Knights."

. . .

Duty called, and Ezra knew he had to move. He should already be out there on his company's boat, talking to the client and his manager, Kent, about the project. It was a big one, potentially lucrative for Easton Salvage. And honestly, Ezra wouldn't mind taking the Knights' money. It would only be a drop in the bucket for them, but it was the thought that counted.

He really didn't want to leave Sam. She'd gone from relaxed to stressed in a heartbeat. And the talk of children left him feeling unsettled. He'd never considered having a child until now. The thought of Sam growing heavy with his child filled him with longing even as the idea made him crazy. How could he protect a mate and a child?

One step at a time. The first thing he needed to do was get the lay of the land. That meant he had to leave his island, something he was never fond of doing unless he was taking to the sea.

He sighed and forced himself to roll to his feet. The day was wasting, and neither of them would relax until they knew exactly what they were dealing with. He held out his hand, but Sam waved it off.

"You go ahead and get ready without me. We both know what will happen if I go to the bathroom with you."

As much as he wanted to deny it, he knew it was true. Sam looked tousled and rosy lying in the sunlight. She also looked pensive. The second he'd stood, she'd grabbed the end of the comforter and wrapped it around herself. He much preferred her naked.

"I'll only be gone as long as I have to." His protective instincts were working overtime. The primal need to guard

Sam was threatening his control and testing his sanity. The dragon in him wanted to drag her off to a cave where no one could find her. The more intellectual part of him knew information was power. Tarrant would be proud, as that was his brother's mantra.

And speaking of his brother… "I'm going to call Tarrant before I leave. See if he knows more about Aaron Dexter, what's going on with the Knights, and what he's learned about the Dragon Guard."

He gathered the clean clothes he needed and headed to the door. "Where are you going?" she asked.

"Guest bathroom. You can use the master bath. I should only be ten minutes. Maybe less." He heard her scrambling to her feet and the bathroom door closed a second later.

He made his way to the guest bath, sluiced water on his face, cleaned himself up, and pulled on his clothes. He was done in under five minutes. He listened and could hear Sam moving around in his bathroom. He liked the sound. It was homey. It felt right having her here, in his private space.

He hurried downstairs to his office and grabbed his phone off the desk. He thought about calling Tarrant but knew Sam would want to hear whatever was said. Food was his second thought. He was still hungry.

He pulled the fixings for roast beef sandwiches from the refrigerator and started assembling a stack of them. Whatever he didn't eat before he left, he'd take with him. He also planned to hit up a drive-thru as soon as he hit town. He checked the time on his phone. He needed to get a move on if he wanted to get out to the *Easton* today.

He heard Sam's footsteps, even though they wouldn't be audible to a regular person. She hovered in the doorway, wearing a long-sleeved cotton shirt that hit her thighs. Her feet were bare, as were her long legs. He stopped in the middle of slathering mustard on the bread just to stare. She had exceptional legs.

"Ah." She pointed to the utility room. "My clothes should be dry." She hurried into the room, and he forced himself not to follow. The sound of her pulling on clothes made him twitchy. He definitely preferred her naked.

By the time she returned wearing her own socks and jeans, he'd made an entire loaf of bread into sandwiches and used every piece of roast beef. He needed to go shopping soon. "You want one?" He motioned to the platter.

"No. I'm still full from earlier. But you go ahead." She looked longingly at the coffeepot. "Do you mind?"

"Go ahead. Make yourself at home." He sat at the counter, pulled the platter in front of him, and started to demolish the large stack of sandwiches. He liked watching her putter in his kitchen. She belonged here with him.

"Did you call Tarrant?"

He shook his head and swallowed before he spoke. "I knew you'd want to be here for it." That earned him a smile that warmed his heart and other parts of his anatomy.

Knowing there was no time like the present, he placed the call and put the phone on speaker. "Everything okay?" Tarrant demanded.

"Yeah. I'm getting ready to head out to the *Easton*, maybe meet Dexter."

"Are you sure that's wise?"

Sam started the coffee machine and crossed her arms over her chest. "I told him it's too risky."

"It's riskier if I don't show. That would be suspicious." He took another bite and chewed. "Besides, as far as they know, I'm just a guy who owns a salvage company." He knew Sam wasn't thrilled with him and quickly changed the subject. "What have you got, Tarrant?"

"Aaron Dexter, thirty-four, former military," Tarrant rattled off the facts. "Spent twelve years in the army, most of them in special ops. Turned mercenary and was recruited by the Knights. Since then, he's been working his way up their ranks. Seems to answer directly to Karina Azarov."

Sam poured them both coffee and joined Ezra at the counter. He silently offered her a sandwich but she shook her head.

"I had a peek at his military record. This fucker is dangerous and smart. Determined, too. So watch yourself around him."

"Yes, Mother," Ezra quipped.

"You can do that?" Sam demanded. "Just have a peek at his military records. Aren't they protected?"

Tarrant sighed. "Why do I put up with such disparagement? Of course the files are protected. Of course I can access them. I keep telling you I'm the best."

"He is," Ezra agreed. Sam was obviously reeling at the idea of someone having that kind of access to heavily protected files. Best not to tell her that Tarrant could reposition every satellite circling the earth if he wanted.

"What are the Knights up to?" Ezra asked.

"They're quiet, which worries me." The sound of clicking came over the phone speaker, and he knew his brother was busy working the keyboard. "There's some chatter about Karina. Seems Temple isn't thrilled with her and is trying to feel out some other members about that."

"You think he's going to mount a takeover?" The Knights were constantly jockeying for power and position.

"I think he'll try." Tarrant was silent for a several seconds. "I don't think he'll succeed. He might think he's ruthless, but my money is on Azarov."

"I probably don't want to know how you know about someone else's phone calls and emails." Sam rubbed her hands over her face before she gulped a mouthful of coffee.

"Best not to," Ezra told her. "The Dragon Guard?" he

prompted Tarrant.

"They're even more secretive than the Knights, which is saying something."

Ezra had to agree. The Knights had public faces they showed to the world, but the private activities of their group were well protected.

"But I am finding some historical references dating back several centuries about a group dedicated to protecting dragons. I'm still looking into it."

"Why don't you believe they exist?" Sam asked. "After all, they approached me."

"You really can't be that naïve, can you?" Tarrant asked before Ezra could shut him up. "It could simply be another branch of the Knights. How better to catch a drakon than to tell him you're trying to save him and his kind."

• • •

Sam thought she was going to be sick to her stomach. She'd never considered, not for one second, that she might have inadvertently been a pawn of the Knights. "Do you really think that is what's happening?" Had they planned to use her skills to try to find a drakon? She'd thought she was the one infiltrating their group to try to disable them, however slightly.

"Doubtful," Ezra said.

"Possible," Tarrant admitted at the same time. Ezra glared at the phone, but she knew Tarrant was only telling the truth. "I'm still looking into it. Until then, I wouldn't trust anyone claiming to be a member of the Dragon Guard."

"But what about Gervais Rames? He told me all about the Knights. Just before he disappeared, he told me he had a lead on a book. He was going to try to steal it from the Knights. Why would he have done that unless it was to protect it from them?"

"So he could use it himself." Ezra's quiet reply hit her like a punch to the face.

She buried her face in her hands. "I played right into their hands, didn't I?"

Ezra's big hand rubbed up and down her spine. "You don't know that. The Dragon Guard could be real."

"They could be," Tarrant admitted.

"But you're still looking into it," Sam parroted. It seemed to be Tarrant's standard line.

"I'm going to the mainland to hit the office before I head out to the *Easton*. I'll have my phone with me. Call if you get any other information."

"Sam's not going with you, is she?" She wasn't sure if Tarrant was worried about her or Ezra.

"Don't be an idiot. Of course she isn't," Ezra shot back. Sam chose to keep her mouth shut. If she thought there was a way she could go without endangering him, there'd be no way to stop her. But the unfortunate fact was she'd be more of a hindrance than a help. The best thing she could do was stay here, rest, and think about the situation and how she might best fake her own death so the Knights would believe her dead. Right now, all they had was speculation.

"If I don't hear from you, I'll call you when I get back." Ezra ended the call and shoved aside the empty platter. He'd demolished an entire mound of sandwiches. "I hate to leave you here alone." He swiveled around on his stool so he was facing her.

"But you have to." As much as she hated the idea of him out there on his own, he was right. Having her with him would only put him in danger. "Don't take any chances." The thought of the Knights getting their hands on her drakon scared the crap out of her.

And, yes, he was her drakon.

"I won't," he promised. "And, hey, you can take the time

to examine all the stuff in my office."

She knew he was trying to lighten her mood, so she smiled, or at least tried to. She knew she'd failed in her attempt when he took her hands in his and brought them to his lips. "I'm going to the office on the mainland and then to the store to get some supplies before I head out to the *Easton*. Once I talk with Dexter, I'll come straight home."

The only thing she could do was not add to his worries. "I'll be fine." She might be stressed, but she'd survive. She'd lived through much worse than waiting in a cozy house with all the amenities. But she'd never had so much at stake before. She'd been ready to sacrifice her own life if necessary to reach her goal of striking back at the Knights. What she wasn't prepared for was having Ezra risk his life.

He had to be safe.

"Go ahead and get ready. I'll clean up here." She eased off the stool and began to tidy the kitchen. Thankfully, Ezra left her to the task. She couldn't talk about it anymore. The faster he left, the quicker he'd be back.

There wasn't much to clean up, but once she was done, she went to peer out the living room window. Ezra joined her, his reflection appearing in the glass. He was wearing jeans and work boots and had pulled a cream-colored sweater over the long-sleeved tee he wore. He had a plaid jacket slung over his shoulder. She knew the heavy clothing was for show and not because he needed it.

"I need clothes." Not what she'd meant to say. Obviously, her brain didn't want to deal with the fear any longer and focused instead on the mundane.

"I'll get what I can."

She shook her head. "No. You can't buy anything around here. Someone might notice." She'd gotten paranoid over the past year, and for good reason.

He rubbed his jaw and nodded. "You're right. We'll order

some things for you online later. Tarrant set it up so I have an account and credit card that are untraceable. Everything will be delivered to a post office box in Bar Harbor. I'll drive down and pick it up as soon as we think it's safe."

Sam had no doubt that if Tarrant had set it up, it probably was safe, even from the Knights. The man seemed to hack military records with ease. Setting up an untraceable credit card was probably child's play. Besides, the Knights didn't know about Ezra. Only her.

"Okay." She really didn't care about clothing. She turned and wrapped her arms around Ezra's lean waist. "If you let the Knights do anything to hurt you, I'm going to be pissed."

He chuckled and nuzzled her hair. "Since I'm more afraid of you than I am of them, I promise I'll be safe."

She didn't want to let him go but stepped back and dropped her arms to her sides. "How exactly are you getting to the mainland? Don't you have to swim to get the boat we used earlier?"

He lowered his head and rubbed the back of his neck. "Ah, not exactly. There is a path I can use. It's rugged, but I can get to the cave from the outside."

"Could I?" She narrowed her gaze and scowled at him.

"Doubtful." He pressed a quick kiss to her lips. "I'll be back as fast as I can, but I'll likely be gone for hours. Try to rest, you're still recovering." He hurried out of the house, leaving her alone. The house felt different without him in it. Bigger. Lonelier.

She stood at the picture window and watched until he disappeared over a rise. Ten minutes later, the small boat she'd been in last night burst into view, jumping over the choppy waves.

She turned her back and headed to his office. She had to do something to pass the time or she'd go crazy. How better to spend it than learning more about the man she loved. Ezra's office offered a multitude of treasures for her to explore.

It even smelled like him in here—sunshine, ocean, and crisp air. The leather chairs were inviting and the desk was substantial, but it was the shelves that interested her. She ignored the slight hum coming from the floor safe. It was mostly muted, and she blocked it out, a skill she'd been forced to learn during the course of her career.

She walked over to a shelf she hadn't examined yet. It held pottery shards as well as some complete pots. It was a cornucopia of history, the pieces coming from various cultures and time periods. She leaned forward and studied the small vase on the first shelf.

Chapter Twenty

Ezra hated leaving Sam behind even if it was the best thing for both of them. He placed an order at the grocery store that would be ready for him to pick up on his way home. That done, he headed to the office next. He kept a truck in a shed by the dock so he had transportation.

His headquarters were little more than a converted boathouse. It was big enough for a small office and to store their gear. He checked the files—because while they had a computer, Kent tended to write things down instead of using the machine—but found little more about the man who'd hired his firm. Dexter was playing his cards close. Not surprising, all things considered. The offices weren't being watched, which was a bit of a surprise. Of course, they had no reason to believe Sam would come here, and they certainly didn't know Ezra was a drakon.

Leaving the office behind, he drove back to his personal dock. His speedboat was tied up there. He planned to take it back with him when he returned home and tow the dinghy behind it. If he needed to get Sam off the island for any reason, the speedboat with its powerful engine was the fastest option. The only way faster was if he shifted and carried her over the waves himself, and since that would definitely cause unwanted attention, he needed the faster boat.

He glanced toward the island and took a deep breath. Knowing Sam was safe was the only reason he was able to be away from her for so long. Their relationship was still so new and tentative.

"Just do it," he muttered. Standing around wasn't going to get him anywhere. He needed to meet with Dexter and try to get a sense of the man who'd shot Sam. If he thought his crew was in danger, he'd find a reason to pull them off the job.

The big challenge would be in not killing the man outright for what he'd done.

Ezra took another deep breath, pulling the salt air into his lungs. He could taste the sea, which never failed to soothe. While it did bring him down a notch, he was still unsettled and knew he would be until he was back home with Sam.

He strode down the dock and climbed aboard his twenty-foot speedboat. It looked like any other recreational vehicle on the outside, was painted blue and white with no fancy or memorable designs. The real difference was in the engine. This baby could move.

He released the lines and started the engine. It roared to life, and he smiled as he eased the throttle forward. Time to get to work. He pushed the engine as hard as he dared, and the boat jumped over the waves. He adjusted the direction to assure the smoothest ride possible. With his feet braced and his hands on the wheel, he threw back his head and laughed for the sheer joy of being on the water.

The only other things that got him this excited were actually swimming in the ocean and being with Sam.

And Sam topped the list.

The spray and mist danced over his skin. Overhead,

several gulls squawked as they dipped and dived into the water, hunting for something to eat. The sun sparkled on the waves. Beneath him, fish and plant life thrived.

He might be on a serious mission, but nothing could stop him from enjoying the ocean. The ebb and flow of the water was in his veins, the pounding of the waves echoed in his heart. He was a water drakon, and the ocean was his home.

The trip still took longer than he wanted. The wreck was quite a distance from his island, which was a good thing. The Knights had no reason to look that far afield for Sam. They probably would, though. They were nothing if not thorough.

As the *Easton* came into view, he studied the deck. There were divers in the water, so he circled around to the opposite side from where they were working and carefully made his approach that way. Kent waved to him from the deck. Ezra waved back but saw no sign of Aaron Dexter. That was disturbing.

The *Easton* was a thirty-eight-foot lobster boat with a fiberglass body and a powerful diesel engine. He'd bought it used a few years ago and had it refurbished. It had a galley and sleeping area for the crew. All the basic comforts of home, a necessity since they often had to stay on site for days, sometimes weeks on end. It was close quarters, but they made it work.

He maneuvered the boat into position and tossed the line up to Kent. "Hey, boss." His business manager, who was also one hell of an experienced diver, caught the rope and tied it off. "I've been expecting you."

Ezra climbed up the small metal ladder attached to the side of the larger vessel. "You know I can't stay away." It was his standard reply and usually true. He normally couldn't wait to get to a dive site. Not this time. He'd much rather be on his island with Sam.

He missed her like he missed the ocean when he wasn't

near it. Like the water, she was a part of him.

"What's going on?"

Kent motioned to Ezra, and they made their way to the port side of the boat. "Bill and Owen are in the water." They were the experienced divers on the crew. "The *Integrity* took a couple of hits. There's a lot of damage to the hull, but it may be possible to patch it long enough to get her out of the water."

"Is the job too big for us?" It was a legitimate question since they were a small salvage operation and might need to subcontract some extra help.

"We'll need some more muscle when we try to bring her up, but we can do the patch job ourselves. It's a big job. The owner and the insurance company might decide to write her off. It won't be cheap."

Ezra stared down into the water. "Find out. If they write her off, we'll salvage what we can for ourselves and sell it." The waves hit the side of the *Easton* in a rhythmic pattern that was music to his ears, but it didn't ease the tension mounting inside him.

He turned away from the water. "Where's Dexter? I figured he'd be onboard watching our every move." The owners or insurance company almost always had someone on board in the early stages of an operation so they'd immediately know what was going on.

Kent shrugged. "He was here, but he took off earlier this morning. One of his guys came out in a speedboat. Dexter left and Calloway, that's the guy who brought the boat, stayed behind." He jerked his head toward the water. "Calloway is a diver and insisted on going down with the team."

Ezra's stomach knotted. He forced himself to remain calm and act natural. He didn't want to do anything to make his crew nervous or suspect there was anything wrong. "You check his credentials?" They'd never let anyone dive without first ascertaining if they were qualified.

"Yup. He checks out."

"What about Dexter? Where did he go?"

Kent shrugged. "He didn't say, but he didn't head back to shore." He pointed out to open water. "He went that way and then he headed northwest." Before Ezra could heave a sigh of relief, Kent continued. "I'm not sure but he might have circled around about an hour ago and headed in the opposite direction."

In the direction of Ezra's home. "What's he doing?"

Kent shrugged. "Who knows? He said something about trying to find a dinghy that went missing the night the *Integrity* sank. But who the hell cares about a dinghy when there's a multimillion dollar boat below us?"

Ezra had to get off the *Easton*. Dexter was looking for Sam. He should have known the Knight would never be satisfied until he found a body.

"I'm heading out."

"Already?" It was no wonder Kent was surprised. Ezra loved to dive. Well, he hated having to use the wetsuit and equipment when his men were around, but he never missed a chance to be in the water.

"Yeah." He raked his fingers through his hair and strode across the deck. "Keep me up-to-date on whatever you find." He turned and pinned his employee and friend with a steely stare. "Be careful on this one." That's the most he would say, all he could say without putting them in jeopardy.

This was an unusual situation since the *Integrity* had been excavating an older wreck and searching for artifacts. The possibility of treasure made some people a little crazy. Best to let Kent think that's where the problem might come from.

"Always." There was a new alertness in Kent's gaze. He hadn't lived to be almost fifty without being smart. The dive business was not for dummies, especially not the salvage and treasure hunting business. "We'll watch our backs."

Ezra vaulted over the side of the *Easton* and landed solidly on the smaller boat. It rocked, but he automatically adjusted his stance and hurried to the wheelhouse. "Call if you need me." Not that he'd be able to come, not with Sam in possible danger.

"We'll be fine," Kent assured him. "We can take care of ourselves."

Ezra waved as he maneuvered the boat away from the *Easton*. How had he missed Dexter on his way here? For one thing, he hadn't been looking. For another, Dexter might have been pulled into any little cove searching for wreckage and Sam's body. Ezra had headed straight to open water to make faster time and because he loved the exhilaration of riding the waves and feeling the cold wind on his skin.

He grabbed his phone and called the work phone that sat on his kitchen counter. It rang and rang. "Pick up." Not that she had any reason to. Even if she heard it ring, she would have no reason to answer, would most likely let it go to message.

Reasoning with himself did nothing to ease the anxiety gnawing at his guts. His dragon wasn't happy, either. The beast wanted out, and it wanted out now. In his dragon form, he could get home a lot faster than he could by boat. It was also day time and there was a risk of someone seeing him. That would put Sam, him, and his crew in danger.

Dexter needed to search every inch of shoreline between here and Ezra's island. Trying to find Sam was like trying to find a needle in a haystack. She should be safe.

But should be wasn't good enough. All Dexter needed was a lucky break, and Sam would be in danger.

Ezra pushed the engine as hard as it would go. If it overheated and shut down, he'd take the risk and shift. Every mile seemed like a thousand, every minute a year.

"Sam," he whispered her name, and the wind snatched it away, pulling it out to sea.

• • •

Sam spent a couple of hours exploring Ezra's office. He had some fascinating items alongside his colorful collection of seashells and sea glass. Like a kid in a candy store, she examined coins and pottery, admired jewelry crafted from beads and metal, and delighted in basic utensils and tools from bygone eras. She liked that Ezra had unique, one-of-a-kind artifacts alongside commonplace shards of pottery. They all had value to him.

The phone in the kitchen rang at one point, but she ignored it. It was the one Ezra used for work, and no one was supposed to know she was here. She was totally cut off from the world. It made her sad and jittery, but she shoved both emotions away and went back to studying Ezra's collection.

For a short time, she was able to suppress her worry. She knew Ezra could take care of himself. But this was different. The Knights of the Dragon were nearby, and it was all because of her.

She left his office and went to the kitchen. She wasn't hungry, even though lunchtime had come and gone, but she wanted some coffee. It had turned into a beautiful day. The sun shining in through the window beckoned to her. It would be chilly outside, it was after all November, but she could bundle up and take her coffee outside.

Leaving the coffeepot gurgling away, she went upstairs to Ezra's bedroom. It was amazing how quickly his home had become familiar to her. She loved that it wasn't too big, but every finish inside had been chosen with care, from the stone countertops to the hardwood floor. Big windows allowed light to pour in and offered wonderful views of the sea from all sides. The outside, made of log and stone, fit with the landscape.

The bed clothes were askew, so she took the time to remake it, smoothing the comforter over the top. This place felt more like home than anywhere she'd lived since her father had passed. She hadn't realized just how much she missed having a real home, instead of just somewhere she slept and kept her stuff.

When the pillows were plumped to her satisfaction, she went to the closet. There was a stack of sweaters on a shelf, so she helped herself to one in a turquoise shade. It wasn't a color she usually wore, but it matched Ezra's eyes and made her feel closer to him. The garment was huge on her and fell to mid-thigh. She rolled back the sleeves, creating wide cuffs on each arm.

The wool was thick and soft and would be warm. She wondered where he'd gotten the sweater, as it didn't seem like something he would choose for himself. It was yet another reminder that he had an entire life she knew little to nothing about. People who cared for him. People she didn't know.

The few she'd had any contact with were just voices on the phone. She wondered if she'd ever meet any of them, or if her time with Ezra would eventually come to an end.

"Stop it," she ordered herself. There was no point trying to predict the future. She left the bedroom and hurried down the stairs. Their relationship was complicated. She gave a snort of laughter. Complicated? That was putting it mildly. She knew most people would think she wasn't in her right mind after all she'd been through, that her feelings for him weren't real. She disagreed.

She loved him. And that meant doing what was best for him, no matter how much he objected.

And where was he? He'd been gone for hours, and she had no idea when he'd be back. The thought of him being around the wreck of the *Integrity* filled her with dread.

"Don't think about it," she muttered. The coffee was done, so she filled a mug and added sugar. The afternoon was waning, and she'd been cooped up all day. It would be smarter to stay inside, but what harm was there in sitting out on the front step, maybe wandering down to the dock to watch for Ezra's return? His island was far away from where the *Integrity* went down. Besides, the Knights had their hands full with the salvage operation. Even if they were looking for her, they wouldn't be anywhere near here. They'd be searching much closer to the wreckage.

Decided, she took her mug and strode to the front door. She hesitated for only a second before she opened it and stepped outside. The sun was beating down on the front deck, warming the area in spite of the bite to the wind.

She sat on the top step and inhaled the salt air. Ezra had created a mini paradise here. She wanted to wander the island and discover its secrets. There were trees in the distance, and she wondered how many different species there were. She recognized birch, poplar, and maple trees. It would be beautiful here in the summer. It was beautiful here now, but it was much starker, more primal. Only the firs and pines retained their needles. At the height of summer, there would be leaves on the trees and wildflowers in the open meadows.

She ignored the longing in her soul and sipped her coffee. But after only a few seconds, the deep yearnings were back. She wanted to sit outside on a warm summer's night in front of the fire pit she'd spied out back. She wanted to look up at the night sky and see the stars. And she wanted to do it all with Ezra.

A lone tear tracked down her cheek. It shocked her, and she brushed it aside. There was no point in crying. What would be, would be. In the meantime, she'd enjoy her time with Ezra and do her best to protect him. Not that he liked that idea. He was all about protecting her.

Filled with a restlessness that wouldn't abate, Sam stood and strolled toward the dock. The wind was much colder once she stepped away from the shelter of the house. She wrapped her hands around her mug, grateful for the warmth.

She wouldn't stay outside much longer, but she needed to walk, to work off some of the nervous tension that wouldn't leave her alone.

The dirt path had become familiar, and it took her little time to reach the dock. Two gulls swooped on the air currents, flying high and then diving back down toward the waves. There was a small stretch of beach on either side of the structure. She wondered if there was any large stretch of beach on his island. She'd always found walking helped her think.

The sound of an engine reached her ears. She put her free hand up to shield her eyes from the sun's glare as it lowered in the sky. Was it Ezra?

She knew sound carried over the water, and it took her some time to find the boat. The small, sleek craft flew over the waves. From this distance, she couldn't tell who was in the boat. She squinted as it got closer and could make out the shape of a single person on board.

Her heart leaped but then sank. What if it wasn't Ezra? She was a sitting duck out here. The chances of it being someone sent by the Knights was slim, but no one was supposed to know she was here. Any locals would know Ezra lived alone, so they'd certainly remember seeing a woman standing on his dock. And if they talked, both her and Ezra would be in danger.

Stupid. It had been foolish to leave the house. She should have at least stayed on the deck.

She turned and hurried back up the path, hoping whoever was on the speedboat hadn't seen her. From the sound of the engine, they were getting closer. They hadn't turned away from the island.

Maybe she was being paranoid. Maybe it was a local out enjoying a sunny afternoon.

Her heart was racing by the time she hurried up the porch

steps and ducked into the house. She leaned back against the closed door and took a deep breath. Then she cursed and glanced out the long, thin window beside the door.

The boat was slowing down, and the man on board was looking toward the house. Recognition came swift and hard. It wasn't a local out enjoying a pleasant afternoon. It was Aaron Dexter, and he'd seen her.

· · ·

Aaron couldn't believe his good fortune. He'd known the bitch hadn't died in the ocean the night the *Integrity* had sunk, but he'd never expected to see her standing on some dock. He had Karina Azarov breathing down his neck, and Sam Bellamy was outside looking like she didn't have a care in the world.

He'd been searching the shoreline for hours, hoping to find a body or a telltale sign of wreckage, something he could use to get the leader of the Knights off his back. His life was hanging by a thread, and he knew it. The Knights of the Dragon did not take failure lightly.

Her distinctive red curls were a dead giveaway. There couldn't be too many women around here with the same wild, out-of-control hair. He'd figured her hair was a sign of a passionate nature. Instead, she'd been a cold, frigid woman, turning aside his every advance.

If he was wrong, and the woman wasn't Sam, no harm done, but he knew in his gut it was her, especially when she turned and hurried back to the house as soon as she had seen him.

It excited him to see her run.

He piloted the boat up to the dock, jumped out, and secured the line. There were no other boats around. He hoped this meant she was alone.

No matter. He checked the Sig Sauer in his shoulder holster and grabbed his Remington rifle. He had more than enough fire power, but it was the Ka-Bar knife strapped to his leg that he planned on using.

Sam would talk before he was done with her. If she still had the artifact from the *Reliant*, he wanted it. And he sure as hell wasn't giving it to Karina. She'd turned on him at the first sign of trouble. No, if he recovered the artifact, he was going to use it to buy his safety in the ranks of another high-ranking member of the Knights.

Maybe he'd find someone to tell him more about it first. If it was a book of some kind, it was most likely written in some kind of code. The Knights were a paranoid, secretive bunch. Aaron wasn't sure he believed in the whole dragon thing. It was outlandish, bordering on crazy. What he did believe in was power. And the Knights had a lot of it.

They had their fingers in every lucrative business on the planet—banking, commodities, technology, communication, and natural resources. They had influence in governments around the world. They had money and power, and he wanted his share of it.

He stepped onto the dock. From what he'd seen, this was a private island, which meant there was no one around to hear Sam scream.

His luck was definitely changing. He smiled as he started up the path toward the house.

Chapter Twenty-One

Sam needed a weapon. She had no idea where Ezra had stored the rifle he'd given her last night, and there was no time to search. Unfortunately, she hadn't seen it during her exploring. There was a locked cabinet in the office, but she didn't have a key.

The Spanish dagger.

She ran into the office. The mug was still in her hand, and she sloshed coffee over the sides. "Damn it." She set the mug on a pad of paper sitting on the desk and grabbed the dagger. It wasn't overly large, but it was sharp and better than nothing.

Sam ran to the window and peeked out. Aaron was on the dock now, and he had a nasty-looking rifle in his hand. She couldn't stay in the house. She was a sitting duck here.

The thought of Aaron inside Ezra's lovely home, his sanctuary, made her ill. But there was no other choice. It would take Aaron time to search the house. While he was busy, she would run and see if she could find the caves where Ezra kept his boat. Maybe he had another one.

"The phone in the kitchen." She raced out of the office,

gripping the knife tightly in her hand. Ezra had taken his cell with him, but the one he used for work was still on the counter. She grabbed it and checked the contacts list. There was only one for work.

Sam felt like crying. There was no way to call Ezra or his buddy Tarrant. And she couldn't get the police involved. That would bring attention to Ezra. She might as well invite the Knights into his home.

Maybe she could convince Aaron she'd washed up on Ezra's island and he'd taken her in out of pity. She'd think of something, but there was no time to waste. She shoved the phone into her pocket just in case she needed it and let herself out the back door.

Aaron had to be close to the house, even if he was taking his time. He had no idea how many people lived here, so he had to be cautious.

The trees she'd admired earlier offered her a haven. Ezra's island was a little more than sixty acres. Not overly large, but hopefully large enough that she could hide. She knew there were caves somewhere. Ezra kept the dinghy there, the one he'd use to get to the mainland.

She was stuck on an island with no way off. Unless he had more than one dinghy. It was her only hope.

Sam took a deep breath and raced toward the tree line, keeping low and praying Aaron was focused on the house. She heard a shout behind her. There went her plan to have him waste time looking for her in the house. She hadn't gotten away fast enough.

As she plunged through the dry, brittle grass, she prayed for Ezra to return. She had no idea how long she could evade Aaron, but she suspected it wouldn't be for long. As former military, he had a hell of a lot more skills than she did, but she had determination on her side.

The grass crunched beneath her sneakers, but there was

no way to soften the sound. She raced between two towering birches and into the shadows created by the trees. The ground was softer here. She jumped over a downed branch and kept going. The wind pulled at her sweater and made her eyes tear up. She swiped at them with her free hand and kept running.

Sam had no idea where she was going. All she knew was she had to keep moving. She zigzagged through the trees, not wanting to give Aaron a target to shoot at. She had no idea if he planned to kill her or if he wanted to *talk* with her first, but she feared it was the latter.

She broke through the trees and stumbled into a meadow. It was too open here. Her lungs were starting to burn, but she knew she couldn't stop. She pivoted and took off to the right. She had no idea if she was heading into a dead end or if she'd end up somewhere she could hide.

All she could do was keep moving. The temptation to stop and hunker down behind a boulder or tree was overwhelming, but it was also dangerous. If she wasn't moving, it would be easier for Aaron to catch her. Of course, he might just shoot her. He'd done it before.

With the dagger still gripped tightly in her hand, she skidded over some slick grass. The surf pounded against the rocks below. There was a twenty-foot drop off here and no way down. Swearing, she veered left. There was another small stand of trees ahead. She'd make for there and keep looking for a secure place where she could catch her breath. She had no idea where Aaron was.

Crack! The bark flew off the trunk of the tree in front of her. Sam ducked and began to zigzag once again. Damn it. Aaron was shooting at her. She didn't know how much ammunition he had but suspected it was more than enough to do the job.

The bark exploded on another tree. This one off to her left. She automatically went right. The bastard was herding her back toward the drop off where she'd have no cover and nowhere to run. Worse, she was letting him.

Sam ducked low and raced deeper into the trees. The sound of him swearing followed her. She dared a glance over her shoulder. She needed to know where he was.

Her stomach dropped and her heart stopped for a brief second before resuming its rapid race. He was right behind her.

She turned back, but not in time. The toe of her sneaker caught on a rock partially hidden by moss and sent her tumbling. She managed to keep hold of the dagger, but that left her with only one hand to catch herself.

She skidded across the ground. Pain shot up her arm and across her knees. She didn't stay down. She popped right back up and kept going. Her ankle hurt, and she was doing more of a skipping jog than a run.

She caught sight of a path off to the right and hurried toward it. It had to lead somewhere, didn't it? It was her only hope.

Aaron was crashing behind her, not even trying to keep quiet. Since no one had come running after the gunshots, he must have rightfully assumed there was no one to come to her rescue.

The path plunged downward. She kept going because there was nothing else she could do, not with Aaron hot on her heels. Oh God, she was heading for the beach. She scanned the distance and felt her heart sink. She'd boxed herself into a corner. There was only one way in and out of this enclosed beach. Tall cliffs ringed it with only the carved path allowing access.

She was well and truly screwed.

Limping now, she picked up her pace, pushing her body as hard as she could. Maybe she'd find Ezra's secret dock. It was a faint hope, but a hope nonetheless.

She hit the bottom of the path and raced onto the beach of small rocks worn smooth by the waves over thousands of years. The only sand was near the edge of the water.

In the distance was sheer rock. She looked behind her. There were cliffs there, too, but she thought there might be a break in one.

"You can't hide," Aaron taunted.

The hell she couldn't. Sam ignored her aches and pains and the blood dribbling down her hand and made a beeline for the crevice. Maybe it was nothing, but she had to try.

She almost tripped but managed to stay upright. Any other day, she would have loved to sit on the beach and watch the waves, maybe explore a little. Today, all her focus was on the break in the rocks.

Her lungs were starving for air, and her heart was threatening to burst from her chest by the time she reached the small cut in the cliff. She felt like crying when she realized it was an indentation only about ten feet deep.

There was no way out. She was trapped.

Then she glanced toward the sea. She wasn't totally trapped. It was insane to contemplate taking to the sea in November. If she didn't drown, hypothermia would take her.

Either option was better than being shot by Aaron. Or worse, if he decided to torture her for information first.

Her thoughts were of Ezra as she plunged into the water. The frigid sea swirled around her feet and climbed higher on her legs.

Aaron was behind her, swearing and calling out to her. She ignored him and kept going.

By the time she was waist deep, she couldn't feel her feet. She took a deep breath and dove forward. And was brutally yanked back. Aaron grabbed her by the hair and dragged her back toward the beach. She tried to fight him, but she couldn't find her footing. Waves washed over her, choking her.

"You stupid bitch." He hauled her close enough to the shore so she was kneeling on the seabed. Through it all, she'd managed to keep hold of the dagger. Aaron was distracted with trying to get her back to shore. It was now or never.

Lunging up, she slammed the dagger toward his heart. Some sixth sense of his kicked in, or maybe he caught sight of the blade. Whatever the reason, he managed to dodge to the right and back. The dagger sank into his thigh.

"God damn it." He slammed his fist into her jaw, knocking her back.

Dazed and cold, she couldn't fight when the waves washed over her. She tried to hold her breath, but her lungs began to burn. She fought, flailing her arms. The sweater that had been so cozy earlier was now water-logged and dragging her down. When a large wave receded, it pulled her with it. She stopped fighting. If she was swept out to sea, maybe she'd have a chance.

"Oh no, you don't." He caught her by the sweater and dragged her onto the shore. Blood poured down the wound in his thigh. He cut off the bottom of his pants with the dagger and used the material to make a bandage.

Sam coughed and sucked air into her aching lungs. She was so cold. Every square inch of her skin hurt. She knew she should move, try to run now that he was hurt. Maybe she could even get one of his guns while he was distracted.

But it all seemed like too much trouble.

She wasn't shivering. She knew that was bad but couldn't quite remember why. An image of Ezra popped into her head. He'd be alone again if she left him. Aaron would find him.

From deep in the depths of her soul, she found the strength to move. She dug her fingers into the damp sand and rock and pulled herself forward. Aaron's rifle was on the ground only five feet away. It seemed more like a thousand miles. She gritted her teeth and dragged herself another couple of inches.

• • •

Ezra went cold when he spied the unknown boat tied up to his dock. Had Dexter found her?

He throttled back and cut the engine. The speedboat was heading hard for the dock. He didn't care. He was already running when it slammed into the side.

He ran for the house and yanked open the door. "Sam!" Silence greeted him. His dragon was going crazy inside him, demanding to be let out.

Forcing himself to stop, he took a breath. If he was going to save her, he needed to be calm.

He stalked back outside and forced himself to listen. The normal sounds of the surf pounding the shoreline, the call of the seabirds, and the *whoosh* of the wind reached him. He was searching for something not quite so normal.

He heard the squawk of the gulls that made their homes along the cliffs of the beach. He could take the boat and approach it from the sea, but he could get there faster on foot.

He moved quicker than he ever had in his life. Sam had to be alive. She had to be. How could he live without her? He couldn't. She'd brought joy into his life, given him a purpose. After thousands of years alone, he was not going to allow a Knight to steal his mate from him.

Sam might not know or accept it yet, but she was his mate, the one who completed him.

He saw them as soon as he broke away from the trees and raced across the open field. Sam on the ground, wet and bleeding. And she wasn't moving.

A great roar broke from Ezra. The ground trembled beneath him.

Aaron Dexter glanced up, his eyes going wide as Ezra

jumped off the cliff. He shifted in midair, giving his dragon freedom to protect Sam. For once, the two sides of him were in total harmony. There was nothing more important than Sam.

His clothes ripped as his wings snapped out. Hard scales replaced his skin. It took seconds, a mere heartbeat for the change to happen. Ezra swooped down and attacked.

Aaron yelled but recovered quickly and grabbed the rifle from the ground. The bullets hit Ezra and fell harmlessly to the rocky beach. Realizing he was helpless against the creature, Aaron turned his rifle on Sam.

"Come any closer, and I'll kill her."

Ezra landed on the beach, making the ground shiver. "You're dead no matter what you do," he informed the man. "It's a question of how much you want to hurt before you die." There was no way Dexter was walking away from this. He knew too much. He'd picked his path when he'd joined forces with the Knights, and it had led him here, to this moment.

He had to give the man credit. His hands were rock steady. He hadn't given up.

"Oh, I think you'll do what I say to protect the woman. Why else would you have helped her?" Dexter seemed pleased with his assessment.

Ezra tilted his head to one side and studied his opponent. He couldn't look at Sam or he'd lose it. Her heart beat was weak, but she was still alive. That was all that mattered.

"She had a book. Now I have it." That was something Dexter would believe. The man lived for power, with greed as his driving force. "A necklace, too." He added that to hopefully anger the man. "You have nothing," he taunted.

He needed to move Dexter a few more feet toward the beach, so he shifted position. As he'd hoped, the man backed up and raised the rifle back toward him, but just as quickly pointed it back at Sam. "Don't move. I need to think."

Dexter wasn't quite as calm as he wanted Ezra to believe. His eyes were wide as he stared at the dragon in front of him in disbelief. Ezra knew he was an intimidating sight. He didn't think Aaron had seen a dragon before. The man was sweating in spite of the chill. The pulse at his throat was fluttering wildly. He might be afraid, but the rifle was still aimed at Sam.

"Take all the time you need." It didn't matter now. Humans tended to forget that drakons had very long tails. He snapped it out, wielding it like a whip. He caught Dexter in the midsection. The rifle went off when Dexter's finger jerked on the trigger, but the barrel was facing up, and the bullet shot harmlessly into the air.

Dexter flew through the air and slammed into the hard, unforgiving cliffs. Ezra knew he was dead before his broken body hit the ground. He didn't bother to check. Sam needed him.

He shifted back to his human form and raced to her side. "Sam. Sam. Look at me, sweetheart." He turned her onto her back. Her face was deathly pale. Her heartbeat was so faint he had to press his ear close to her chest to be able to hear it. She was much too cold.

He lifted her into his arms and hurried up the path. He'd deal with Dexter's body later. As far as he knew, Dexter had been alone in the speedboat. He hadn't seen another boat or signs of another person. The Knights tended to keep secrets, even from each other. Right now, Sam took priority over everything else.

Ezra took a deep breath and sent out a controlled blast of heat around him. Anything too hot would only hurt her. He needed to bring her core temperature up slowly. "Sam. I'm here." She didn't stir, didn't even moan.

Her breathing was shallow and labored.

Naked, he ran with his precious burden cradled in his arms. The trees passed in a blur, and he gave a sigh of relief when the house came into view. He hurried inside and took her straight up to his room.

A sense of déjà vu hit him. This was the third time he'd carried her cold and limp body into his bedroom. He could measure the length of time he'd known her in days, a pinprick of time considering how long he'd lived. But she'd changed him forever.

He set her down on the bed and stripped her wet clothes from her body. A cell phone fell out of the pocket of her jeans. It was his work phone. Had she tried to call anyone? She wouldn't have been able to contact him because he hadn't thought to leave her the number. That was on him.

It would never happen again. He'd never leave her without resources to protect herself, that's if he ever managed to make himself leave her side again.

Her skin was clammy and still far too cold. He climbed onto the bed and rested his back against the headboard, settling Sam between his legs. He dragged the comforter over her, using the blanket and his body to warm her and sending another controlled blast of heated breath over her.

"Sam, sweetheart, open your eyes." He hugged her, trying to infuse his heat into her. Hypothermia was no joke. It was a deadly killer. Her knees and one of her palms were scraped and bloody. She had bruises everywhere, but he didn't think anything was broken.

"Sam?" Why wasn't she waking up? Her heart skipped a beat. When it started again, the rhythm was erratic. "Sam!" Was she going into cardiac arrest?

He couldn't take the chance. Desperate times called for desperate measures. He had no way of knowing how she'd react to what he was about to do, not physically or emotionally, but he had to try.

He manifested a claw on his right index finger. It was usually more difficult to hold a single part of his dragon form.

When the creature wanted out, it wanted out. But they were both working in harmony toward the same goal.

Ezra dragged it over his forearm. Blood trickled from the wound. He brought his arm to Sam's mouth. "Drink. It's medicine, Sam." He hoped she was too out of it to notice she was drinking blood from his arm. He had no way to know how she'd react to such a revelation, and he had to get her to swallow. "Drink your medicine. You'll feel better."

She was so still, so quiet, nothing at all like the vibrant woman he'd come to know. With his own heart pounding so loudly he couldn't hear hers anymore. "Sam. Drink. You fucking drink. Do you hear me?" He yelled and cajoled. Something blurred his vision. He ignored it and kept the seeping wound by her lips.

He tilted her head back and prayed some of his blood dribbled down her throat.

"Please, Sam." He switched from yelling to pleading. "You have to drink." Desperate, he tried another tactic. "The Knights are coming for me, Sam. You have to help me." He called out to her over and over, one minute threatening and the next entreating her to come back to him.

Chapter Twenty-Two

Sam heard someone calling to her from a great distance. She was cold all the way to her soul. Was she dead? If she was dead, why was she so cold? Heaven would be like a lovely balmy day, wouldn't it? And hell would be hot.

While she pondered these questions, the voice grew more insistent. She wished whoever it was would be quiet so she could think.

There was something wrong. Something she had to do.

"Knights—Sam—drink." The conversation was broken up, and she only caught the occasional word. She recognized the voice. It made her feel warm inside and drove back some of the chill.

She needed to get closer to the voice.

Something was running down her face. Tears? No, that wasn't right. It was around her mouth. She managed to part her lips the slightest bit and something trickled in. It wasn't salty like tears or the sea. This was rich, like chocolate and red wine. It was also warm.

It was difficult to swallow, but she managed a small one.

That tiny action exhausted her. She felt as though she were encased in a block of ice that muffled all sound and made it almost impossible to think.

Where was she? What had happened?

"Sam—"

There was something about the voice that made her heart ache. The organ fluttered in her chest before resuming a slow, ponderous beat.

There was something she needed to do, wasn't there? She'd been doing…something.

"—fucking drink." The voice was more insistent now, but beneath it she heard a tinge of fear. "The Knights—"

More of the delicious liquid slipped down her throat. Whatever it was, it was the best thing she'd ever tasted. She parted her lips and tried to get more of it. Maybe this was heaven, this floating feeling coupled with whatever it was she was drinking. Could be worse.

The liquid settled in her belly, and a slow warmth began to expand outward, seeping into her blood and flowing toward her extremities. If she could bottle this stuff, she'd make a fortune, but she wasn't sure she would ever want to share. Maybe with Ezra.

Ezra! Panic shot through her, and adrenaline surged through her veins. Aaron had found her, chased her, caught her. Where was he? And where was Ezra?

Sam bolted upright, gasping for breath, choking on whatever she was swallowing. The source was quickly cut off.

"I've got you, Sam."

The deep male voice made every cell in her body sing. She knew it as well as she knew her own. "Ezra." It was hard to speak, but she forced the word past her lips.

His lips grazed her temple. "You're safe."

She licked her lips and fought through the numbness and fatigue that permeated her. "Aaron?"

Ezra stilled, and his grip on her tightened significantly. "He's no longer a problem."

Which meant he was dead and they had an even larger problem. "Knights?"

He ran his hands up and down her arms, sharing his warmth with her. "Don't you worry about that. There's plenty of time to deal with the Knights."

She wasn't sure she liked the sound of that. She had to make Ezra see reason. Before she could form her next thought, the heat of a thousand suns blasted through her. Her entire body jerked, no longer under her control. Her back arched, and she cried out.

Ezra swore. "Stay with me. It won't last long."

Any longer than one second was too long. Sweat seeped from her pores. Pure agony shot through her limbs. Her organs felt as though they were being roasted over an open flame.

She had died and was in hell. There was no other explanation.

"Go," she urged Ezra. She didn't want him here with her, didn't want him hurt. Every inch of her skin hurt. "Save—" She cried as the pain became unbearable. "Save yourself."

Maybe Ezra wasn't even here. Maybe he was nothing more than a figment of her imagination, brought on by the pain and longing enveloping her.

"You're safe," he crooned. "We both are."

She didn't believe him, not with her entire body being tortured. As quickly as it began, it subsided, leaving a rush of coolness in its wake.

Panting hard and fast, almost hyperventilating, she forced herself to take slow, deep breaths.

"I'm so sorry." Ezra lifted her onto his lap and rocked her. "I'm so damn sorry. I should have been here. It's my fault Dexter hurt you."

She was confused, her thoughts jumbled. It was her fault

Aaron had found her. "Not your fault." Sam didn't want Ezra taking the blame on himself. "Went down to the dock to watch for you."

She licked her lips and tasted salt from the sea and the amazing drink Ezra had given her. Energy zinged through her veins. She was getting stronger with each passing second.

"I should have warned you to stay inside." Ezra seemed determined to take this on himself. She wasn't having it.

"I'm a grown woman, and I should have known better." She'd known the Knights would have someone searching for her or her body. If not Aaron, then someone else. "When I saw the boat, I thought it might be you."

Ezra heaved a huge sigh and buried his face against her hair. The curls were wild, damp, and stiff from the salt. She patted his chest, wanting to reassure him. She shifted position slightly, and something rolled along the top of the comforter covering her. She saw the flash of blue and grabbed whatever it was before it fell onto the floor.

It felt warm in her hand. She uncurled her fingers to see what it was and was shocked. It was the size of a dime, the blue impossibly deep. "Is this…is this a sapphire?" She turned her head to look up at Ezra. He rubbed his hand over his face and his cheeks grew red. Was he blushing?

"Ah, that's a drakon tear."

"A drakon tear," she repeated, not quite sure she was hearing him correctly. "Like the ones in the necklace."

"Those were rubies from a fire drakon."

"You're a water drakon," she pointed out, still not quite able to wrap her head around what she was seeing.

He began to pick more of them off the comforter. She was shocked to see there were so many. Ezra held them all in his hand. He had a fortune in gems sitting there. When she started to add the one she held to the pile, he shook his head. "They're yours."

"I don't understand." How could she understand anything with everything that had happened? "And what exactly is a drakon tear?" She thought she knew but wanted to be sure.

"Put your hands together." When she did as he asked, he poured the mound of perfect gems into her palms. "Drakons rarely ever shed a tear." He closed her hands over the stash of valuable stones. "They only do so in times of great sorrow."

She turned her hands over, letting the gems fall onto her lap. She didn't like the idea of Ezra hurting in such a deep and profound way. "I'm sorry you were hurt."

He shook his head and cupped her face between his big hands. "I was hurt because I thought you were drying. You can never do that again." His big body shuddered. "Promise me that will never happen again."

She wanted to. But the fact of the matter was she was human with a limited lifespan. "I'll live as long as I can." It was the best she could promise him. "But I'm human, and you're not." That was putting it mildly. Ezra was practically immortal.

He pressed his lips against hers, driving out the last echo of the cold and pain she'd endured, replacing it with pure pleasure. They were both alive, both safe. It was more than she'd hoped for.

He slipped his tongue into her mouth and stole her breath away. Not that she minded. He was warm and gentle and made her toes curl. As much as she wanted to continue, there were things that needed to be dealt with.

She reluctantly sat back, and her gaze fell onto the perfect sapphires glittering on her lap. They were a tangible sign Ezra had deep feelings for her. He might not have said it directly, but if drakon tears were rare, then maybe he loved her. She knew she loved him and had told him so. Maybe this was his way of telling her he felt the same. And maybe she was grasping at straws.

"What happened with Aaron?" She had to know.

Ezra's gaze grew shuttered and remote. "I took care of it."

"Where's his body?" The world she now lived in was a violent one. If she hoped to have a relationship with Ezra, she had to accept that. The Knights and the drakons were at war.

"On the beach."

"We need to get rid of it. And all the evidence." She'd never thought she'd hear herself utter such words, had always been a law-abiding citizen. The normal world had no idea there were creatures like Ezra, or that there was a powerful, secret society hunting him and his kind. The rules of human civilization didn't apply to this situation.

"The dagger." She'd forgotten all about it.

"What dagger?" Ezra trailed his fingertips over her bare shoulder and down her arms, leaving goose bumps on her skin in his wake.

"The one from your desk. The Spanish one. I couldn't find the rifle. I stabbed Aaron with it. It has to be on the beach. It might be lost."

"I don't care about the dagger, only that you're safe." He kissed her forehead, cheekbones, and lips.

And that was something else that didn't make sense. She stared down at her palm, the one she'd caught herself with when she'd fallen, the one that had been scraped and bleeding. There was nothing but smooth skin.

She raised her hand. "How is this possible?" She wasn't imagining things. She'd hurt her hand and her knees and twisted her ankle. She'd been bruised where Aaron had struck her jaw. Now, she didn't feel any pain at all. Just the opposite. She felt amazingly good. "What did you do?"

Ezra's brows lowered and his lips thinned. "I did what I had to do."

There was nothing that could heal wounds this quickly, no miracle drug to not only heal her injuries but energize her as well. She remembered the taste of the delicious liquid in her mouth. Her fingers flew to her lips. She'd thought it medicine, and in a way, she supposed it was. Just not the kind you could get a prescription for or buy from the drugstore.

"Drakon blood," she whispered. That had to be the source of the heat that had roasted her from the inside out before healing her. It was the reason the Knights hunted his kind. What had he done?

• • •

Ezra gave a single nod, not willing to lie to Sam. He'd done what he'd thought best and wouldn't change his decision if he had it to do again. "The hypothermia was making your heartbeat erratic."

Sam nodded. He wished he knew what she was thinking, if she was angry with him or okay with what he'd done. "I see."

"I'm not sorry." How could he be when he had Sam alive and well in his arms. "It was the best way to save your life. I couldn't take you to a hospital, could I? Not with the Knights running around on the mainland."

She continued to stare at him with her vibrant green eyes. When she licked her lips, his cock stirred. Now that she was out of danger, he was very aware of both of them being naked in his bed. They were both alive, and it was natural to want to celebrate that fact in the most natural way. He wasn't sure she'd be amenable to his suggestion right now. Best to keep it to himself.

"Thank you for taking care of me."

He waited for the "but" he was sure would follow. When she said nothing else, he prompted her, "But?"

"I'm sorry you had to go to such extreme measures. That's my fault for allowing Aaron to see me."

"Bullshit." He lifted her so she was facing him. Sapphires

spilled everywhere, some of them falling to the floor. He didn't care. All he cared about was Sam. "Dexter would have checked out the island even if he hadn't seen you. At least you saw him coming and he didn't take you unaware." He shuddered to think of what might have happened if she hadn't been able to run, to buy enough time for him to get here.

His cock was throbbing now, wanting inside her warmth. All he had to do was lean forward and his chest would be brushing her breasts. With her straddling him, he could easily lift her and slide his shaft inside her.

She placed her hand on his chest, looking sad and hurt. Some of his arousal died. "I'm sorry you had to give me your blood."

Didn't that just make him feel like crap. Did the idea of having his blood inside her upset her that much? "You needed it." He couldn't be sorry he'd done it. He was just sorry about her reaction.

"I don't want to be like them." Her whispered confession confused him.

"Like who?"

"The Knights." She slid her hands up his biceps and over his shoulders. "They want you for your blood, the healing ability. They want you for wealth and power." She picked up one of the sapphires and held it between them. "I don't want you to think I'm like them. I don't want anything from you. I just want you safe and happy."

He palmed her shoulders and lightly shook her. "You make me happy. Your safety makes me happy." He released her and closed her palm around the sapphire she held. "These belong to you. I belong to you."

She flung herself against his chest, clung to his neck, and whispered the words he'd wanted to hear again since she'd first said them, mostly to make sure he hadn't hallucinated them. "I love you."

"You are mine." He tunneled his fingers into her curls. "Mine to protect and keep." A drakon always protected what was his. "You are my treasure." He stared into her eyes, wanting her to understand how much she meant to him.

"Oh, Ezra." She sighed and then kissed him.

Elation washed over him in waves. Sam was safe, she was healthy, and she wasn't mad at him for feeding her his blood. Drakon blood was powerful, and not everyone reacted well to it. There was always pain, always a price to be paid for accelerated healing. Sometimes it was too much for a human body to bear, and the person died. But the benefits outweighed the risks, especially in this case where Sam's life had been in danger.

There were many things that needed to be done, the least of which was getting rid of Dexter's body and the boat he'd arrived in. He also had to check in with his brothers and the crew of the *Easton*. The Knights were still out there. That hadn't changed.

But it could all wait while he kissed Sam and strengthened the physical and emotional bonds between them. He took his time to map every crevice of her mouth. She'd almost died, could have been lost to him.

Inside him, his dragon roared. No one would take Sam from him. He'd lay waste to the world if he had to.

He suddenly understood his brothers a lot better, especially Tarrant, who after centuries of hiding and staying out of the Knight's way, was now taking the fight to the Knights. The group had gotten bloated on its own power as the drakons kept to themselves and tried to evade the greedy bastards. That time was at an end.

He held the world in his arms. Sam was the sweetness he'd been missing for so many years. She filled a void inside him, one he hadn't realized was there until she'd come into his life. She was passion and love and friendship all rolled into one sexy package.

Since her safety came before all else, even his need for her, he eased her away. It pained him to do so, but it was necessary. "I have to take care of things." There was a dead body in the small cove and a strange boat tied up at his dock.

"I can help." She started to climb off his lap, but he clamped his hands around her waist and held her in place.

"Absolutely not." He was putting his foot down about this. She didn't need to deal with Dexter's body. It was better if she wasn't reminded how easily he could take a life. If the man had been an innocent, his death would prey on Ezra's conscience, but he'd been a Knight. Ezra wouldn't give him another thought once he'd gotten rid of the body.

Sam frowned. "I am going with you. Either I'm part of your life, or I'm not. I'm not part of your collection. You can't just put me on a shelf and tell me to stay there."

He'd known she was going to be trouble. She was a strong, independent woman. And while he admired those qualities, at times he wished she was a little less so.

"You don't have any clothes to wear." Her jeans were soaking wet in a pile on the floor.

"That's okay." She climbed out of bed and hurried to his closet. He watched, totally bemused and charmed as she pulled out a thick cotton sweater and dragged it over her head. He hated that she covered her delectable body, but it was probably for the best.

He shoved aside the comforter and stood. Sam's gaze widened as her eyes focused on his arousal.

"You're going to need more than a sweater," he informed her.

"There are sweatpants in the dryer." She took a step toward him and pointed a finger at his erection. "Is that going to be a problem?"

He growled at her playful teasing. "I can manage until

you can take care of it later."

Sam started toward the door but turned back and stepped into his arms. "Thank you."

He banded his arms around her and lifted her right off her feet so he could hold her against his chest. "You're everything to me."

She stroked his jaw and kissed his cheek. "I'm starting to understand that." He hoped she was, because neither of their lives would ever be the same again. She patted his chest. "Put me down."

He didn't want to. He wanted to carry her around with him for the next century or so until he recovered from seeing her near lifeless body on the beach with Dexter standing over her. If there was any way he thought he could convince her to let him keep her glued to his side, he'd try.

He forced himself to set her back on her feet. Sam was going to complicate his life, change how he lived, how he did everything. He was looking forward to the challenge.

She darted toward the door. "I'll be back. Get dressed. We have things to do." She paused and gave his erection a pointed look. "Sooner we get them dealt with, the sooner I can take care of that."

Her laughter trailed behind her. In spite of being aroused to the point of pain, Ezra was happy.

Chapter Twenty-Three

Sam hesitated for the briefest of seconds when she reached the top of the path leading down to the beach. The sun was sinking below the horizon. If they didn't hurry, it would be full dark. Not that it would matter to Ezra, but it would make it virtually impossible for her to see. She had a flashlight tucked in the jacket pocket. It was Ezra's and fell all the way to her knees. With the sleeves rolled up, she knew she looked ridiculous, but it was warm, so she didn't care.

He'd been silent on the walk here, but he hadn't ignored her. No, he'd been there to help her over any obstacle and to make sure she was right beside him. He was in full protective mode.

She knew he would have much preferred if she stayed back at the house, but she needed to be a part of dealing with this mess. Not that she had any experience dealing with a dead body before, not outside of a formal funeral setting, and this wasn't anywhere near the same thing.

"You can go back, and I can handle this." Ezra stepped in front of her to block her view down to the tiny cove and the body on the beach.

That he wanted to spare her meant a lot. "I need to do this." She wanted him to understand. She had to stand beside him through the good and the bad, otherwise they'd never have a shot at a real relationship.

He nodded, turned his back on her, and started down the path. She followed and tugged the zipper all the way to her neck. The wind was whipping up, and she was grateful for the heavy jacket and the sweater beneath it.

Sand had blown over a part of Aaron's body. His eyes were wide open, and his features were locked in an expression of pain. She felt a twinge of sorrow for him before reminding herself he would have killed her in the end. It had been his life or hers, and Ezra had made the choice.

"What do we do?" She slipped her hand into his and gave it a squeeze to remind him they were together.

He rubbed the back of his neck. "I'll move him back to his boat, take it out to sea, and toss his body overboard. If it's ever discovered, I'm hoping they'll decide that the injuries are consistent with his body being tossed against the rocks."

It should work, because that was exactly what had happened, except it had been Ezra and not the ocean waves that had done the tossing. She glanced at the blood on Aaron's leg. "What about the wound I gave him?" She looked at Ezra. "Won't they notice that if his body is found?"

He shook his head and his jaw firmed. "Doubtful. They'd most likely assume it was caused by a sharp rock. If he's in the water for any length of time, the marine life will feed on him, and it won't be a problem."

She shuddered and tried not to think about it. "What can I do to help?"

"Look for the dagger and anything Dexter might have dropped. We can't leave anything here." Ezra began to unroll the tarp he'd brought with him.

Sam was glad to be away from the body. She wasn't squeamish, not usually, but seeing the body was a little off-putting. "I'm on it."

Since the sun was virtually gone, she dug out the flashlight and began to shine it along the shore, trying to remember exactly where they'd fought. The light caught a flash, and she hurried toward it.

The Spanish dagger was sitting just beyond the reach of the waves. She picked it up and examined it. The priceless artifact seemed to have sustained no damage, other than the blood still staining the hilt.

Sam shuddered and walked to the edge of the water. She couldn't let it stay there. Nothing could link Aaron with them. When the next wave rolled in, she bent down and let the water wash over the blade. She held it there as the ocean covered the blade again and again until it was finally clean.

She wiped the blade on the leg of her pants and tucked it into her pocket. She was glad they'd found it. It was one of Ezra's treasures. In spite of the fact she'd used it to stab a man, she loved the piece. It had allowed her to fight back, had given her hope.

She scanned the beach with the flashlight, walking up and down the area, scuffing out any sign of Aaron's footprints as she went. She was very aware of Ezra wrapping the body and gathering Aaron's rifle.

"I don't see anything else," she told Ezra. He had much better vision than her. He could have found the dagger faster than she had. She knew this was his way of allowing her be a part of things.

Ezra stood beside her. He narrowed his gaze and scanned the sandy and rocky shoreline. He stopped abruptly and moved his gaze back a few inches. When he walked away, she followed, wanting to know what he'd seen.

A scrap of fabric covered in blood fluttered in the wind.

He didn't bother to pick it up, and her skin prickled. The rise in energy was unmistakable. He leaned forward and blew softly. It wasn't warm wind he blew this time. It was fire. The fabric caught and burned, disappearing into nothingness. The blood stain disappeared, leaving only darkened sand behind.

"Wow, that's impressive." That was putting it mildly. "I didn't know you could do the fire thing." Made sense, though. In every legend about dragons, they had the ability to discharge fire from their nose or mouth.

"It's a challenge to control it in this form, but I can do it. We all can." He wrapped his arm around her and led her back to the base of the path. "Drakon fire destroys completely. The only thing it can't destroy is another drakon. Our scales are too tough. Only a drakon's own fire can destroy them."

"So drakons can't use it to destroy other drakons." From an evolutionary standpoint, that made sense.

"Right, but we can still beat the hell out of one another." On that pleasant note, he left her to retrieve the body. She had so much to discover about Ezra and his culture and was eager to learn. The fact she couldn't share it with anyone was somewhat of a disappointment. She was an archaeologist, after all. But nothing was more important than protecting Ezra.

"Let's go." He had the tarp over his left shoulder and indicated with his free hand that she should lead the way.

She really needed the flashlight now and focused the beam on the ground in front of her. "Do you think the Knights will send someone else?"

"Yes. They already have another man on board the *Easton*. Even if they buy Dexter's death as an accident, they'll investigate. They don't know what happened to you."

"What are we going to do about that?" The race for her life had seemed so much longer earlier today, but they weren't too far from the dock. It was actually a pleasant walk with

Ezra beside her and the moon rising in the darkened sky. If it weren't for the dead body, it might even be considered romantic.

"You have to die."

Sam stumbled to a halt and swung around, aiming the flashlight right at Ezra. "What?"

He threw his hand over his eyes. "Can you point that damn thing away?"

She knew he hadn't meant it literally, or at least she hoped not. No, she was certain he would never harm her. Her nerves were just frayed from the happenings of the day. The dead body certainly wasn't helping settle her. She lowered the flashlight until the beam hit the ground. "Care to explain yourself?"

He sighed, grabbed her free hand, and started walking again. "I have to retrieve the damn dingy you stole from the bottom of the ocean. I'll need some of your clothes, too. Your jacket for sure. Your sneakers, too."

"You're going to stage my death."

"Yes." They walked out of the woods and started across the meadow. The light from the house shone like a beacon. "And no, you can't help. I sunk that boat deep in a crevice so it would never be discovered. I wasn't thinking ahead. I only wanted to destroy any evidence that might lead the Knights to my home."

Sam refrained from commenting. Ezra had assumed she'd been working with the Knights when they'd first met. It had made perfect sense to get rid of any evidence. Sort of like what they were doing now.

She followed him down the path to the dock. The sound of their shoes against the wood seemed to echo unusually loud. Or maybe that was her imagination acting up. After all, they were disposing of a dead body.

Ezra stepped on board Aaron's boat, his balance never

wavering. He might have been walking down a sidewalk for all the difference it made to him. He set the tarp down and then stepped back onto the dock.

"I don't know how long I'll be gone."

She understood. "Okay. I'll make coffee or something." She winced, feeling rather useless.

Ezra brushed his fingers over the side of her face. "There's nothing you can do, but it means a lot to me that you want to help."

Sam nodded. What could she say to that? It was the truth. She couldn't exactly dive down and retrieve the boat like he could. She couldn't be in the cold water like he could. She huddled in his jacket, feeling totally useless and not liking the sensation at all. She was a doer and not used to sitting on the sidelines.

He put his thumb under her chin and raised her head. "There are things I can physically do that you can't." That was certainly blunt but accurate. "But having you here makes me stronger, more determined. You have strengths of your own, knowledge, experience. Never doubt your value."

He brushed a kiss over her lips. "You have more courage than any other woman I've ever known." He gave a rueful laugh. "If it were up to me, I'd lock you inside and surround you with guard dogs." He brushed a curly, windswept lock behind her ear. "But I know you wouldn't stay. And that's what makes you special."

Her throat tightened and her eyes filled. She swallowed and blinked back tears, praying he would believe her watering eyes were caused by the chilly wind. His words touched her heart.

She cleared her throat. "Go. Do what you have to do and come back."

He gave a curt nod and began to strip off his clothes. She shivered when he removed his sweater and then his jeans. The dipping temperature had no affect on him. He might as well have been on an island in the Caribbean instead of off the coast of Maine in November.

He folded his clothes and handed them to her. "Can you take these inside for me?"

That she could do. "Absolutely." There were other things she could do as well. "I'll have something cooked for when you get back." He'd be expending a lot of energy and would be hungry.

"I'll hurry," he promised.

Sam shook her head. "I'd rather you do it right and safely than fast."

He flashed her a grin. "You and Tarrant are going to get along famously. You're a lot alike."

"A man of infinite wisdom and sense," she shot back. If she didn't tease him, she'd probably cry.

"I'm not telling him you said that." Ezra stepped back on board Aaron's boat. He was a shadow in the dark, but his tattoo seemed to shimmer beneath the gloom. "Stay inside." He paused and pinned her with his patented stare, the one that would reduce most men into jabbering idiots it was so fierce. It made Sam smile.

"The phone for my office is broken."

She winced, knowing that was her fault. She'd had it with her when she'd fled the house and Aaron. The salt water had destroyed it. "Sorry about that."

"I'm not. I only wish you'd had my phone number." He handed her his phone, which he'd retrieved from the beach. His clothing hadn't survived the shift to his dragon form, but his phone miraculously had. "Charge it and use it if you have to."

"I will," she promised, even though she couldn't foresee a situation where she would. Ezra would come home and the Knights had no idea where she was. If she stayed inside, she should be fine.

"I need your sneakers." He'd mentioned he'd need some of the clothing to stage a shipwreck, but it was suddenly more real.

"Oh, right." It was harder than she thought to slip off her sneakers and hand them to him. The chill from the thick wooden planks seeped through her thin socks. "What about my coat?" He'd mentioned using that, too.

Ezra glanced away and then back to her. "I put it aboard the boat earlier when you were getting ready."

"I see." Ezra was one step ahead of her, always thinking.

She shivered and huddled deeper into his coat. She knew he only wore it when he went to the mainland. He didn't need it for warmth. But it still held his scent, and that comforted her.

She'd thought she'd be fine here on Ezra's island, but Aaron had found her.

"I'll be back as soon as I can," he promised.

He cast off the line, started the engine, and backed away from the dock. He waved before he set a course out to sea. She wanted to stay and watch but knew it was safer for them both if she was inside.

The island seemed lonelier, darker, and more ominous without Ezra beside her. She hurried toward the house, using her flashlight to guide the way. The last thing she wanted to do was trip and fall.

If she did, would she injure herself or would Ezra's blood, which was flowing through her veins, heal her?

She had so much to learn.

She heaved a sigh of relief when she hit the porch stairs. She bolted through the front door and closed it behind her. The lighting in the room wasn't overly bright. More for ambiance than anything.

She removed the jacket Ezra had loaned her and hung

it up in the closet by the front door. She needed coffee. And if she was being truthful, more light. She hit the switch in the kitchen and the room was bathed in a warm, bright glow.

She stood there and took several deep breaths before going to the coffeepot. She tried not to think too much while she filled the machine and set it to brew. Once she was done, she stood in the center of the kitchen, not quite sure what to do.

Her life was irrevocably changed. There was no going back to the normal world, whatever that was. She was in love with a drakon, a mythical creature who wasn't supposed to exist. She was also in the middle of a war, one that had been waging for centuries.

She began to sway and grabbed the edge of the stone countertop. "Get a grip." She needed to keep busy, otherwise she'd lose her mind while waiting for Ezra to return. She'd already studied his collection earlier. Not that there wasn't more to see or learn, but she wasn't in the right frame of mind to enjoy it.

She needed physical activity.

When all else failed, there was always housework. She left the coffee brewing and headed upstairs. She'd change the bed and gather all the dirty clothes. Once she had the laundry sorted out, maybe she'd clean the bathroom. She needed to make something for Ezra to eat. Soup was always quick and easy and could be heated whenever he returned.

Filled with purpose, she strode into the bedroom. All the bedclothes needed washing, even the comforter and blankets. She went to pull the comforter off the bed and stopped. Shimmering on top of it were large sapphires.

"Oh God." Sam dropped onto the mattress and picked up one of the sparkling gems. It caught the light, and she stared into the heart of the stone. No, not a stone, a tear. Her drakon's tear.

She closed her fingers around the gem and held it to her heart. He'd shed them for her. She took a deep breath and then another. Every time she thought she was calmly accepting the situation, something else would remind her things were anything but normal.

But that was okay. Normal was overrated. If having to deal with a bunch of crazy stuff meant she got to have a life with Ezra, she'd gladly take it.

She set the drakon tear on the bedside table and then started searching for the rest. They were sprinkled on and between the blankets and sheets. Several had fallen on the floor. When she was satisfied she had them all, she stripped the bed and gathered all the dirty clothes.

As she dragged the bundle downstairs, she glanced out the window by the door. Where was Ezra? What was he doing?

Chapter Twenty-Four

Ezra stopped Dexter's boat and let it drift on the tide while he unwound the tarp. It would be so much easier if he could just burn Dexter's body, but dumping it was the wiser option. He'd chosen a place not too distant from where the *Easton* was anchored. With the tides, it was possible Dexter's body would eventually wash up on shore. Or it might not. It was a gamble either way.

He eased Dexter's body over the side and let it slide into the inky depths. He felt no remorse. The world was better off without him. Any man who'd join the ranks of the Knights and had risen as high as Dexter had done his share of killing. There was no way of knowing how many people he'd murdered doing the Knights' dirty work. He'd also laid his hands on Sam, would have killed her if he'd had the chance. For that reason alone, he deserved to die.

Maybe some people would find Ezra's attitude brutal and callous, but he wasn't all human. Only half of him was. His other half was all dragon. Being a drakon wasn't easy. It was a constant tug-of-war between his two sides. Even though his human body was his base form, he was just as comfortable in his dragon form. But there was a difference. His awareness, how he saw the world, differed slightly depending on which form he was in.

But one thing remained constant. He'd protect his brothers with his life. And nothing and no one would be allowed to harm Sam, not as long as there was breath in his body.

He bundled Sam's coat and sneakers into the tarp to make them easier to transport. Then he took one last look around to make sure he wasn't missing anything. There was no GPS on the boat, for which Ezra was grateful. The Knights were paranoid about such things and rarely used them.

When he was positive there was nothing to point the Knights in his direction, he dove over the side of the boat. It was full dark now. Sam was home alone, probably worrying about him.

It was strange to have to consider someone else's feelings, but it was nice, too. He and his brothers loved one another, but that was different. They all lived their own lives, came and went as they chose. But it was different with Sam. He was aware of her every emotion.

He could picture her in the kitchen. She'd promised to cook something for him. He growled in pleasure at the thought. He had no idea if she was a good cook and didn't care. Whatever she made, he'd eat.

The darkness didn't hinder him as he dove into the water and shifted into his dragon form. His big body cut through the water like a stealth missile. He had to retrieve the dinghy Sam had used to escape the *Integrity*.

It took him a lot less time to reach his destination than it had using the boat. He could move so much faster. He rose to the surface and made a complete three-sixty sweep to make sure he was alone. Then he took a deep breath and dove.

The water pressed around him. It would crush most humans at this depth, but to Ezra it was like a warm, comforting blanket wrapping around him.

The dingy was jammed in a crevice in the rocks, just where he'd left it. He pulled the boat out, being careful not to gouge it with his claws, which was no easy task. He shoved the small craft toward the surface and followed it up.

The dingy wasn't in great shape, but it would do what he needed it to. Ezra shifted back to his human form long enough to unroll the tarp and put Sam's coat and her sneakers on board. He'd toss one of the sneakers over the side once he was closer to shore. He knew the perfect place to dump the dinghy. There was an area that was notorious for its jagged rocks. He'd run the boat aground there. It would account for any gouges.

He shifted back to his dragon form and swam toward shore, dragging the dinghy behind him. He had way too much time to think while he was swimming. Usually, nothing could distract him from his enjoyment of the water, but he was worried about Sam.

She loved him, he reminded himself. That meant she had to stay. It also meant she'd no longer be able to do the job she loved. Not that she'd be able to do it with the Knights after her, and they'd been on to her before she'd met him.

Still, he was worried. What if she wasn't happy on his island? What if she wanted to move...inland? His blood ran cold, and a shiver ran down his spine. He needed to be near the ocean.

He needed Sam more.

Everything inside him settled. He was a drakon, had lived for thousands of years. He'd do whatever it took to make Sam happy.

He could hear the gulls and other seabirds squawking from where they nested along the shoreline. The waves pounded against the rocks, the spray shooting twenty feet in the air before plummeting back down again.

He retrieved a lone sneaker and shoved the dinghy toward the rocks. It slammed into them again and again, each hit damaging it more. He turned his back on the rocks and swam closer to shore. This late at night, there was no one around. He tossed the sneaker onto the shore. Someone would eventually find it. Whether they identified it with Sam or not was another thing. The Knights were more likely to keep her disappearance to themselves, especially since they hadn't reported her missing.

He didn't want to take the tarp home, but he couldn't dump it in the ocean. He'd only do that in extreme cases. He swam back over by the rocky outcrop where no one could see him. Even though he was alone, he figured it was best to be safe.

He tossed the tarp onto a rock, opened his mouth, and breathed fire. It was easy in his dragon form. Fire bellowed from his mouth, lighting up the night. The tarp caught fire and disintegrated almost instantly. Nothing burned hotter than drakon fire. Maybe the sun, but that was about it. A fire drakon could produce flames hotter than molten lava.

Feeling lighter than he had in days, Ezra turned his back on the remains of the boat and headed toward home. He dipped and dived, but made a straight line to home, to Sam.

• • •

Sam stirred the thick soup. The fragrance of rosemary and thyme mixed with onion and other vegetables. The chicken soup she'd made smelled delicious. The dryer buzzed. She glanced at the clock. Ezra had been gone almost four hours.

"Patience." She went to the utility room and removed the latest load of clothes from the dryer. The sheets were done and back on the bed. So were the blankets and comforter. The towels were back in the bathroom and linen closet. She'd done the linens before she'd tackled the clothing. Ezra had clothes he could wear, and she could borrow another sweater or sweatshirt or something.

She pulled the warm clothing from the dryer before putting a mound of wet jeans and sweatpants into the machine. She folded each garment carefully and placed it in the basket. Ezra was a big man and all his clothing was oversized. She hugged one of his sweaters before tossing it on top of the rest.

She'd showered in between loads of laundry and making soup. She'd even cleaned the bathroom when she was finished. Now she'd run out of things to do.

Coffee, she'd have another cup of coffee. It didn't matter she was running on caffeine and nerves as it was. She rubbed her hand over the flannel shirt she wore. She was down to underwear and a pair of tattered jeans. The rest of her clothing had either been sacrificed to make her disappearance believable, or been ruined.

She left the utility room and closed the door behind her. The kitchen looked and felt homey with the soup on the stove and the table set. She'd decided to make it a little more formal than sitting at the counter like they usually did.

She wandered over to the window and looked out. Not that she could see much of anything. The moon spilled over the water, but the waves were still impenetrable. Ezra was out there somewhere. She turned away and wrapped her arms around herself, trying to stave off the worry mounting with each passing minute.

The handle of the front door jangled. Fear and hope warred inside her. The wooden panel pushed open, and Ezra strode inside. His hair was damp and tousled. A single bead of water flowed down the center of his chest, right along the edge of his tattoo. He looked more handsome than ever with his broad shoulders, rippling biceps, and massive chest.

She scanned him from head to toe, searching for any injury. It was still jolting to see the almost iridescent tattoo bisect his body completely from neck to ankle. "Thank God," she breathed. He was safe and unharmed. Sam ran toward him. Ezra opened his arms wide and lifted her right off her feet.

"I'm home," he murmured. He ran his big hand down her spine.

She grabbed his face and kissed him, pouring all her anxiety into it. He groaned and kissed her back. He took two steps to the left and spun around. Her back hit the wall. She wrapped her legs around his bare flanks, needing his touch, his heat, to drive away the lingering fear.

He growled and pushed his hips inward, rubbing his erection against her core. With only a thin layer of fabric separating them, the sensation was exquisite. She kissed his neck and face before diving back toward his lips.

If she was hungry for him, he was ravenous for her. He devoured her, stealing the air from her lungs, running his hands over her thighs and up her sides. She gasped when he shoved his hands beneath the neckline of the shirt and cupped one of her breasts.

"We should talk," she managed to get out between kisses.

Ezra pulled back and stared at her like she'd lost her mind. "Later." He dove back in and stole her next thought. She traced the bulging muscles of his biceps, the broad line of his shoulders, and down the furrow of his spine. He was big and warm and all hers. She didn't think she'd ever get used to touching him.

He was special. It was more than him being big and handsome, even more than him being a mythical creature. It was his intellect, his dry sense of humor, the way he looked at her as though she'd hung the moon. Then there was the unexplainable spark of passion that kindled each time they were together.

He was naked, and she was only wearing one of his shirts. He shoved the garment up and rubbed his shaft against her sex. She was wet and more than ready. And she didn't want to wait. She'd already been waiting for hours.

"Now." She gripped his shoulders and tried to maneuver herself into position. Ezra held her with one hand and positioned himself with the other. His turquoise gaze met hers, and he drove himself home.

She sucked in a breath as he filled her. Each time was like the first. They'd only known one another for such a short time. The kind of connection she felt with him should be impossible. But it wasn't. There were times she felt as though they'd known one another forever.

"Sam." He sprinkled kisses on her forehead and cheeks before following the line of her jaw. "My Sam." There was a wealth of possessiveness in his words, and they amped up her already bottomless need for this man.

"My Ezra," she shot back.

He growled and began to move, driving his shaft deep before almost withdrawing. She tightened her thighs around him, not wanting to let him go. He slammed home once again.

She gasped and writhed, not able to get enough of him. He leaned one forearm against the wall and pumped his hips faster. Pressure built between her thighs. She was so close. She tried to move, tried to help, but Ezra was out of control. All she could do was hang on and enjoy the ride.

He angled his hips and his pelvis stroked her clit, driving her over the edge and into oblivion. She cried out, digging her fingers into him. Heat flashed through her, over her. Every breath she took was filled with the scent of the sea and Ezra— fresh, wild, and masculine. It was mingled with the deeper notes of their arousal. He growled and worked his hips faster.

Harder.

He threw back his head and roared his release. Every window in the house shook. Something shattered in the kitchen. She buried her face against his shoulder and clung to him. Emotion too deep to name enveloped her. It was more than just love. It was an unbreakable connection.

His tattoos began to shimmer, almost as if they were alive. Fascinated, she reached out and stroked his bicep. The ink seemed to almost rise toward her fingers. Shocked, she pulled her hand back.

"What is it?" He was still hard and pulsing inside her, but he never seemed to lose his awareness of her. If anything, their lovemaking seemed to sharpen it.

"Nothing." It had to be her imagination.

Ezra took her face between his hands. "What is it?" he repeated.

"It's crazy, but I thought your tattoo tried to move onto my skin."

He frowned. "Really?"

"Yeah. That's not normal?"

He shook his head and looked mildly concerned. "No, it's not. At least it's never happened with me before."

She shrugged. "I probably imagined it." She didn't want to dwell on it, to spoil their lovemaking. She draped her arms over his shoulders. "Hi. Welcome home."

A slow grin spread across his face. "If that's the welcome I'm going to get each time I leave home, I'll be going away more often."

She laughed and rubbed her nose against his. He cupped her butt and squeezed.

She wanted to ask him what had happened, but they needed their time together first. She patted his arm. "I have soup waiting on the stove. Why don't you put on some clothes, and I'll dish us up some."

He studied her face, looking concerned. "You're sure?"

"I am. Everything else can wait until you've cleaned up and eaten." He lifted her away from the wall but kept her in his arms. He was still hard inside her. She moaned and tightened her grip on his hips.

"We could go upstairs," he murmured in her ear.

She wanted to, she really did, but they did need to talk about what had happened. "After," she promised.

He sighed and disengaged their bodies before releasing her. She hated the separation. "Go on," she told him. "I'll get everything ready."

He gave her one last smoldering look before heading up the stairs. She watched his tight buttocks and the heavy muscles in his back and thighs as he took the steps three at a time. When he disappeared into the bedroom, she released a pent-up sigh. She was still decently clothed, with only two of the tops buttons undone. They barely touched one another, their need to great to allow for anything but the most basic joining.

She took one last glance up the stairs before heading to the downstairs bathroom to get cleaned up. Once she was done, she went to the kitchen and turned up the heat on the soup. She'd found some frozen rolls in the freezer earlier and thawed them. Now she popped them into the microwave.

By the time she had the rolls and butter on the table and the hot soup dished up, Ezra was back. He'd taken a quick shower and donned only a pair of jeans, which were zipped but not buttoned. How was she supposed to form coherent sentences with him looking so hot and sexy?

"Smells delicious." He kissed the top of her head and held her chair for her. She was unused to such gestures, but she liked his old-fashioned manners. He cleared his throat as he sat. "The table looks nice, too."

She hadn't found a tablecloth but had dug up a few

placemats. They made the table look a little less bare. "I hope you like it." And could their conversation be anymore stilted? They sounded like two people on a first date.

She lifted her spoon and tasted the soup. It was hot and delicious, but she really wasn't hungry. She set her spoon back down and leaned her elbows on the table. "What happened?"

Ezra had only had two mouthfuls of soup. He looked longingly at the bowl but lowered his spoon.

"I'm sorry. Eat first." She could wait a few minutes longer.

"I should call Tarrant and the others. That way I only have to explain things once. They need to know that Dexter found you."

In other words, his friends needed to know he'd killed for her and disposed of the body. Not exactly the best way to endear herself to them. "Eat first." The longer she could put it off, the better.

He nodded and went back to eating. When he emptied his bowl, she moved hers in front of him. He raised his eyebrow in question, but she just shook her head and motioned for him to keep eating. He devoured the dozen rolls and the entire pot of soup. She'd have to learn to adjust quantities when she cooked. What would be a meal with leftovers for most people was a snack for Ezra.

He placed his spoon in the empty bowl. "Thank you. That's the most delicious meal I've ever had."

"I doubt that, but you're welcome." It was only chicken soup. He'd probably eaten all over the world and tasted dishes by some of the world's best chefs.

"No." He reached out and took her hand in his. Her hands were rough from work and strong, but they looked delicate next to his. "It's the best meal I've ever eaten because you made it for me."

Her heart turned over in her chest. The things he said to her made her feel special, and loved, damn it. He might not have said the words, but she knew he loved her. Or if he didn't, he was close. That was more than enough for her. His actions spoke louder than any words ever could.

"Then you're welcome. There's more where that came from," she assured him.

He winked and gave her a roguish smile. "I was hoping you'd say that."

She laughed and withdrew her hand from his. "Make your call." Then she glanced at the clock on the stove. "It's not too late, is it?" It was well after midnight.

He shook his head. "Not for this bunch. Besides, if I wake them, they can always go back to sleep later."

While she ferried the dirty dishes to the kitchen, Ezra retrieved his phone from the charger and placed the call.

. . .

Birch was waiting for Karina when she stepped inside her New York home. She'd spent the evening at the opera and then had drinks with some associates afterward. She hated the opera but attended regularly. She was, after all, considered a patron of the arts, a rich dilettante who played at business while her management team handled everything.

If they only knew the truth.

But they never would, and she was more than content to leave it that way. She'd given Birch the night off, had insisted on it. He'd never take any downtime otherwise. He'd sent four men with her. A little excessive for the opera, but she didn't object. When it came to her security, she trusted no one like she did Birch.

"What is it?" She handed her fur coat off to the maid who took it and scurried away.

Birch walked over to her office door and held it open. This was serious. She walked across the marble floor, her heels tapping against the expensive stone flooring.

She wanted a drink and then about six hours of uninterrupted sleep. She had a headache coming on. Things had been more difficult than usual lately.

Birch waited until she was inside and then closed the door. "No one has seen Dexter since he took off in a speedboat from the salvage ship this morning."

Karina frowned and walked over to the decanter. She definitely needed that drink. "He was supposed to supervise the salvage operations." Or at least the crew.

Birch stood in front of her desk, strong and solid as his namesake. "Dexter left Calloway in charge and took the boat he arrived in. According to Calloway, Dexter was keen to search for Doctor Bellamy."

"I can't fault him for that." She poured the amber whiskey into the crystal glass. "Unless of course, he's hoping to find her and keep the artifact for himself."

"That's the concern."

She sipped the whiskey, letting the mellow liquid slide down her throat and warm her stomach. Why couldn't the Knights focus on what was important—finding and capturing dragons? Instead, they spent much of their time infighting. It was a waste of time and manpower.

But it had to be dealt with.

"Find him. If he has the artifact, retrieve it. I want to know if it's worth salvaging the *Integrity*, or if I should take the insurance money." She walked over to her desk chair and sat. Even alone with the one person she trusted most in the world, she never truly let down her guard.

"You don't think there's more than one artifact in the wreckage of the *Reliant*?" Birch didn't even glance at the guest chairs, so she motioned him to one of them. He sat.

Karina took another sip of her drink. "Doubtful. Travel was iffy in those days. I can't see the Knights risking two powerful artifacts on one ship. They'd want to split them up in case of a wreck." She tapped the side of the crystal glass. "And if the archaeologist took the one big find, it's doubtful there is another one there."

Birch nodded as though he'd expected her to say that.

"What do you think?" He was the only person she would ask something like that. Anyone else would see it as a weakness and exploit it.

Birch didn't reply immediately. He sat and seemed to be considering every option, every scenario. She knew because she always did the same. He was the one who'd taught her how.

"I think you're right. Either Bellamy is dead and the artifact is lost, or Dexter will find her and retrieve it. And I don't think you'll get it back if that's the case." He rubbed his hand over his jaw and nodded as if coming to some decision.

"I think word has leaked to Temple by now."

Karina felt like growling. Herman Temple was a thorn in her side. "No doubt it has."

"Let him do the work for you. He'll send one of his people out to search for Dexter and the woman."

That was actually rather clever, not that she expected anything less from Birch. He was a big man, and fast on his feet when he needed to be. Because he never had much to say, many people made the mistake of thinking he wasn't very bright. They couldn't be farther from the truth.

"And the *Integrity*?" she asked.

"Keep Calloway on the job until the insurance people have come and gone. Then take the money. No need to waste more time and manpower. You can always get a new research vessel."

Birch was right, as usual. Karina rose, leaving her half-full glass on the desk, and Birch immediately came to his feet. "I'm going to call it a night. Let me know if you hear anything."

Chapter Twenty-Five

Ezra wanted this call over and done with so he could enjoy Sam. He'd been all over her practically as soon as he'd stepped inside the front door. He'd taken her against the wall with no preliminaries at all. Just a wham, bam, thank you, ma'am. And she'd fed him soup. Soup she'd made for him from scratch.

He wanted to take her to bed so he could worship every inch of her amazing body before he made love to her again. But first, he had to deal with his family and the situation with the Knights.

"If you leave the dishes, I'll get them when I'm done." She'd cooked. Didn't seem fair for her to have to clean up.

"That's okay. I've got it. This time," she added.

He grinned. His Sam was no pushover. While she piled the plates and bowls and cutlery into the dishwasher, he dialed Tarrant. It was earlier on the West Coast, so the rest of them should be awake. Tarrant and Valeriya were in Washington State, Darius and Sarah were currently in Arizona, and Nic was in Nevada.

"What?"

Ezra put the call on speaker and set the phone on the table. "It's lovely to hear your voice, too."

"What's happened?"

"Two whole words." He knew he shouldn't tease Tarrant, but sometimes it was just too easy. Silence was followed by a low growl. "I need to talk to you all at once."

The phone went dead.

"He sounds angry." Sam squirted dish liquid into the pot and filled it with water. He could sense she was worried and didn't like it. If his brother was nearby, Ezra would kick his ass.

"Ignore Tarrant. He always sounds that way. I don't know how Valeriya puts up with him."

Sam left the pot in the sink and wiped her hands on a kitchen towel. "Is that his wife?"

Ezra wasn't quite sure how to answer that. Wife? Mate was more accurate. The phone rang and he held up his index finger. "Hold that thought. Yeah?"

"I've got everyone connected," Tarrant told him.

Ezra took a deep breath. "A lot has happened since we last talked." He was aware of Sam listening as he told his family about his trip to the *Easton* and coming back to the island to find Dexter hurting Sam.

She was standing in the kitchen with her arms wrapped around herself. She looked so alone. He stood and went to her. She looked up at him and mouthed, "I'm sorry."

"It's not your fault," he whispered.

"Hey, we're still here," Tarrant pointed out.

Ezra threw his arm around her shoulders and brought her back to the table with him. "Sorry about that." He wasn't really, but best not to tell his brother that. He sat back in his chair and pulled her down onto his lap.

"You destroyed Dexter's body." It wasn't so much a question as a statement of fact. He knew it's what Darius would have done.

"Not exactly. I took his boat out to sea and dumped the body overboard. If it ever washes up, it will appear as though his body was battered by the ocean."

"Smart." Tarrant gave his approval.

"I also hauled up the dinghy that Sam stole when she escaped the *Integrity*."

"Let me guess," Nic interjected. "Another wreck?"

"It happens at sea." Maybe two was a little suspect, but the Knights would eventually have to accept both people were gone—Dexter dead and Sam off the grid with him.

"It's a little too neat and tidy, but it's the best you could do."

Ezra didn't take offense to Tarrant's observation. He knew his brother was worried about him. Sam was getting tenser by the second. If her spine got any stiffer, it would snap.

"I'm sorry," she blurted out. "To all of you. All I can do is promise to never divulge Ezra's secret."

The silence was deafening.

"It's not your fault." It didn't surprised Ezra that it was Valeriya who spoke first. She, of all of them, knew what it was like to feel guilty about having an association with the Knights.

"I did what I thought best," Sam told them all. "But if I'd believed for one second that the stories Gervais Rames told me about dragons were true, I would never have gotten involved with the Knights. I just wanted to enact some kind of revenge or justice or whatever you want to call it for my friend. He was the only family I had."

Ezra nuzzled her neck, wanting to comfort her. He also wanted to change the subject. What was done, was done. There was no changing it. "Tarrant, I need the name of the jeweler you and Darius used?"

He wished he could see his brothers' faces. He knew they

had to be shocked. Sarah gave a squeal of delight and he heard the clapping of hands.

Sam swiveled so she could look directly at him. "A jeweler."

He nodded. "Those sapphires belong in a necklace, for you."

There was both fear and wonder in her eyes. "Like the one from the fire drakon?"

"A more modern setting. Silver or platinum, I'm thinking."

"What the hell happened?" Darius demanded. "You've never given up drakon tears before."

He was grateful to his brother for not saying he'd never cried his eyes out before. Saying he'd never given tears up made it seem more manly.

"Sam was hypothermic, her heartbeat erratic." Ezra ran his fingers through her wild curls he loved so much, over her delicate cheeks, and finally across her lush lips. There was so much about her that he admired beyond the physical.

He eased his hand under the hem of the oversize shirt she wore. His shirt. He felt like beating his chest, but he didn't think that was a particularly wise course of action. Her thigh was warm and supple. He coasted his hand over the curve of her hip and into the slope of her waist.

"Welcome to the family." The dry undertone in Darius's voice jolted Ezra. His damn brother knew what he was doing. Maybe not exactly, but he knew where Ezra was heading. He had to get off the phone before he ended up making love to Sam while his family got an earful.

"Thank you." There was a tentativeness in Sam's voice but also pleasure. "And Ezra's secret is safe with me."

"It better be." Tarrant was as gruff as ever. "Hurt Ezra, and we'll end you."

Ezra was more amused by his brother's warning than furious, especially since Sam was smiling at him. "I can live with that," she told them all. "I do have a question." She pushed off of Ezra's lap, something he wasn't overly pleased with, and began to pace.

"Shoot," Tarrant told her.

. . .

It was both thrilling and intimidating to be a part of this group. She still didn't understand the intricacies of all their relationships, but they were family in every sense of the word. She sensed they shared a deep history and that there wasn't anything they wouldn't do for one another. That was love. That was loyalty and commitment.

It was what she'd always wanted.

Having Darius confirm Ezra had never shed drakon tears before awed her. Her drakon might never give her the words, but there was no doubt in her mind that he loved her.

If she was a part of this group, this family, she needed to understand things better, maybe even find a way to help them to offset all the trouble she'd brought with her.

"You've lived for years. Centuries. Right?" she asked him.

"Yes, about four thousand," Ezra confirmed, "give or take a decade."

She still had a hard time wrapping her brain around a number that large. Ezra had seen the rise and fall of the great civilizations of history. Drakons understood the ancient world better than any living scholar. They'd lived it.

Maybe it was her background in archaeology, the years she'd spent studying various cultures that gave her an insight they might not have considered before.

"Why now?"

Ezra frowned and leaned back in his chair. With his legs kicked out in front of him and his hands behind his head, he was the epitome of the relaxed male. She knew that could change in a heartbeat and he'd be ready to fight, to protect. Her Ezra was a warrior at heart, but he was also a scholar.

Sam began to pace. Walking always helped her think better. "Maybe I'm out of line, but I know Darius is also a drakon. In our last conversation, he referred to the Knights as hunting *us*, and not *you*," she pointed out to Ezra.

"Fuck," Darius muttered. "I did. So?"

"So"—Sam ran her fingers along the edge of the wooden table—"I gather you and Sarah haven't been together for long."

"Again, so?" Darius was obviously not happy with the turn in the conversation. Neither was Ezra, if his sudden frown was any indication.

"Bear with me. Please." She gripped the back of one of the chairs. Maybe she was poking her nose into an area it didn't belong, but if her theory was right, the rest of the drakons out there could be in for a rough road unless they were prepared.

"Go on," Ezra encouraged.

She nodded and took a deep breath. "I don't know if you're human or not, Tarrant."

"You know," he told her.

She did. In her heart, she suspected all the men were drakons, including Nic. "And you and Valeriya haven't been together for long?"

"No."

"Why now?" Nic sounded thoughtful. "That's what you mean, isn't it? Darius and Tarrant hook up with women, and now Ezra."

"Exactly. Why now, after four thousand years? If it was only one of you, I wouldn't even question it, but three drakons finding a connection with women in such a short period of time after all these years is significant. Do you think there's a reason?"

"I want to say coincidence, but it pushes the boundaries

too much." Tarrant sighed. "Any ideas?"

"Maturity." As she'd expected, she'd stunned them all silent. "It makes sense. You guys live a long time."

"Undetermined," Ezra told her.

"So what if you needed four thousand years or so to reach sexual maturity."

Nic laughed. "Sweetheart, I've been bedding women since I was fifteen. Or was it fourteen. Things were a lot different back in those days."

"I'm not talking about sex, but the need to mate, to settle." And she certainly didn't want to think about the thousands of women Ezra must have slept with. She warmed to her subject and started pacing again. "Maybe all of us women have something in common?"

"Like what?" Darius demanded.

She was thinking out loud, something she often did when she was working. "I have no idea. It's nothing more than a question at this point."

"You think other drakons will be experiencing this drive, this need to mate, as well?" Tarrant asked.

"Maybe. I don't know. It's just a thought, a theory."

"Why four thousand years?"

"Well," Sarah interjected. "Men mature more slowly than women." Valeriya laughed and Sam couldn't help but grin.

"There is that." She walked around the table to Ezra. "Like I said, it's something to think about." She stopped several steps away from him. If she got any closer she'd probably end up in his lap again. Not necessarily a bad thing, if they weren't talking with his family. "Nic needs to be careful," she blurted.

"Why?" Nic asked.

"If the Knights discover drakons are eager to mate and can figure out what kind of woman calls to a drakon—" She couldn't finish the thought.

"They'd set a trap," Ezra finished. "Like staking out a

virgin like they used to in the old days."

"They actually did that?" Sam was both appalled and curious. "Did it work?"

Ezra scowled and shook his head. "No, it didn't work."

She shrugged. "I had to ask. How else will I learn?"

"We all need to think about this," Tarrant pointed out. "In the meantime, Nic be careful if you're attracted to any woman."

"I'm attracted to many women," he quipped.

"Don't be an ass." Ezra leaned forward, his fingers touching the edge of the phone. She thought he wanted to reach out and touch his friend. "You be extra careful. If I have to rescue you from the Knights, I won't be pleased."

"Maybe I'll come for a visit. Meet the lovely Sam in person."

Ezra growled, the low rumble vibrating through the floor and up her legs. "You're always welcome."

Sadness tinged Nic's laugh. "But not as welcome as I was before."

Ezra shook himself. "No. You're always welcome. Come and meet my Sam."

A shiver of longing snaked down her spine at the possessiveness in his tone. She could tell he was concerned for his friend. She took the few steps necessary to bring her to his side. She rubbed his shoulder, and he leaned into her.

"I will. Not sure how soon I'll get there, but soon."

"Watch for Knights," Tarrant reminded him. "Ezra's neck of the woods is going to be lousy with them for the next while."

"Do you think they'll buy the whole boat wreck and lost at sea scenario?" Darius asked. "For both Dexter and Sam?"

"No." Ezra rubbed his chin across her stomach. Even through her clothing, it sent tingles all the way to her toes. "They'll send someone to investigate. Several of the high-ranking Knights might send men loyal to them to check things out. Eventually, they'll have to give up, but they'll always have one eye open for Dexter and for Sam."

And wasn't that a happy thought? Sam was tired of the Knights and their deadly games. She wanted to spend time alone with Ezra and learn more about him. She wanted some semblance of a normal life, whatever the new normal was going to be.

"You two must be exhausted," Darius pointed out. "Best to get some rest."

"I doubt they'll sleep just yet." Nic chuckled. She couldn't take offense since he was probably right.

"Let me know if you hear anything." Ezra was watching her now. The heat from his gaze was warming her all the way to her soul.

"What about the book?" It was Sarah who reminded them they still had a deadly artifact in the safe in Ezra's office.

"I think we should destroy it." As much as it hurt Sam to even think about destroying a piece of history, the book was a threat to Ezra. "It's too dangerous to simply leave there, even if it is locked away."

"Do you feel any affects from it?" Sarah asked.

"What do you mean?" She wished she could talk to the other woman, to all of them face-to-face.

There was the briefest of hesitations before Sarah continued. "The book I discovered kept growing in power the longer it was around Darius, around me."

"Really? You could sense that?" Sarah obviously had talent. "Ezra mentioned you have a gift for psychometry, but I'm not quite sure how that works."

"He did, did he?" Darius was obviously not pleased.

"Yes, he did." Sam plunged onward, sensing they were getting closer to learning some things they needed to know. "I can find artifacts, but I have an affinity for those associated with arcane rituals, mythical creatures. It's like a hum in my blood that gets louder the closer I get."

"My talent is magnified around books," Sarah offered.

Valeria cleared her throat. "I can sense danger around me. My instincts tell me when to hide, when to run, basically the best way to deal with it."

Sam met Ezra's gaze. Could they have discovered the link that easily? "Maybe that's it. All of us women have a little something extra, some sort of extra ability that so-called normal people don't have."

"What do you think?" Ezra asked the others.

"I think we need to do more research," Tarrant told him. "It's too soon to draw any conclusions."

"I agree," Sam told him. As a theory it was worth investigating, but it was still only a theory.

"I'll keep my eye out for a good-looking psychic," Nic assured them. The men chuckled, but the women were silent.

"Just be careful," she told him. She didn't want anything to happen to any of Ezra's friends.

"You, too. I'll see you soon." Nic left the conversation.

The others quickly said good-bye, and Ezra turned off the phone and stood. "It's time for bed.

• • •

Ezra knew Sam had a million questions. He could see them in her eyes. He tucked his phone back in the charger and held out his hand. She took it and they walked through the house and up the stairs. "This is getting to be a habit."

"What is?" She yawned, her green eyes tired. She'd been running on adrenaline for days. In spite of ingesting some of his blood, her body had been through a lot. What she needed more than anything was unbroken rest, nourishing food, and time.

"Going to bed when the sun is coming up." Through the

bedroom window, he could see the sun rising over the water. It never failed to stir his soul. Didn't matter how many times he'd seen it.

"Yeah, I'm beginning to feel like a vampire." She crawled onto the bed, and he sniffed and caught a whiff of his laundry detergent. "Up all night and sleeping most of the day."

She yawned again and pulled the covers over her. He tossed aside his jeans and climbed in beside her. For the first time since he'd met her, he started to relax. Sam was safe, the immediate threat to her was gone, and the Knights had no idea where she was. He nestled her head on his chest and ran his fingers along her arm.

"Tell me about your friends, your family." Sam's sleepy query startled him. He expected her to fall asleep instantly.

"What do you want to know?" He loved having her beside him. Being able to touch her when he wanted, able to inhale her unique fragrance.

She ran her fingertips over his bare chest. "I know Darius and Tarrant are drakons. I expect Nic is, too."

"Yes, they are." If he expected her to share his life, he needed to be honest. "The Knights suspect Darius is a drakon. They made a run for him and Sarah."

She bolted upright, her eyes as wild as her curls. "But they're safe where they are, aren't they?"

He eased her back down and started stroking her again. "They're safe. Darius will take care of them. And Nic is close by."

She shuddered and clung to him. "I hate the Knights."

"We all do." It was easy to forget how much she'd lost to them. They'd killed her mentor and altered the course of her life, leaving her no safe place to call home until he'd found her. "They're my brothers," he blurted.

Sam popped upright again and stared at him with disbelief. "Your brothers?"

He tried to draw her back down, but she wasn't having any of it. She sat cross-legged beside him, all signs of sleep banished. He should have kept his mouth shut until after she'd had some rest, but it was too late now.

He stacked his hands behind his head knowing she wouldn't sleep until he'd given her some of the details. "Same dragon sire but different mothers. Tarrant and Darius knew about one another. They were from the same village."

"Where?"

Ezra shrugged. "It doesn't matter. It's been nothing but dust for centuries."

She placed a hand on his chest. He knew she meant it to be comforting, and it was, arousing, too. "I'm sorry."

"Don't be. That was a long time ago. After our sire left this world with the other dragons, we had to figure things out for ourselves, who we really were, what we really were." That hadn't been an easy time. Humans had either wanted to revere them as gods or slaughter them. There never seemed to be much in-between.

"So how did you all find one another?"

"Darius. He's the oldest. We were all born within the span of a couple years, but he was first. He figured if there were two of them in their hometown, there might be more of us in nearby villages. He was right."

"Wow. Do you think you found all your siblings?"

He'd never really considered they might have missed a brother, that there might be another drakon out there that belonged with them. "I don't know."

He sat up and raked his fingers through his hair. "Darius and Tarrant found me first. Then we found Nic." They'd stopped searching once they'd covered the immediate area. "We were thinking like humans."

"What do you mean?" Sam scooted closer and touched his arm. He wrapped his hands around her waist and lifted her so she was straddling his lap. If he had to talk about a subject he'd much rather forget, he'd at least like the pleasure of being able to touch Sam.

He blew out a breath. "We were all lost when our sires abandoned us. After it became obvious we weren't exactly like them, that we were more human than dragon, they decided their grand experiment was a failure and left. They went back to the dimension they'd come from."

Sam's jaw dropped. Ezra put his index finger under her chin and pushed until it closed. "That's…" She trailed off, obviously not knowing what to say.

"So there I was all alone with a mother who hated me. She was frightened of what I was becoming. There was no way to hide it in the beginning. I was too young. We all were. My village cast me out."

"That's horrible. And your mother didn't stop them?" She bit her bottom lip and concern filled her eyes.

"No." That day was burned in his memory, as fresh as if it had happened only yesterday. "She led them."

He'd felt so totally alone that day. Hurt and bleeding, he'd stumbled into the wasteland beyond his village, no longer sure he wanted to live.

"Darius and Tarrant found me wandering in the desert." It turned out he was a lot harder to kill than he'd thought. His physical wounds had healed quickly. "At least it wasn't as bad as what Darius and Tarrant went through. Their mothers tried to poison them. When that didn't work, the entire village tried to kill them."

"That's so unfair. It wasn't your fault. How could your mothers do such a thing?" She sat back and cupped his face in her small, capable hands.

"They were afraid." He'd come to terms with his mother's failings long ago. "My mother was alone in the world with a son who wasn't totally human and no man by her side. She didn't know if we came from the gods or demons. She did what she had to in order to survive."

"You were a boy."

Ezra shook his head. "No, in those days I was considered a man." Still he'd felt the loss of home, such as it was, he'd belonged somewhere.

"Did your sire tell you nothing about what you were?"

"He was mostly absent when I was young. He told me what he was, what I was, when I was twelve. Then he watched me for a couple years to see if his dragon genes would dominate. But we were all something completely different."

"And what about Nic?"

"After Darius and Tarrant found me, we went to every village within two hundred miles. We found Nic half buried in the desert." No need to mention he'd been curled into a ball crying for his mother. He was the youngest of them all. He'd been lying on the burning hot sand surrounded by rubies.

Nic had been wary of them at first and then overjoyed to have family. It was Darius who'd gathered the rubies and made Nic take them. His brother's tears had gotten them their start in life, enabling them to purchase the supplies they'd needed to survive.

"Poor little boy," Sam murmured. "All of you."

"But we stopped looking. We were thinking like humans. We knew how far apart our villages were and how often our sires visited. We thought we'd found everyone."

They might have lived for thousands of years, but once they'd found one another, they'd simply given up the search. Sure, over the years they'd come in contact with others of their kind. Tarrant actively tried to find drakons, wanting to be able to reach out to them if he felt it necessary. But they'd never gone looking for another blood brother. He didn't know if that made them stupid or simply complacent. Not that it mattered. The results were the same.

"You didn't factor in the fact he could fly."

Ezra closed his eyes. To think he might have another brother out there on his own—maybe even more than one—made his soul ache. They all knew what it was like to be alone. "Drakons are solitary creatures by nature, but having family helps anchor us."

"You were all children and you'd been through a trauma. It's amazing to me that you found one another at all."

He knew she was right, but that didn't stop the sick feeling deep in his stomach. "I'll have to talk to the others. But it's time for you to sleep now."

· · ·

"No, it's time for me to love you." She whisked the shirt over her head and tossed it aside. The sun shining through the window warmed the space. It was chilly outside, but here in Ezra's bedroom it was cozy. This was a safe place for the two of them.

Talking about his past had been difficult for Ezra, but he'd done it. For her. Nothing could change his past or erase what he'd been through, but his future would be different. She would see to it.

"What are you doing?"

She placed her hands on Ezra's bare chest and traced the contours of his abs. "If you have to ask, I must not be doing it correctly," she teasingly repeated what he'd said another time they'd made love.

He ran his hand over her hip. "You're not doing a damn thing wrong, but you've been through a lot. You have to be tired."

She was, but her need to comfort Ezra, to love him, overrode everything, even the need to rest. "Touch me." She needed his hands on her.

"Baby, you never need to ask." His voice deepened, his amazing turquoise eyes darkened. He stroked upward, caressing her sides.

She moaned. His hands felt so good, so right whenever and wherever he touched her. She wanted to make love to him, but more than that, she wanted him to know he was loved.

He was hers for the foreseeable future.

But what about when she started to age and he didn't? She ignored the doubts that slipped into her mind. She wouldn't start looking toward the end when they were just beginning.

"What is it?" he asked.

She didn't want to talk about her stupid fears and insecurities. "It's nothing." To distract him, she stroked her fingers over his chest.

"You know I love it when you touch me." Her heart skipped a beat when he said the "L" word. "But, Sam, don't pretend there isn't something bothering you." He trailed his fingers over the side of her face. She turned toward his warmth.

"It's stupid," she muttered. She really didn't want to talk about it.

Ezra shook his head. "It's not stupid if it's upsetting you."

So much for being a femme fatale, able to seduce a man whenever she wanted. She was stark naked on his lap, and he wanted to talk.

"Are we in a relationship? Are we exclusive? Permanent?" Boy, that came out sounding needy. "I just need to know where I stand," she clarified. "Should I be getting ready to leave, or am I staying?"

Ezra jerked back as though she'd hit him. He stared at her for so long she began to fidget beneath his intense scrutiny.

"I'm sorry."

Sam closed her eyes and promised herself she wouldn't

cry. She'd always believed she wouldn't be here for long, although she'd begun to change her mind, to hope. She should have known better. "That's okay," she began, but he cut her off.

"No, it isn't." He framed her face between his big hands. "Look at me." She didn't want to. She wanted to crawl into a closet somewhere and have a good, long cry. She finally looked up at him.

His eyes practically glowed. So did his tattoo. He pulsed with a tangible energy, and she could feel the fine hairs on her body standing on end.

"I'm sorry you had to ask me that. You are my everything." He shook his head. "If you try to leave, if you wanted to leave, I'm not sure I could let you." He ran his thumb over her bottom lip. "Are we in a relationship? Most definitely. Are we exclusive? Absolutely. Are we permanent?" He leaned closer, caught her bottom lip between his teeth, and gave a gentle tug. "Forever."

She shuddered and felt a tear slip from the corner of her eye. He caught it on his tongue. "Salty. I love salty."

She surprised herself by laughing. So many emotions were battering her right now.

"I shed drakon tears for you." They both glanced at the small fortune in gems piled on the nightstand. "They're the equivalent of a human wedding ring, only more binding. A drakon will only shed tears in the most extreme of circumstances, and only for love."

She sucked in a breath, not sure she was hearing him right. "You love me?" She groaned and buried her face in her hands. "Ignore me, please."

He chuckled. "That's one thing I won't do. You love me." He peeled her hands away so he could see her. "You told me so."

"I do." There was no one like him.

"And I love you." He placed one of her hands over his heart. "Forever."

"I'm human. I'll get old, and you'll still be young and hot." That startled a laugh from him. She smacked his chest. "That's not funny." She sighed. "You're right. I need to focus on the positive. We have forty or fifty good years to look forward to. Maybe more. Hey, I'll be a cougar in a few years, and you can be my boy toy."

He started to choke. "Boy toy?" he sputtered.

She shrugged. "That's what everyone will think." She winked at him. "I'm fine with that."

"Sam," he began.

"No. I'm done talking." Fatigue was starting to wear on her, and she wanted to make love with him before she fell asleep. She kissed him, pushing all else aside but their lovemaking. It was tender and sweet and filled with passion.

When they'd both found release, he collapsed to the side, dragging her with him and curling his big body around her. Sunshine filled the room, but she knew that wouldn't keep her awake. She was beyond exhausted. She was also strangely content.

It didn't matter that the Knights of the Dragon would never stop looking for her. She had Ezra. Any risk was worth it to be with him. She'd had a price on her head before he'd met her. That she'd found him and he loved her was more than she'd ever expected.

A low rumbling sound rose from deep in his chest. She snuggled closer and closed her eyes. She smiled when she felt the comforter being thrown over them. That was Ezra, always thoughtful, always thinking about her.

"Sleep," he murmured. "We'll talk more later. But know this. You're never leaving me. Not while I have blood in my body."

She knew there was some significance to what he was

telling her but she was too fatigued to make sense of it. Later. She'd think later.

He kissed the top of her head and they snuggled together as the sun bathed the room in a soft glow.

· · ·

Talking with the authorities always gave Karina a headache. "No, I had no idea anyone was missing from the crew. Aaron Dexter was in charge of the operation and he assured me everyone was fine. Obviously, he lied to me. Now not only is he missing, but you're telling me the archaeologist I hired is also nowhere to be found."

Karina was nothing more than an innocent victim. At least as far as the police were concerned. Having them show up at her home to question her was something else she could blame Dexter for. If he wasn't already dead, he soon would be.

"Is there anything else I can do for you?" She kept her tone light when she really wanted to scream. "I don't know any more than I already told you. I funded the expedition to explore the wreck of the *Reliant*, but the research vessel sank. As far as I know, they suspect a whale rammed the boat, puncturing holes in the bow."

"It was insured?" the detective asked.

"Of course it was. Everything I own is insured. It's also a great nuisance to have to buy and outfit another research vessel."

"But you plan to?"

"Of course." She wanted to be ready in the event there was another artifact to be salvaged somewhere in the world. She glanced at her watch. "If that's all, I have another engagement."

"We appreciate your cooperation." The detective stood,

as did his partner. Karina remained seated. "Thank you for your time," he added.

"Whatever I can do to help. I hope the authorities find both Doctor Bellamy and Mr. Dexter. I have questions for them both."

The men turned and walked away. Birch, who'd been standing just inside the office, walked them to the front door. Karina was up and pacing by the time he returned.

"I want to know if Dexter is dead or alive." She paused and smoothed down her Channel suit. Classic clothing never went out of style.

"We've got a man on the coast guard vessel. We'll know as soon as they know anything."

"Good." Karina paused by the window, but she barely noticed the view of the city. "If Dexter isn't dead, I want him questioned before he's disposed of. He might have tried to fake his own death. We don't know what he found. He might have been lying about what Doctor Bellamy discovered among the artifacts of the *Reliant*. Bottom line is we can't trust anything Dexter told us."

"Agreed. What about Bellamy?" Birch asked.

"I suspect she's dead. Dexter probably killed her. He either stole the artifact from her or it was already lost. Either way, we watch the area for the next few months, we also watch the other Knights, especially Temple, in case he's gotten his hands on whatever it was they found."

"You're writing off the *Integrity*?"

"Yes. The insurance adjuster says it'll cost a small fortune to refloat her, and all the high-tech equipment on board will have to be replaced regardless."

"Have you contacted that local company, Easton Salvage?"

"Not yet," she told him. "I haven't had time. Call them. I want any artifacts they can find on board the *Integrity*, just to be safe. After that, she's theirs to salvage."

"I'll take care of it." Birch left her alone, closing the door to her study behind him.

All her plans had been upended. It was time to make new ones.

Epilogue

Sam tugged at the hem of her sweater. Well, actually it was yet another one of Ezra's sweaters. The only things she wore that actually belonged to her were her underwear and jeans. Her wardrobe was severely limited. Not that she'd ever been much for fashion, but she needed more than two pieces.

She peered out the front window of Ezra's home. Her home now. She might not have lived here for long, but she already loved it, and she was looking forward to watching the island go through all four seasons.

Right now, she wanted to be on the dock watching for Ezra to return, but it wasn't safe. It probably wouldn't be safe for her to venture out much in the daytime for the next few months. She was okay with that if it kept the Knights away and Ezra safe.

It had only been a week since he'd told her he loved her. She wrapped her arms around her waist and hugged herself tight. He loved her. She could still hardly believe it.

It had been a week of learning how to live with one another, of settling into a routine. It had been frighteningly easy to do. Already, she could barely remember her life without him.

He'd been busy during that time. He'd taken the sapphires, her drakon tears, but hadn't told her what he'd done with them. He'd stocked the refrigerator and freezer with what he called "women food." Why he'd consider fruit and vegetables to be gender specific, she had no idea, but she loved him for it.

Her man was a meat and potatoes guy all the way, and you could mostly hold the potatoes. Not that he complained when she cooked. Just the opposite. He ate everything she made and praised her efforts to the high heavens.

She glanced out the window again and her stomach dropped when she saw the speedboat heading toward the dock. Ezra was back, and he'd brought one of his brothers with him.

Nic had decided to come and visit. It had also been decided that Ezra shouldn't buy or order any clothes for her to wear. There was still too much of a risk of the Knights skulking around. Instead, Sam had gone online and made her selections and Ezra had sent the list to his brother. Nic had purchased everything and was bringing her new clothes with him.

It was all very cloak and dagger, but unfortunately very necessary.

Sam would never make the mistake of underestimating the Knights again, and neither would Ezra or his brothers.

Nic stepped onto the dock. He was as big as Ezra, maybe a touch larger, which made him at least six-eight. She tugged on the sweater, wishing she was wearing something nicer, but beggars couldn't be choosers.

She'd been busy since yesterday cooking and baking. She had a vat of chili, another filled with marinara sauce, as well as pots of both beef stew and chicken soup on the stove. Since Ezra had left this morning, she'd made an apple pie, banana bread, and a chocolate cake. It had kept her too busy to worry about meeting Nic.

Nicodemus Wilde—Ezra had chuckled when he'd told her his brother's chosen last name—was a gambler and a collector, buying and selling artifacts all over the world when he wasn't gambling in Vegas, Monaco, or other exotic locations around the world. He was also a fire drakon. Most importantly, he was Ezra's brother.

The two men shouldered several large duffle bags and made their way up the path from the dock. Sam wiped her moist palms on her jeans. "Everything will be fine." It had to be.

She went to the front door and opened it. Ezra scowled at her, but Nic smiled. He hurried his step, beating Ezra to the door. "Hello, Sam." He dropped the duffle bags to the floor and lifted her right off her feet.

Ezra slammed the door shut. "Put her down, you idiot." He didn't wait for Nic to release her, and yanked her out of his arms. She felt like one of those duffle bags.

Ezra planted a quick, hard kiss on her lips before he set her down. He kept his hands on her shoulders. "This is Sam." She could hear the pride in his voice and it made her smile.

"I got that." Nic gave her a courtly bow. "Nicodemus Wilde, my lady. At your service."

"Idiot," Ezra muttered.

Sam held out her hand. "It's a pleasure to meet you. If you're hungry, I've got plenty of food."

Nic sandwiched her hand between two of his. "You are my sister now." The vow brought tears to her eyes. "You're family."

He was lonely. And why wouldn't he be? In spite of his bravado, all his brothers had found mates and he was still alone. "I am." She turned her hand in his and squeezed it. He gave an abrupt nod and released her.

"I assume my room is ready." He grabbed one of the bags and motioned to the rest. "Those are yours. I made a few adjustments to your list."

Nic left her standing in the foyer with Ezra, her mouth hanging open as he disappeared up the stairs. "All these are filled with clothes for me." There were three large duffle bags.

Ezra frowned. "You don't have anything. You'll probably need more. This is just to get you started."

Sam couldn't help herself. She started to laugh. "Why in heaven's name do I need so many clothes? The seabirds won't care. Neither will the fish or the whales." She'd seen a humpback breaching just off the dock yesterday. It had stayed there until Ezra finally joined the massive animal for a swim. How cool was that?

His frown deepened. "I'm sorry, Sam."

She shook her head, not wanting him to have regrets about anything. "About what? I don't need to go anywhere or do anything. About the Knights? That's not on you."

He sighed and lifted her right off her feet. She wrapped her legs around his waist and twined her arms around his neck. He smelled like fresh air and the ocean, scents she would forever associate with him. "I'm happy here with you."

"I have something for you."

It was her turn to scowl. "You wouldn't let me pay you for the clothes Nic bought."

"You're not paying for the clothes. And this is different," he assured her.

"How?"

He walked over to the kitchen and sat her on the edge of the counter. He reached inside his jacket pocket and pulled out a velvet bag. "Here." He thrust it at her, forcing her to take it.

She had a sneaky suspicion she knew what it was before she opened it. Her hand shook as she pulled the drawstrings open. Ezra grew impatient and tipped the bag up. Sapphires set in platinum spilled over her fingers. The chain would go around her neck twice and still hang low. It was worth a small fortune.

"It's beautiful." When the gems had gone missing she'd half wondered and half hoped he was getting them set into a necklace, like the one he'd found in the wreck of the *Reliant*.

"Not nearly as beautiful as you," he told her. He dropped the long chain over her neck and then doubled it so there were two long strands hanging down the front. The gems caught the light and sparkled.

"Oh, Ezra." She was at a loss for words.

"I love you."

She raised her face, and he bent down. Their lips met in a tender kiss, filled with the love they shared. The necklace was a tangible reminder of that. Sadness gripped her.

"What is it?" he asked when he pulled away. He tucked one of her curls behind her ear. "I sense your sadness."

"I was thinking about the necklace in the safe." She played with the white-colored chain. "They must have loved one another, the drakon and the woman who wore his tears."

Ezra rubbed his chin over the top of her head. "I'm sure they did. They were lucky enough to find one another, even if it didn't last forever."

"How could it last forever? She was human. Maybe she died, and he never took the necklace back." That was better than imagining the Knights killed them.

"Sam." Ezra held her face with his hands. "He wouldn't have let her die. He'd have fed her small amounts of his blood to keep her young. I told you I wasn't letting you go, that this is for forever."

She knew her mouth was hanging open. "What?"

Exasperated, he took a step back and set his hands on his hips. His glare would have frightened the most battle-hardened men. Sam just glared back.

"I don't recall agreeing to this," she pointed out.

His expression went blank, but he couldn't disguise his hurt, not from her. "You want to leave me?"

She shook her head. "Of course not, but I'm not using you, either. That would make me no better than the Knights."

"They take what is not offered. I'm offering you my blood so we can be together."

She was being an idiot. "You're right." When he made an exaggerated expression of surprise, she scowled. "Don't expect me to ever say that again."

"But it sounds so sweet." He nuzzled her jaw. "Tell me again."

She knew when she was beat. "You're right. I'll take enough of your blood so I can stay alive." She teased her fingers over his chest. "I don't want to leave you. Just promise me if there ever comes a day when you don't want to be with me any longer, you'll take me somewhere I can grow old alone."

"It will never happen." He dragged her off the counter and into his arms. His grip threatened to suffocate her.

She tapped his arm. "Ease up."

He set her on her feet and released her. "I'm sorry. Did I hurt you?"

Sam sucked air into her lungs. "I'm okay. No harm done." She knew he didn't quite believe her, so she picked up the long chain around her neck and studied the sapphires. "Thank you for the amazing gift." She looked straight into his turquoise-colored eyes. "The necklace is beautiful, but what it represents means more. Thank you for the precious gift, but most of all for your love."

• • •

Nic quietly let himself out the front door. He knew Ezra heard him leave even if Sam didn't. He hadn't meant to listen to their conversation, but with his enhanced hearing, it was difficult not to.

All his brothers had found women of their own. Was Sam's theory right? Was it the right time in their development to want to settle down? Were they attracted to women with special gifts?

He honestly didn't know.

He wandered toward the woods and through the trees. He liked it here well enough but missed the hot climes of the desert. He was all about heat.

He broke through the trees and peered down at a secluded cove. This had to be the place Ezra had told him about, the place where Dexter had almost killed Sam.

Nic sat on an outcropping of rocks and rubbed his hand over his face. He was tired, and not just physically. It was getting harder and harder for him to stay interested in living.

He knew what it meant. These were the warning signs that the Deep Sleep was close at hand. It was something that happened to their kind when they decided they no longer wished to dwell in this world.

They'd settle somewhere isolated and hidden in their drakon form and sleep. But it wasn't a normal sleep. No one knew if they could even wake as none ever had. Over time, they eventually turned to stone, blending into whatever environment they'd taken shelter in.

Only his love for his brothers had kept him in the world this long. It was the reason he spent all his time among humans, gambling, buying and selling artifacts, anything to keep him interested.

It was getting more and more difficult, especially now that his brothers no longer needed him. They were happy with their mates. Maybe it was time to let go.

He pushed himself off the rock and turned his back on the sea. "But not today," he whispered. He made the trek back to Ezra's home, taking his time to allow his brother the privacy to make love with his woman.

Nic smiled as he imagined how Sam would react if he walked in on them. Might be worth Ezra's wrath just to find out.

Acknowledgments

Writing the book is only the first step in the journey toward publication. Thank you to my amazing editor, Heidi, for your expertise, hard work, and advice. I love working with you. And thank you to the amazing team at Entangled. You are the absolute best.

About the Author

N.J. Walters is a *New York Times* and *USA Today* bestselling author who has always been a voracious reader, and now she spends her days writing novels of her own. Vampires, werewolves, dragons, time-travelers, seductive handymen, and next-door neighbors with smoldering good looks—all vie for her attention. It's a tough life, but someone's got to live it.

www.njwalters.com

Discover the **Blood of the Drakon** *series...*

DRAKON'S PROMISE

DRAKON'S PREY

Discover more Entangled Select Otherworld titles...

THE WAY YOU BITE
a novel by Zoe Forward

When King Werewolf shows up in veterinarian Vee Scarpa's ER, she's livid. Her father, North American head honcho vampire, has threatened a chilling *or else* if she "accidentally" helped a wolf again. But she's tempted by the sexy wolf. And his deadly blood calls to her... A promise to his brother in arms obliges Lexan Dimitrov to rescue the aristocrat vampire before her family discovers her secret. What he didn't expect was to find her sexy-as-hell. He's not into vamps, yet the inescapable heat building between them is a delicious temptation guaranteed to end in total disaster.

NEW MOON
a *Moon* novel by Lisa Kessler

Jaguar shifter Sebastian Severino is an enigma. He lives alone, works alone, and will die alone. But the night he's attacked by a female werewolf, nothing will ever be the same. Sebastian, the deadliest assassin Nero has ever produced, will be forced to choose a side. Isabelle Wood has never taken the easy path as a bounty hunter and now a bitten werewolf without a mate. The night she gets the opportunity to take out their enemy, with her blade at his throat, her wolf discovers her mate in the last person she can be with.

THE RED LILY
a *Vampire Blood* novel by Juliette Cross

The Black Lily needs a larger army if they are to defeat the vampire monarchy. In order to do so, former lieutenant Nikolai must seek help from the red-hooded temptress he needs to avoid, for the secret he carries could prove dangerous for her if she gets too close. But Sienna will do anything for the Black Lily…

WHEN DANGER BITES
a *Bravo Team WOLF* novel by Heather Long

Buttoned-up Corporal Kaitlyn Amador is dangerous on every level. Marine Captain Jax can survive the temptation for only so long before his wolf takes over and pursues what it wants.

65544103R00192

Made in the USA
Lexington, KY
15 July 2017